The Last Pirates

by

Cynthia Breeding

The Last Pirates

Cover Art by *Debbie Taylor*

The Wild Rose Press, Inc.
PO Box 708
Adams Basin, NY 14410-0708
Visit us at www.thewildrosepress.com

Publishing History
First Edition, 2024
Trade Paperback ISBN 978-1-5092-5403-3
Digital ISBN 978-1-5092-5404-0

Published in the United States of America

The Bayou Prince: Chapter One

Christian Picard kept an eye on his target, Fiona Gordon, standing by a potted palm near the French doors that opened onto the veranda of the governor's ballroom. Even if she had not had hair the color of a pumpkin, she would have been hard to miss in this crowd of young Southern belles swirling in their white and pink tulle dresses to the fashionably new quadrille. The young woman was nearly a head taller than the other girls and somewhat gangly, as though she hadn't quite become accustomed to her height. Her dress, a somewhat drab gold—or perhaps it just looked drab next to the flaming color of her hair—had a high collar and fitted waist, unlike the smooth lines and low *décolletage* worn by the debutante society of New Orleans. Not that Fiona's modest dress hid the fullness of her breasts, he noted with interest.

"Are you going to gawk at her all night or make a move?" his friend, Andre Dubois, asked with a grin.

"What do you suggest I do? I cannot simply walk over to her and introduce myself as one of Jean Lafitte's privateers, can I? We have all been declared outlaws…and her aunt, Mrs. Claiborne, is her chaperone, to boot."

Andre's grin widened. "Jean was tempted to attend this ball himself, just to see the governor's wife again…even if she only knows him as 'Mr. Clement.' "

"Unfortunately, Governor Claiborne knows Jean only too well," Marc Rochelle, Christian's other friend, said with a chuckle.

"With his brother, Pierre, rotting in jail, Jean couldn't take the chance of joining him," Christian said, "even though he chafed about not being able to outwit Claiborne again."

"That's why we—or specifically you—are here," Andre answered. "That girl is staying right here in the governor's mansion. Her father is Captain Harry Gordon, serving under Commodore Patterson. Patterson is no friend of Jean's either. We need to keep tabs on him, too." He grinned again. "The girl can be a gold mine of information for us."

"Not to mention, with the British burning Washington D.C. last week, Jean needs to know where the English navy is as well," Marc added. "Barataria is defensible; hell, even Patterson can't navigate the bayous and swamps, but British ships patrolling the Gulf waters would interrupt our…er, *trading* business."

Christian looked over to Fiona again. She had not moved, nor made any attempt to smile at the one or two still wet-behind-the ears swains who had headed her way only to veer off.. Did she not have a dance card? His eyes roved down her figure. She had nicely flared hips, perfect for providing a soft, comfortable cushion for a man if she were on her back with her legs spread… He forced his mind off that subject. He already felt like a louse for having to concoct a cover story and gain her trust only to use her for deceptive means. But there was a war on. The British were rapidly winning, and New Orleans was divided between the aristocratic French and Spanish families and the Americans—a population the

Creoles didn't think much better than the British.

Ah. Yes. There was the dance card dangling from her wrist. He wondered why Mrs. Claiborne had not bullied the young men into signing it. Surely, being the niece of the governor's wife had some advantage. Just as he was thinking that, a young man did approach Fiona, taking her card and pointing to his name. Christian watched as she shook her head and turned incredibly red—the curse of anyone with such fair skin as she had. The young man bowed stiffly and stalked off. She had refused to dance? That was unheard of in Society. He saw the color drain from her face, and she turned quickly to hurry out onto the veranda.

"There's your chance, man. She's all alone." Marc slapped him on the back. "She may not be the most attractive woman in the room, but she's no crone, either."

"Think of it as duty to your country," Andre added with another big grin. "There are worse assignments than stealing a kiss or two to enthrall a fair maiden."

Christian shook his head and left his two friends chortling about Fiona and a dark veranda. From the little he had observed of her, he did not think she was easily *enthralled*. She had the look of a woman who knew her own mind.

And his challenge was to change it.

****

Fiona leaned over the banister and drank in deep gulps of the humid night air. The room had been stifling, and her dress clung to her as though she had stepped out of her bath and not toweled off. How any of those girls could *dance* in that heated room and not have those silly little ringlets they all favored look like wet, limp pasta she didn't know. But then, she did not understand why

3

they acted silly in the first place, batting their eyelashes and fans at young boys barely old enough to shave and old men alike. In fact, any close male presence seemed to launch them into fits of giggles. The leader of that group of girls was Caroline Frazier, a petite, dainty thing with golden hair, blue eyes, and a china-doll complexion…the epitome of everything Fiona was not. Of course, she did not *understand* half of what any of them said either, since they spoke rapid French.

She missed Boston. This late in August, the morning air would already be cool and *dry*. In a few weeks, nature would produce a stunning array of red, yellow, and orange foliage. The first frost would bring a decidedly crisp smell to the air. Here, the cypress trees hung heavy with Spanish moss. Strong winds off the Gulf brought the stench of the swamps with them.

Worst of all, she missed not being able to visit her mother's grave at Granary Burying Ground at Park Street Church. The pastor had assured her the grave would be well cared for, but she would miss placing flowers by the tombstone as she had for the past ten years.

Even the cemeteries were different here. The dead were buried above the ground in boxlike structures stacked one on top of the other. Her aunt told her it was because the earth was too water-soaked below the surface to keep caskets buried.

Some things were similar, though: The French Market on Decatur Street reminded her of the indoor market in Faneuil Hall, at Dock Square. The mighty Mississippi wound its way around the *Vieux Carré* much like the Charles River did Boston. The majestic steeples of the Basilica reminded her of the white steeples of Boston's churches, too.

Fiona sighed. She and her sixteen-year-old brother, Cory, had been here less than a month. Her father told her it would take time to adjust to the South, but he had not really prepared her for such drastic change.

Her aunt had been kind. She had taken the time to arrange for introductions and outings with many of the girls who were at tonight's ball, but after stilted attempts at conversation, Fiona realized she had little in common with the debutantes, especially fragile-looking ones like Caroline. When Fiona told a group of them she did not dance, they stared at her as though she had grown another head suddenly. Nor was she particularly interested in whether the next batch of bonnets from Paris would include feathers or whether gown fashions would change now that Napoleon had been defeated by the British. But her true fall from grace had been admitting that she could fire a musket and toss a knife. She was shunned as swiftly as though she had developed a case of their much-feared yellow fever.

It didn't take long for the gossip to spread that there was something *odd* about her. She was not usually approached at these society functions. Not that she cared. Most of the boys were as silly as the girls…competing with each other to lavish ludicrous and outlandish compliments on each and every dance partner, swearing they would call any man out to duel should the lady of the moment ever be insulted. God's blood! In all her twenty years, she had never heard such blathering. She'd had to grit her teeth the first time one of them had tried that with her. How could anyone believe such trivial fluff?

But three men had arrived a short time ago and gotten her attention, along with the giggling debutantes.

The men were, perhaps, no more than five-and-twenty years of age, but they had a look about them—a bold and roguish presence—that made them stand out. Even the gray-haired chaperones had noticed them, dashing subtle glances in their direction before looking anxiously for their own charges, to be sure they were safe with some young man from Society. All three were strongly built, with broad shoulders, their waistcoats firm over flat bellies, trousers fitting well-muscled legs. Their faces were bronzed from the sun. One had sun-bleached hair while another's was raven black. But it was the man in the middle, with chestnut-colored hair and dark eyes, who caught her true attention. He had watched her, not bothering to look away as a gentleman should when she'd glanced at him. In fact, a corner of his mouth quirked up ever so slightly instead, and she had felt…*something*.

Fiona lifted her loose mane of hair off her shoulders, hoping for a touch of coolness. Tonight, a light breeze carried the sweet smell of magnolias and honeysuckle from the garden around the corner.

"Are you offering me your neck to kiss?"

She jumped and spun, her long hair whipping across her face, and then gaped. Almost as if she had conjured him, the intriguing man stood only a few feet behind her.

He smiled. "I did not mean to startle you, Mademoiselle Gordon."

He knew who she was? Finally finding her voice, she managed, "You did not…I was lost in thought. How do you know my name?"

Taking two steps toward her, he reached over and brushed strands of her hair from her face, the backs of his fingers grazing her cheekbone. The light touch was tantalizing, as was his scent—soap and leather and something uniquely *him*—Fiona suddenly became aware of how very close he stood and how very isolated it was in this corner of the veranda. She shivered in the warm air, a strange tingle of anticipation washing over her. His eyes, so dark they looked black in the dim light, glimmered, as though he knew the effect he was having. His mouth quirked up in that little half-grin again. This was so totally improper that if Fiona had any sense of propriety, she would step around him and get back into that well-lit room before her reputation was completely ruined. And yet...

As though sensing her dilemma, he dropped his hand and stepped back and gave a little bow. "I asked. You are the niece of Mrs. Claiborne. I would have arranged for a formal introduction, but, at the moment, I am not in good graces with the governor. I am Christian Picard, captain of the schooner *Dorada*."

No wonder he was so bronzed! She frowned slightly. What was it the governor had said about ships in the area? Something about pirates. Christian did not look like a pirate—weren't they supposed to be a rough lot, armed with curved swords and gold hoops in their ears? She tilted her head. "Why are you not in good graces?"

Christian shrugged. "A duel a fortnight ago. The governor frowns on dueling."

Fiona felt her eyes widen. "You called a man out? Why?"

"He insulted a lady friend of my acquaintance. Her father is dead; she has no brothers. Someone had to stand for her."

A sharp twinge shot through her at the thought of his

defending this unknown woman, which was ridiculous, considering he was a complete stranger. Even though it was not her business, she found herself asking, "Is this lady your betrothed?"

He looked amused. "No. She's someone I've done business with in the past."

A businesswoman? Fiona knew a few women, mainly widows, who had small stores in Boston, but here? And what kind of a business would a woman have with a ship's captain? The docks were dangerous places. "What kind of trading does your ship do?"

"Imports from many places."

Fiona frowned again, thinking that her uncle said the U.S. Customs was losing money from illegal entry of goods that were not taxed. "You are not a pirate, are you?"

For a moment he looked startled, and then he laughed. "Are you always so blunt, *Mademoiselle*?"

Fiona felt her face heat. She'd inherited the trait from her father, and it was probably one more reason the Southern belles shunned her. Still…it was who she was. "Yes. I've been told so."

"And painstakingly honest as well." His smile faded and he studied her. "Admirable traits, both of them."

She stared back at him. "They are? My father wouldn't think so. He says ladies are—"

Christian placed a fingertip against her lips. "Ladies are devious—although delightful—creatures. Among themselves, they purr like cats finishing a bowl of cream, while their claws are sharp as lethal weapons. They drip sweet, honeyed words on their worst enemies. I have found they often say the opposite of what they mean. Woe be the man who believes a woman who says nothing is wrong when her eyes are shooting daggers." His finger traced lightly down Fiona's jawline. "I find it quite intriguing when a woman actually speaks her mind."

How could such calloused fingertips have such a feathery touch? They traced gently along the curve of her cheek. Fiona wanted to close her eyes and lay her head against that hand. Her body seemed quite detached from her brain. Christian had moved closer again; she could feel his body heat and something that almost irresistibly pulled her toward him, even though he had dropped his arm and was not touching her. Never had she reacted like this with a man. She was a sensible girl, not given to romantic notions of sultry, perfumed night air and dark verandas with a handsome stranger who could be a prince from a children's faerie tale…or a pirate. She straightened, coming out of her near-trance.

"You didn't answer my question. Are you a pirate?"

Inside the ballroom, the music stopped. Fiona almost cursed—another trait her father did not approve of—if the musicians were taking a respite, the veranda would soon be flooded with people. Her aunt would be mortified to have her found out here. Fiona turned to go.

Christian grasped her arm and pulled her against him. Before she could protest, he angled his mouth across hers in a soft, sensual kiss that lingered just long enough to hold promises of much more to come. He released her just as quickly.

"If you want to know about pirates, *Mademoiselle*, meet me in the City Park tomorrow, midafternoon. Right now, I must save your virtue and be gone."

With a grin, he vaulted over the low banister and disappeared into the darkness of the garden, leaving

Fiona breathless and tingling in spots she did not know *could* tingle. Her shaky fingers went to her puffy lips. A dizzying sensation swept over her as she recalled the feel of his mouth claiming hers. He had taken advantage of her and she had let him. She should be indignant...or at least, mortified by her own behavior. But she wasn't.

She was curious.

She wanted *more*.

Chapter Two

"I don't know why you want to go the park today," Cory grumbled as he slapped the reins over the horse's rump and the cabriolet lurched forward. "It looks like rain."

"It always looks like rain in the afternoons," Fiona replied. "There is so much humidity in the air I can practically wring water from it." She dabbed at her damp face with a linen handkerchief. The groomsman had looked incredulous when she'd requested the open carriage in the middle of the afternoon. Apparently Southern girls stayed indoors and did not allow the sun to strike their peaches-and-cream complexions. She sighed. No doubt another rumor would go out about her oddity.

But that would dull in comparison to her aunt or father finding out she was on her way to meet a man she didn't even know. She glanced at Cory, wishing she had not had to bring him with her, but ordering a carriage *and* going out on her own was not an option. The head groom would have refused or, just as bad, sent her off in an enclosed coach accompanied by a driver and two footmen. Even if Christian would recognize and approach her, news of her liaison would spread like wildfire once they returned.

Fiona spotted him as soon as they entered the park. He was astride a magnificent dappled-gray stallion, whose full, crested neck with its thick, dark mane and finely sculpted head bespoke the breeding of a Spanish Andalusian. Christian's pearl-gray jodhpurs and black riding coat blended in with the horse's coloring, giving him a regal appearance. He lifted the reins slightly and the horse broke into a graceful, rocking canter as they headed toward the carriage.

"That's some piece of horseflesh," Cory said approvingly.

As much as Fiona was taking in the way the sun glistened burgundy over Christian's flowing hair and the wide breadth of his shoulders in the well-fitting coat, she couldn't help but also notice how well he sat the saddle. He rode as though he were an extension of the horse. She waved.

Cory looked startled. "Do you know that man?"

"He was at the ball last night. Didn't you see him?"

Her brother looked back at the rider. "Wasn't he with two other men?"

"Why, yes, I believe he was."

His eyes narrowed as he looked back at Fiona. "I do not remember seeing him introduced to you."

"Well, of course he was, silly. How else would I know him?" Fiona cleared her throat, hoping Cory had not noticed the slightly high pitch her voice had taken.

He looked like he wanted to argue the point, but Christian had arrived, bringing the gray to a stop with a half-rear. He bowed slightly from the saddle.

"Mademoiselle Gordon. How nice to see you taking the air this afternoon."

"It is a lovely day." Fiona ignored her brother's astonished look. He knew she detested the humidity. "I hated to be cooped up inside." At least that much was true. She loved being outdoors. "Cory, may I present Mr. Picard? My brother, Cory."

Christian nodded his acquaintance. "A brother is a fine person to have as a chaperone. No one can be more protective, *non*?"

Cory straightened. "That's right, sir. I am *very* protective of her."

Fiona managed to keep from rolling her eyes. Most of the time her *little* brother thought she was a bossy, pushy, older sister who gave too many orders. Why was he puffing up like a bandy rooster with his feathers all ruffled?

But Christian only smiled as he tossed a leg over his saddle and slid down. "I would very much like to take your sister for a walk in the gardens over there. With your permission, of course."

Cory sputtered, looking like he didn't know what to say. Christian handed the reins of the gray up. "I would appreciate it, *mon ami*, if you watch Jupiter for me while we are gone?"

That settled it for Cory. He practically preened at being given the opportunity to be responsible for the horse. Fiona was pretty sure he had forgotten that he was supposed to be protecting *her*.

Christian's eyes glinted mischievously as he reached up to help her down. His warm, strong hands encircled her waist, lifting her and setting her down beside him, his fingers lingering only slightly too long, not enough to be noticeable to Cory, who was gazing with star-struck eyes at the gray. Christian's mouth quirked up in that way that Fiona was beginning to think was really, really alluring, and offered his arm.

"Shall we, *Mademoiselle*?"

Fiona placed her hand on his arm and felt the hard, corded muscle beneath the superfine of his riding coat. Her fingers ached to travel up his arm to his expansive shoulders and down his chest. She felt her face heat at such a thought—where had that wanton thought come from?—and lifted her hand only to find Christian closing his fingers over hers, holding her hand in place.

"I rather like your touch," he said, amusement in his voice as he guided her down a winding garden path.

Fiona looked down, unable to meet his eyes, sure that her face was flaming. Thank goodness he did not know where her fingers had wanted to go. Or…did he? The thought was truly mortifying. Was he laughing at her? She stole a look upward to find him smiling at her. He lifted a brow.

"I will not bite you, *Mademoiselle*. Unless you ask me to, of course." Christian gave her his lopsided grin. "But you must ask very nicely or I won't consider it at all."

Fiona stared at him and then she began to laugh. He was teasing her!

His grin widened. "You have a very nice laugh, Fiona. Do you mind if I call you Fiona? I know we have just met, but—"

"I do not mind if you call me Fiona," she interrupted. "I think it is rather silly to be so stilted and formal."

"Good. Then you must call me Christian." He tilted his head, his dark eyes looking into hers. "You are different from most women."

Fiona's smile faded. "I know. Everyone thinks me odd."

His finger traced the curve of her cheek lightly. "Not

14

odd. Different. Not afraid to speak your mind and, I suspect, you mean what you say. You have no idea of how refreshing that is. Now smile for me, *s'il vous plaît*."

She felt herself relax with him. It was as though he understood her somehow. That it was all right to be herself…that he would not judge her on her outspokenness. She gave him a trembling smile.

"That's better," he said as they approached a gazebo. He gestured to the bench inside. "Would you care to sit? I believe you wanted to know about pirates, *non*?"

Once they were seated—close, but not touching— she began. "My uncle says the waters around the mouth of the Mississippi, and especially Barataria Bay, are infested with pirates. Since you said you were a ship's captain… I should not have been so blunt as to ask if you were a pirate."

Christian brought her hand to his lips, brushing a light kiss across her knuckles before letting go. "I admire your bluntness. As I said, you are unique."

Fiona's hand tingled and she decided she rather liked these little, fleeting touches. Christian made her feel feminine—and she usually felt too tall and gangly— and yet, he did not take advantage of her. Unless she counted last night's kiss. Her eyes strayed to his full mouth, wondering what it would be like to kiss him again, and then tore her thoughts away. What was getting into her? Christian did not appear to have noticed, thankfully.

"Your uncle, the Governor, has had a long-running feud with Jean Lafitte, a privateer who owns a fleet of boats."

"Uncle William says he's a pirate. A condemned

one. That a Grand Jury met and there were witnesses who told of murders and taking of ships."

"It is true he has been labeled as such. Even now, Pierre Lafitte sits in the Cabildo and there is a price on Jean Lafitte's head. It's the reason he can no longer operate his blacksmith shop or handle his wares at Maspero's."

"Wait. Are you saying that these—pirates—actually have legitimate businesses?"

"They did."

"Uncle William spoke of illegal auctions of stolen goods that were held at someplace called the Temple."

Christian lifted a brow again. "And how would the governor know the goods were stolen? The Lafittes have always called themselves privateers, since they sailed under a Letter of Marque from Cartagena. That would give them the legal right to stop any ships flying the Spanish flag and collect whatever bounty that was aboard."

"But they did not pay taxes at the Customs office," Fiona said stubbornly. "That is illegal."

"I can see your uncle has filled you in on quite a bit about pirating," Christian replied, "but if you were to talk to other people, you might hear another side to that story."

"Like what?"

"It would take much too long to even begin today," Christian answered. "I do not want to worry your brother by keeping you gone too long."

Fiona almost rolled her eyes. "Cory probably has forgotten I am even in the gardens. The Irish love for horses is strong in him. Nothing would suit him more than to run a horse farm in Kentucky, so I am sure your

Jupiter has wiped all sense of my presence away."

Christian laughed and stood, offering his hand to help her up. "Even so, there is no need to risk your reputation by being seen in a man's company for too long without a chaperone lingering nearby."

"I told you, Society already thinks me odd. I suspect no one cares about my reputation."

"I do," Christian said solemnly.

Fiona swallowed hard as she stared at him, a slow warmth spreading through her. Christian actually *cared* if her reputation was sullied? He really was like a faerie-tale prince come alive…or maybe a prince from a nearby bayou. She almost giggled.

"I would like to see you again, Fiona," he said, his fingers stroking her palm lightly. "I wish I could ask to pay court to you properly, but I am sure your uncle would not agree to my suit." He looked apologetic. "Could we meet here again in two days' time?"

He wanted to court her! The warm feeling turned into heat that lounged deep in her belly. It was totally improper of course…but even as a child, Fiona had been headstrong. And she remembered the duel Christian said he'd had because of a woman who had no male to defend her. He had done a noble thing, especially since he indicated the lady was merely a business acquaintance. So how could Fiona fault him for not being able to take the proper route to courtship? Her uncle, she had already learned, was not wont to change his mind once it was made up. Besides, Christian Picard intrigued her like no man had ever done.

"I will find a way," she said.

He smiled, his eyes lingering on her mouth. He bent down, his mouth mere inches from hers. "You are a woman I am going to enjoy kissing," he said.

Her stomach muscles clenched and her breath hitched. Oh, how she wanted him to do just that—

"But not today," he said as he straightened and took her arm to lead her back to the carriage. "I intend to show you every respect I can."

Fiona tried not to let the disappointment show. She did not understand these new feelings of desire that Christian brought out in her. She should be grateful he was gentlemanly enough to care about her virtue.

But, somehow, that did not make up for not being kissed again.

Chapter Three

Christian eased the pirogue alongside the dock on Grand Terre and nimbly jumped off, securing the line to a cleat before he proceeded up to the house where he knew Jean waited. Probably not very patiently, either, for the Boss hated not being able to walk openly in New Orleans any longer. As Christian climbed the steps to the porch, he cursed the ex-lieutenant, again for sinking the American merchantman in the Gulf. Jean had strict rules never to attack an American ship. Prior to that incident, Governor Claiborne's attempts to break Jean's stronghold had been merely threats…he had no grounds to find that a crime had ever been committed. The governor had been like a terrier worrying a bone ever since.

Still, Christian was surprised to see Jean's three other lieutenants, along with his banker waiting in the study where a refreshing breeze from the Gulf blew through the open French doors. From the frowns on their faces, he had a feeling there was bad news.

"What's wrong?" he asked as Dominique You handed him a snifter of brandy.

Jean shuffled some papers from his desk. "I have had a visit from the British," he said.

Startled, Christian almost dropped his glass. "The British are *here*? So soon? New Orleans is not prepared—" He stopped when Jean held up a hand.

"Only one English brig, the *HMS Sophia*. I had the *privilege* of entertaining her captain and two of his naval officers for breakfast and lunch," Jean replied.

"*Mon Dieu*! Why?"

Jean picked up one of the papers. "This is a letter from the commander of the English forces. It *asks* that all Louisianians of French, Spanish or British blood join with the English to fight the Americans. That the English are only at war with Americans. However, if we do not comply, we will be attacked by Her Majesty's ships and the Indians will go back on the warpath." He laid the letter down and picked up another. "This one is addressed to me as "Commandant of Barataria"—it offers me a position as a captain in the British Navy and more land than I already own…as well as thirty thousand dollars once the war is won." He pointed to a third piece of paper. "That one *requests* that my men guide the British throughout Barataria. I am to meet their captain aboard the *HMS Hermes* in Pensacola once this is done. And this one," he said as he slid a fourth paper toward Christian, "kindly states that if I refuse, the British will destroy Barataria."

"We can defend the pass by putting men on both Grand Isle and here," Christian said. "The British must have seen how narrow that pass is."

"Perhaps. But the British have plans to sail up the Mississippi directly to New Orleans. We cannot defend the whole delta. There are too many passes and we are quite outnumbered."

"What are the numbers?" Christian asked.

"Fifty ships," Jean-Baptiste answered, "and the English are twelve thousand strong."

Stunned, Christian set his sniffer down. "And

they're as close as Florida?"

"Yes," Nez Coupé replied, his scarred face with its half-nose taking on a sinister look. "There's more. The damn *batards* are not going to stop at New Orleans. They mean to conquer the entire United States by sailing up the river."

"They would be sitting ducks, doing that," Christian said with a laugh. "Troops on the banks could fire on them at will."

"Remember that most Indians are willing to fight *against* the Americans, who have taken their lands," Dominque replied, looking as grim as Nez. "The redcoats are planning to free the slaves, as well. Free Negros willing to fight their former owners would keep everyone off the riverbanks."

Christian turned to Jean. "What are we going to do?"

"What we are *not* going to do is assist the British, although I have told them I need time to think about it. I have written two letters. One goes to John Blanque, requesting his assistance."

Christian nodded. Blanque was a Creole legislator and friend of Jean's. "And the other?"

Jean smiled wryly. "Blanque will deliver it to Governor Claiborne. I am going to offer him my ships and the services of my men, including myself."

"You will be hanged! The man hates you."

"Does he hate me enough to give up New Orleans? Jean-Baptiste tells me the governor petitioned one of the generals for troops but was told hel could only spare seven hundred to defend New Orleans."

"Against the twelve thousand English," Nez added.

"There has been a rumor that General Jackson won his battle with the Indians at Mobile and that he might come," Jean-Baptiste said, "but can we count on it? And if he does not arrive in time, it will not matter. I think we have a chance with the governor."

"With your help," Jean said, "and that of the governor's niece."

Christian had a sinking feeling in the pit of his stomach. He knew the reason Jean had picked Andre, Marc, and himself to be his eyes and ears in New Orleans. None of them could be directly tied to working with Jean. And Christian knew, too, why Jean had chosen him to gain Fiona's trust. Andre was too much a charmer and a Yank wench would be suspicious of the flattery Southern women accepted as their due. Marc had not the patience or inclination to play the wooing game. So it was up to him to use Fiona and find a way to get Pierre out of the calaboose. And now this.

"You have met her?" Jean asked.

"*Oui*. I made her acquaintance on the veranda at the ball. Stole a kiss and vanished, just as we planned." He remembered how soft and surprisingly pliant Fiona's lips had been under his, for that brief moment.

"Works nearly every time. A bit of flattery, a bold move, and then a step back before the lady feels threatened," Jean said as the men all grinned, "and leaving her to wonder what might have been."

"Women are contradictions in logic." one of the lieutenants who had not taken part in the previous conversation said. "They have no interest in bedding with a man who pays them court and plays by the rules Society sets. Yet if a man simply *takes* a kiss, without asking and without apologizing, and *leaves,* the woman wants *more*. She will deny it, of course, but she will also be gasping for breath…wanting *more*."

"Well, if anyone has experience in playing the rogue, it is you," Nez answered and clapped his friend on the back. "How many bedroom windows have you had to jump out of? It's a good thing dueling is outlawed, or you'd be meeting irate husbands at *Place d'Armes* most mornings."

René shrugged. "It puts some spice into my life, *non*?" He looked at Christian. "And it should work doubly well with this Irish female. She's a bit plain and not too graceful, from all accounts. Probably not a woman men pay much attention to in the first place."

Christian felt his jaw clench. He might have thought Fiona rather ordinary when he first glimpsed her, and maybe even a bit awkward, but in talking to her at the park, he also found a young woman who knew her mind and was not afraid to speak it. And…he really *had* wanted to kiss her in the gazebo, even if his first intention had been to tease and withdraw to gain her interest. The steady, straightforward look in her brilliant green eyes had stirred something in him. Yet…this was an assignment. No more than that. He forced himself to relax his jaw and smile nonchalantly.

"I met her in the park yesterday," he said, "and we have a rendezvous tomorrow."

Jean raised an eyebrow. "Very good. Is Mrs. Claiborne her chaperone?"

The men all laughed at that. Christian knew that Jean had once actually met the governor's wife after a price had been put upon his head. The quick-witted Creole lady whose plantation he was visiting when Mrs. Claiborne came to call shooed all the servants away except for a trusted Negress and introduced Jean as "Mr. Clement." And to Jean's delight, Mrs. Claiborne had spread word among Society that she had met the most brilliant, charming, and fascinating Frenchman on her visit.

"*Non*," Christian said. "Her chaperone is her brother, a young lad of six and ten, who happens to have the sense to recognize good horseflesh when he sees it. I suspect Jupiter will keep him quite entertained during future meetings."

"Even better," Dominique replied with a chuckle. "Old enough to escort his sister but young enough not to be aware of your intentions."

Christian wasn't sure he liked the sound of that either. He had no wish to dupe the boy, but he had to gather any information he could about the governor's plans regarding Pierre.

As if reading his thoughts—a skill Lafitte seemed to have—Jean spoke quietly, quelling all laughter. "If the governor turns down my offer of assistance, he may very well proceed with Pierre's hanging. So far, the citizens of New Orleans have fond memories of the good that the Lafitte brothers have done, and the governor knows it. But if twisted word of this British offer gets out, the winds of Fate may blow from another direction. Time is of the essence, I fear. Do whatever you must, Christian."

He straightened his shoulders. "I will not let you down. You can count on me."

But as he rowed the pirogue back through the bayous later that afternoon, Christian wondered what the final cost of this assignment was really going to be.

Chapter Four

"I do not understand why this Mr. Picard cannot pay you proper court," Cory said as he drew the cabriolet to a halt by the park's entrance. "If Aunt gets wind of this—"

"We are simply going for a drive," Fiona interrupted. "Aunt can hardly object when she has been trying to get me to be more social. It is perfectly proper to visit the park, especially since my brother is my chaperone."

"Perhaps I should actually accompany you into the garden this time," Cory said darkly.

"And who would watch the horses?" Fiona countered swiftly. "I doubt Mr. Picard would want to keep that magnificent horse of his tethered to a pole unwatched."

Cory's eyes lit up. "That is some horseflesh! Do you think Mr. Picard might actually let me ride Jupiter sometime?"

Fiona smiled. "Perhaps. But first you need to prove to him that you are responsible around animals. He *did* entrust you with Jupiter last time."

"Aunt is entrusting your safety with me," Cory said stubbornly.

From the look on his face, Fiona could tell he was warring with himself. The boy in him really wanted to stay with the horse. But her little brother was nearly a man, too.

She patted his hand. "I will be fine. I hardly need a bodyguard for a stroll through garden paths in broad daylight."

"I still do not see why Mr. Picard cannot call on you at the house."

"I explained that. He had to defend a lady and dueling is illegal. Uncle William would not approve. He might even have Mr. Picard arrested, and then what would happen to Jupiter?"

Cory looked like he was about to argue the point. Fiona sighed. She had considered asking Uncle William about duels and perhaps bringing up the one that Christian had been involved in, but she decided it was too risky. Over the past two days she had spent hours thinking about Christian, remembering his first kiss and how close he had come to kissing her in the gazebo. Her body tingled at the thought, her nipples pebbling, and she felt a strange new throbbing between her legs. She did not know why her body reacted like that, but it was much too pleasant a sensation to not want to experience it again. If the governor even suspected she was meeting Chrisitan, she was quite sure her social drives would be over.

Luckily, Christian's arrival, in a flurry of gravel as he pulled his horse to a stop beside their carriage, halted any argument that Cory was about to make. His eyes were riveted on Jupiter.

"You mentioned your brother would like to raise horses some day?" Christian asked as he and Fiona entered the gazebo and sat on the bench.

"It is just a silly dream that he and I had, growing up," Fiona replied.

26

"You had the same dream?"

"I love horses and riding," she answered.

"And I will wager you prefer to ride astride rather than with a proper sidesaddle?"

Fiona felt herself blush. She looked down at the floor and nodded. "Just another thing that makes me odd."

Christian slipped his hand under her chin and tilted it up. "I told you before that I do not think you are odd. Frankly, I do not see how a female stays on a horse all unbalanced like that." He smiled, his dark eyes looking deeply into hers, and let his thumb follow the curve of her lower lip before he dropped his hand. "That makes you a very intelligent lady, in my book. Be proud of who you are."

A different kind of warmth spread through her, beginning with the swell of her lip and washing over her, making her breasts feel suddenly heavy and full. His words, with his soft, low French accent, were music to her ears. He thought she was smart! And, better, he thought it was all right for her to be smart!

"Actually," he continued, apparently unaware of her physical reaction to him, "plantation owners are always looking for pure-blooded horses to race and hunt. I considered it myself once, but I am out to sea too much to oversee such an operation."

"That is the same thing my father said when Cory talked to him about it. Of course, we were in Boston then, and Cory was too young to handle it by himself. I offered to help, but he wouldn't hear of it. I think he still has hopes that someday I will act like a lady. At any rate," she said, changing the subject before she blathered on about her failure to please her father, "you promised to tell me about pirates. Jean Lafitte, in particular."

"So I did." Christian eased back, stretching his long legs out in front of him and crossing his feet. "To begin, you have to understand that the area between New Orleans and the open waters of the Gulf is treacherous, filled with swamps and bayous that are home to gators and water moccasins. Streams curve around mud flats and *chênières*—islands of white shells and oak trees— and what appears to be solid ground, if stepped upon, can suck the unwary into a bog of quicksand. The swamps are a haze of blue-green mist. But men have managed to live in what we call 'the trembling prairie' for years."

"Why? Because they are criminals?" Fiona asked.

Christian shrugged. "Some are. Some may be fugitives for other reasons. Still others prefer the solitude. Regardless, though, all men need to make a living, and many of them sign on as crew for the captains of the brigantines, caravels, and galleys that pass through here. Trade with the Caribbean is brisk and profitable."

"Slave trade, you mean? You know, we do not favor such in the North."

"The North does not have hundreds of acres of cotton needing to be picked, either," Christian said with a smile. "The very backbone of the South would break if slave ownership was not allowed. However, there is a trade market for many other things as well, such as French silks and imported wines, along with the fine china and crystal you see in the governor's mansion. Those things were not made here."

"You are saying that all this trade is legitimate?"

"I do not know about all of it," Christian said, "but with Napoleon's war, much of the goods New Orleans wanted were no longer available. And what did come through the English blockades was priced so high few could afford the luxuries, especially after the United States taxed the imports as well."

"But the States have the right to tax imports. It is illegal not to do so."

Christian smiled again. "You forget, *chèrie*, that most of New Orleans does not consider itself *American*, even if Louisiana recently became a state. French culture is ensconced in our blood. When Jean and his brother, Pierre, arrived here several years ago, they understood the need to restore the luxuries the Creoles were accustomed to having."

"Uncle William says it is not right that auctions of untaxed goods are held at some place in the swamps called the Temple. He says Jean Lafitte is holding them."

"He did in the past. By not sailing all the way into New Orleans, he could make the argument that the goods were not on American *soil* and avoid the customs taxes. Plantation owners and businessmen alike were delighted that prices became more affordable at these auctions. It might surprise you to know that many of the leading dignitaries of New Orleans attended them. I've been told it was quite the social thing to do."

Fiona tilted her head to one side, studying Christian. "So you are saying the Lafittes were well liked by the citizens?"

"Very much so. Let me tell you the story of what happened when a young seaman named William tried to blame the Lafittes for piracy."

Fiona turned slightly, tucking her legs up under her and smoothing her skirt. Christian quirked a grin at her. "I know this a totally improper way for a lady to sit," she said, "but whenever my father tells me a story, this is how I sit. Do you mind?"

His grin widened. "Not at all. You can be as improper around me as you like."

Fiona felt her face heat. "I did not mean—"

He shushed her. "Nor did I. I like to tease you to see you blush. It is most becoming. But, at any rate, I want you to be comfortable with me. You do not need to heed all of Society's little proprieties if you do not want to."

Her eyes traveled to his full, sensual mouth before she could think *not* to look there. She really, *really* wanted to find out what another kiss would feel like…

"Fiona?"

She forced herself to look into his eyes. "Yes?"

"If you keep looking at me as though you would like to devour me, I may not be responsible for my actions."

This time her face flamed and she averted her face. "Dear God. I do not know what has gotten into me."

Christian took her hand and brushed a kiss across it before releasing it. "I think I do, but for now, perhaps I should continue with the story I was going to tell?"

"Yes, please," she whispered, not quite sure she could face him.

Christian didn't press her. "One Saturday night about two years ago, a young sailor named William was rescued when the *Independence,* an American merchantman returning from the African coast, was attacked by pirates as it made its way from Havana toward New Orleans. The Americans in the city blamed the Lafittes. In fact, your uncle met with William the next day, along with John Grymes, the district attorney, to see what could be done.

"That same afternoon, Jean and Pierre came into town, strolling quite publicly through the Basilica square, dressed as gentlemen, tipping their hats to the ladies. Some bold man stopped them and asked if they had heard an American ship had been attacked by pirates and that the lone survivor was at the governor's even as they spoke. Jean politely replied that he hoped they caught the scoundrels and continued on his way. Gossip spread quickly through the *Vieux Carré* that the Lafittes had incredible nerve, bravery, and courage to appear on the streets when they had been accused of such treachery. Just as quickly, the Creoles decided the Lafittes would never have done such a thing. They were honorable men, attacking only Spanish galleons under a Letter of Marque that made it legal, much to your uncle's dismay."

Fiona turned to him, forgetting her embarrassment as she listened to the tale. "What finally happened?"

"It seems that your uncle—or Mr. Grymes— realized the tension and loyalty building among the Creoles, and this was not a battle they wished to fight. The sailor disappeared, not to be heard from again." Christian shrugged. "And the auctions continued."

"Until Pierre Lafitte got arrested for piracy."

"Perhaps it was a foolish thing for him to be walking about the old square in front of the cathedral. He was easy prey for soldiers to surround." Christian paused. "Or, perhaps, he was innocent of the charges and refused to be cowed into submission."

Fiona frowned. "Uncle William says Pierre Lafitte can rot in jail."

"Is that what the governor plans for him then? No hanging?"

Fiona widened her eyes. "Hanging?"

Christian hesitated, as if to weigh his words carefully. "That can be the punishment. It would be a pity if the man were truly innocent."

"I wonder if my—" Fiona was interrupted by a sudden shout from her brother, calling her name.

Christian stood up and held out his hand. "It seems I have kept you too long from your very protective brother."

Fiona placed her hand in his, swinging her feet around as Christian helped her up. "Cory had better not have left Jupiter and the carriage unattended."

Christian peered around the foliage that surrounded the gazebo and laughed. "He is standing at the very edge of the garden, holding the reins of the team."

"We had better move quickly, then, before someone chases him away—or worse, recognizes the carriage and reports us to my aunt." She moved toward the opening in the railing.

Christian blocked her. "I think I would take that kiss from you first."

Fiona stared at him, trying not to notice how close his mouth was to hers. "What kiss?" she asked, her voice a little breathless.

"The one you were wanting before."

"I was not—" The rest of her feeble protest was lost as he drew her close against him and angled his mouth over hers, his warm lips firm yet caressingly soft as he nibbled first her upper lip and then drew her lower one gently between his teeth before placing a full kiss to both of them and releasing her, leaving her slightly dizzy from the experience. She caught her breath. "I really should not let you do this."

"Why not? Did you not like it?"

Her face warmed. "Of course I did."

Christian laughed. "So honest. And how

refreshing." He tilted her chin up. "If you like my kissing you, then why should you stop it? It pleasures both of us and brings no harm. What can be wrong with that?"

Looking into his dark, mesmerizing eyes, inhaling the male scent of him, feeling her body tingle in places that had never tingled before, Fiona could not, for the life of her, think of a single reason.

Chapter Five

"I must say, dear, that your attitude about attending tonight's ball is much more positive," her aunt said to Fiona as they entered the foyer of Edward Livingston's mansion.

"I think it is the fresh air I have been taking in the afternoons," Fiona replied, trying not to bobble her head to see if Christian was there. "I do enjoy being out of doors…I am even adapting to the heat."

"Yes, well, be sure you wear a bonnet." Her aunt peered at her. "You have such fair skin. You do not want to freckle."

Fiona almost snickered, but caught herself. She spent most of the time "out of doors" in the shade of the garden gazebo with Christian. But that was her secret…and Cory's.

Her brother had turned into quite an accomplice in her several-times-weekly forays to the park. On the second visit, Christian had asked Cory to exercise Jupiter while they strolled. Cory could not believe his luck. He was most happy to ride about for an hour, leaving Fiona to enjoy Christian's company.

Fiona blushed, remembering the intensity of the last kiss. She'd had no idea of how velvety soft a man's tongue could be, or that it would feel so good exploring her mouth. Next time, she was going to be bold enough to return the favor. Since he had not mentioned the next date to meet—the pleasure of kissing being interrupted by another couple approaching the gazebo—she could hardly wait to see Christian tonight to find out when. And maybe—she looked to the outside wall of the ballroom… Yes! French doors opened onto a veranda here also—maybe they might be able to slip out there a bit later!

"Edward and his wife are such good friends of William and me," her aunt said as they moved through the receiving line. "Since you lived in Boston, did you know that his brother helped draft the Declaration of Independence?"

Fiona plastered a smile on her face. "I do not recall, but it sounds interesting." She tried not to swivel her head too much, but the room was crowded and she had not spotted Christian. Surely, he would attend. She had told him she would be here. He always seemed interested in her personal life and asked so many questions about both her uncle and her father. He told her each time they met how much he enjoyed her company. She even envisioned attempting to dance with him. The thought of his arms around her sent shivers up her spine despite the warm air. She scoured the room once more with her gaze but did not see him or either of his friends either.

Her aunt introduced her to the Livingstons, and she murmured something appropriate, but when her aunt stopped to talk with another friend a short time later, Fiona excused herself. She could not very well hide behind another potted plant if she wanted Christian to find her, so she wandered over to the punch bowl. Holding a cup would give her the excuse of refusing to dance…that is, if any of these immature boys were foolish enough to ask. Luckily, the musicians were taking a break, and the bevy of giggling girls followed Caroline into the powder room.

Fiona recognized John Grymes, the district attorney, as he strode through the wide foyer and into the ballroom without waiting to be announced. He had paid several calls to Uncle William, which usually resulted in her uncle calling for a brandy when he left. Mr. Grymes was Mr. Livingston's law partner, so perhaps he did not stand on protocol here. But then a hush fell over the room as he said something to Livingston.

"Pierre Lafitte has escaped?" Livingston asked into the silence.

Before Grymes could reply, Governor Claiborne was shouldering his way through the crowd. Fiona didn't think she had ever seen him so pale…or so angry, if the way his jaw was set and his eyes had become glittering slits was any indication.

"How could he escape?" her uncle demanded when he reached the pair. "He has been in chains the entire time. Chains which are attached to the wall!"

"They were cut," Grymes replied.

"What of the jailers? There were to be three guarding that cell at all times."

Grymes shrugged. "They have disappeared. The jailer arriving for duty found an empty cell. Two empty cells, actually. Three Negroes escaped also."

Her uncle's face went from pale to flushed and then paled again. "It's Jean Lafitte's doing. It is just like him to let those slaves go, to rub my nose in the dirt."

"We cannot be sure of that," Grymes answered. "There is no proof."

"Proof! Just go to Grand Terre! You'll find the whole thieving band of pirates there, including Pierre, no doubt laughing at my expense."

Mrs. Claiborne approached the trio and their voices subsided, even as a general buzz rose about the room. Two gray-haired matrons standing close to Fiona nodded their heads sagely.

"Governor Claiborne is quite put out," one of them said.

The other nodded. "It all goes back to last year when the governor sent that revenue officer and the dragoons to capture the Lafittes, but they fought them off and vanished into the swamps."

"Almost like will-o'wisps," the first one said with a smile. "Some say they are protected by a voodoo queen."

The second one sniffed. "Those quadroon sisters may live in sin with Jean and Pierre Lafitte, but I doubt they know anything about voodoo. Most likely it's gold pressed into palms of men that keep the brothers protected."

"Well," the first one said practically, "the governor offered a five-hundred-dollar reward for the capture of Jean Lafitte, and that did not seem to help."

"And what did Mr. Lafitte do? Took down all the posters in the middle of the night and replaced them with offers of fifteen hundred dollars for anyone who would capture the governor and take him to Grand Terre!"

The ladies both laughed at that and moved away, still talking. Fiona frowned. Was that why her uncle was so determined to rid Barataria of the men who lived there? From what Christian had told her, the Lafittes had never attacked an American ship and the *Dorada* was free to come and go without interference, as were other ships.

The musicians were back, striking up a cotillion for

their last set. Fiona looked around the ballroom again, hoping to see Christian's dark head, but he was not there. The ball was nearly over. Disappointed, she walked out on the veranda and inhaled the sweet fragrance of magnolias. They reminded her of the trees near the gazebo where she and Christian had been meeting. In spite of the warm night, a little shiver went up her spine that had nothing to do with the air around her, and everything to do with remembering his kisses and caresses. No man had ever made her feel attractive and feminine before. She sighed.

Where in the world was he? Why had he not come?

****

Christian swirled the brandy in his snifter and watched as Dominique, Nez, and Beluche all clapped Pierre on the back, chortling about what a coup they had managed. The smell of roasting boar mingled with a sugary-cinnamon scent coming from some concoction that Jean's chef was preparing to welcome Pierre back to Grand Terre.

"You did a fine job," Jean said as he joined Christian near the window looking over the dark waters of the bay. "I am in your debt for getting Pierre out."

"You should have seen him," Pierre said. "Walked right in and asked the guards if they would like to leave New Orleans before the British arrived. Said he had barely outrun the English brigs bringing his ship in…they were coming up the river. *Sacrébleu*! He almost had me believing the story! Said with the governor and every important dignitary at Livingston's ball tonight, it would be easy for the British to lay claim to New Orleans without firing a cannon."

"A piece of information you got from the bit of fluff

you've been romancing," Beluche said with a laugh. "Have you bedded her yet? Women talk even more once they've spread their legs for you."

Christian felt a muscle twitch in his jaw. He had been reporting to Jean whatever pieces of information he could glean from Fiona about Pierre's fate, any strengthening of forces that the governor might use to attack Barataria, and even what her father's—which also meant Commodore Patterson's—orders were, as far as she might know. He also felt guilty in using her because he had actually come to look forward to their visits. She was honest, forthright, and intelligent…and learning to respond quite nicely to his kisses. It had been a long time since he had been with anyone quite so innocent.

"The girl's a virgin. I see no need to ravage her."

Jean lifted an eyebrow slightly and studied him. Christian hoped Jean was not about to ask if he was developing feelings toward the girl. He was not. Privateering was a dangerous career, albeit a lucrative one. When he was on the high seas pursuing a Spanish galleon, he needed every bit of his attention focused on that, not thinking about some woman waiting for him. Andre, Marc, and he had all agreed on that point. Better to enjoy an experienced woman or a lonely widow than to become an unwilling victim of the parson's noose. Not that he hadn't wondered how Fiona would respond, lying naked under him in a soft bed. Hell, he was a man. Still, he would hold himself in check.

"I need more information from her," Jean said, looking at him steadily. "I have not had any response from the letter that Blanque delivered to Claiborne."

Christian held his gaze. "I do not think she knows about that."

"Probably not. He would be a fool to turn down my men, ships, and supplies when so little help is coming from the government. All I ask in return is pardons for all of us."

"Even though the crimes we are accused of committing are falsehoods," Nez added. "The *batard* should be grateful we like Americans!"

"Too bad you cannot have another conversation with Mrs. Claiborne." Dominque laughed. "She could persuade her husband to agree to terms."

Jean smiled. "I had already given that some thought, but it is too risky right now to have even 'Mr. Clement' make an appearance." He turned back to Christian. "If you present the story right, perhaps your…friend…might be able to persuade her aunt to speak to the governor about New Orleans' lack of defense."

"I will talk with Fiona about it," Christian answered.

Beluche gave a half-snort. "Talk? What woman understands war? I tell you, it is easier to persuade one to do your bidding once she's had the pleasure of—"

"Enough." Jean held up his hand to silence his lieutenant. "I have faith in Christian. He will do what needs to be done. *Non, mon ami?*"

Christian took a deep breath. "*Oui. Je comprends.* You will have your information." He slanted a look at Beluche as he left. "I'll do it my way."

****

Fiona forced herself to keep her hands folded demurely in her lap two days later when the rain from a sudden storm finally stopped and it was pleasant enough to take the carriage to the park. She did not want Cory to realize how nervous she was. Would Christian be there?

Since the night of the ball, she'd had no word from him. She knew he could not call at the house. There was still the pending matter of a duel having been fought, although she could not remember Uncle William mentioning it. Then she chided herself for making excuses. Yet, like a silly schoolgirl, she had hoped for some message. She was as foolishly romantic as those sausage-curled debutantes who giggled and batted their eyelashes. Maybe worse. A woman of twenty years ought to have more sense. And she did. Common sense had always been one of her strengths. It helped combat the fact that she was not pretty and petite, with dainty little feet and hands, or that her hair was not soft, golden curls but rather a wild mane of orange copper. But somehow, Christian made her forget those things by the way he looked at her, his gaze intense and never leaving her face to stray to other women who strolled along the garden paths…the way his warm, strong fingers caressed her cheek or arm, brushing just close enough to make her nipples pebble and her breasts ache. Yet his hand did not stray there, and she found herself wishing it would. A blush crept over her—she could feel the heat of it. When had her thoughts turned so utterly wanton and loose?

"I do not see Jupiter," Cory said as he slowed the cabriolet near the park's entrance.

Her hands clenched tighter and she managed to keep her voice neutral. "Why don't we ride the road around the park, then? The sunshine is welcome after that endless downpour." Humid and damp, she really wanted to say, but at least the stifling heat of summer had passed into early autumn. Or what substituted for autumn in a place where everything stayed green year round.

They had made a half-circle around the park when

the thundering of hooves came up behind them. Turning, she nearly wept as relief flooded through her. Christian! She felt slightly giddy at the sight of him, and even lightheaded when he dismounted and gave Jupiter's reins to Cory before climbing onto the bench next to her in the small carriage. His bulk took up most of the seat, his thigh pressed against her skirts, his arm against hers, just the slightest brush of coat fabric grazing the side of her breast. Her breath hitched.

"My apologies for not attending the ball," Christian said as he tapped the reins to the carriage horse and they ambled on. "I had to take care of some business. And then the blasted rain for two days!" He glanced over at her, his dark gaze intense. "I missed you."

She could lose herself in the depth of his eyes. They were a deep color of chestnut, appearing almost black in contrast to the dark auburn streaks in his hair.

A corner of his mouth quirked up in that endearing half-grin. "You are staring."

Fiona blinked, bringing the world back into focus. "I am sorry—"

"Do not be," he said as the quirk widened into a grin. "I rather like the attention."

She felt her face heat again. What was it about this man? "Well, you missed some real excitement."

"Oh? What happened?"

"Pierre Lafitte escaped from jail! Mr. Grymes brought the news to Mr. Livingston. It was quite the gossip for the rest of the night."

"I can imagine," Christian replied. "What did your uncle say?"

"He was furious. He is sure Jean Lafitte is behind the escape and that both brothers are at some place called

Grand Terre. Do you know where it is?"

"Every sailing captain does," Christian answered as he maneuvered the carriage around a small group of boys playing in the path. "There is a pass between Grand Terre and Grand Isle that leads into Barataria Bay. It is a more direct way of getting to New Orleans than sailing the river with its currents and twists and turns. Faster, that is, if you know the way. The swamps can be treacherous." He glanced down at her again. "So what effort is being made to find the Lafittes?"

"Uncle William met with the Collector of Customs yesterday. They are sending a dozen men down there."

Christian raised an eyebrow. "A dozen men? It's rumored there are more than a thousand men living in Barataria, none of whom are too fond of the government, let alone Customs inspectors. Who is the brave man in charge of this?"

Fiona shrugged. "Some man named Stout. Uncle William says he has knowledge of the waterways and can surprise the Lafittes."

"Ummm." Christian said. "When is this supposed to happen? I do not want the *Dorada* getting caught in the middle of a skirmish."

"I am not sure. They were waiting for the rain to stop. Maybe tonight."

"I see." Christian brought the carriage to a halt as they made a full circle of the park. "In that case, I had better get down to the docks and tell the quartermaster we will stay in port one more day. The men won't mind an extra night of liberty."

Christian looked into her eyes again and then let his gaze travel to her mouth. He leaned slightly toward her and Fiona parted her lips slightly, her body beginning to tingle in anticipation of his kiss. But he stopped and took her hand instead, brushing a kiss over her knuckles. "Unfortunately, the day's delay in departure means I am going to have to redo charts and calculations, so I will not be able to come here tomorrow. Could we meet the day after, about this time?"

"I am sure I can arrange that," Fiona murmured, aware that he still held her hand.

Christian grinned as Cory rode up on Jupiter. "Until then…and next time we will return to the gazebo where I can give you a very thorough kiss."

That thought stayed with Fiona as Cory drove her home. She much preferred the gazebo herself, and next time, she might just surprise Christian with a very thorough kiss of her own.

Chapter Six

It rained for almost a week, thanks to a late season storm in the Gulf. Fiona alternately cursed under her breath—her father would probably be shocked and her aunt would swoon that she even knew such words—and paced the floor of her room with frustration. Getting out in the buggy, even a covered one, was out of the question. Uncle William had been in such a foul temper the past few days she dared not even risk asking a groomsman to prepare a carriage.

And she knew why. Three days after the Customs collector sent Stout and his men to Grand Terre, a bedraggled youth who had accompanied the party came back with a message from Jean Lafitte. He was sorry, he said, that the group had chosen to fight the Baratarians, but unfortunately, Stout had been killed and the rest of the troops were now "guests" at the Temple.

Prisoners in the slave stockades, or so her uncle had raged.

Fiona sighed, looking out at the gray drizzle that dripped down the glass panes and made everything smell mildewed. The governor had appealed to the state, and this time a heavily armed militia was organized to go into the swamps once more. None had returned and no message came. Her uncle was fit to be tied.

And so was she. Fiona hurled another epithet at the miserable weather and turned away from the window.

Christian had ridden by the mansion the day after they were to have met; in fact, he and Jupiter had huddled across the street, the horse's head hanging down to avoid the worst of the rain, but Christian had let it wash down his face, his chestnut hair plastered to his head. When she had appeared at the window, he grinned, made a gesture with his fingers of rain falling and then opened his arms wide to express the sun and pointed in the direction of the park, indicating they would meet once it stopped raining.

Or at least that's what she though he meant. Was the *Dorada* still in port?

Christian had told her he needed to make a run to the Florida panhandle, but he was probably waiting for better weather.

The rain finally thinned to a soft mist two evenings later, as they sat down to dinner. "I do not think I will ever welcome sunshine as much as I will tomorrow morning," Fiona said to Cory as they took their seats.

He gave her a conspiratorial glance. "It should be a fine day for a carriage ride. I'm sure the horses need exercise."

"Too muddy," her uncle said. "The buggy will get mired down."

Damnation! Fiona managed to refrain from saying it by biting her cheek. Christian would be expecting her in the park. She almost missed what her uncle was saying except that Cory's laugh had been turned quickly into a cough. Her uncle narrowed his eyes at her brother.

"You think it funny that the militia returned without the Lafittes?"

The pirates again. Did her uncle think of nothing but defeating them? And why was it so personal to him anyway? But Fiona did not like the way he was looking at Cory. "Was anyone hurt this time?" she asked.

Her aunt tried to give her a warning look, but it was too late. Her uncle's face turned a bright shade of pink. "No," he sputtered, "not this time. The whole dam—the entire militia returned, whole and hearty. Not only that, but that dam—the pirate loaded them down with expensive gifts and wine! The dam—the whole lot of them have nothing better to say than that they were feasted beyond belief. Even Stout's men came back."

"Dear, do not get so upset," Mrs. Claiborne said. "You know it is not good for your digestion."

The governor took a deep breath. "That pirate is making a laughingstock out of me! One of the French newspapers even mentioned the incident this morning!" He put his napkin down. "But do not worry, my love. I have already planned my revenge."

Fiona's aunt looked wary. "What is it?"

"I have ordered Commodore Patterson to take the schooner *Carolina*, along with six gunboats, to Barataria Pass. Colonel Ross and his soldiers will accompany them. They are to demolish and destroy everything on Grand Terre and Grand Isle. I will be rid of those pirates once and for all, and God help any other ship that gets in our way!"

Fiona stared at him. The *Dorada* was to sail through that pass. She did not care what happened to these pirates that her uncle hated, but she had to warn Christian not to sail. She kept her eyes averted, lest her uncle see the determination in them, but her chin lifted. Just before dawn broke, once all the drunks were passed out and her relatives still asleep, she would make her way to the docks and find Christian.

****

Christian poured the last of the Muscatel into Andre's glass as Marc lifted his own in toast. "Jean did it again. Tweaked the governor's nose by sending his own men back laden with riches and singing the praises of such fine hospitality as is found on Grand Terre! *Bonne santé*!"

Christian raised his glass as he sank into the bolted-down armchair in the *Dorada's* main salon and looked around at the burnished teak paneling. Even the Customs collector did not know the ship was Jean's. "I just hope it was not too much of a trek this time," he said.

Andre paused, his glass half the way to his lips. "What have you heard?"

"Nothing. That is the problem. This storm has kept me from a rendezvous with Fiona for nearly a week. I have not been able to find out what her uncle's inclinations are."

Marc frowned. "There is no way you can send a message for her to meet you elsewhere? The shop on Rue Royal, perhaps?"

"I tried. The day we were to meet, I sat in the rain until she appeared at her window and I signaled to meet in the park when the rain ended. Two days later I tried again, only to have the butler sent out—and not happy about getting wet, either—to inquire why I was loitering on RueToulouse."

Andre nodded. "With Pierre's escape, the governor will be itching to put anyone he thinks might be connected to Jean in the calaboose. The *Dorada* has made some lucrative runs."

"But that does not prove Christian is linked to Jean," Marc said.

"True. But the men on Claiborne's Grand Jury who swore false witness statements about piracy can just as easily point fingers at *us*. The *Dorada* sails through that pass unmolested," Andre replied.

"And she was supposed to sail three days ago," Christian added. "Now that the wind is down, I plan to leave at daybreak."

"You cannot hold off another day in order to meet Claiborne's niece?" Marc asked.

Christian shook his head. "The Cuban slaves are already in Florida. Slavers will not hold them for long. They are probably already on half-rations. Time is of importance."

His thoughts went to Fiona. Aside from needing information about her uncle, he had missed their little interludes. He found it refreshing to be with a woman who was bluntly honest and his slow, tantalizing teasing of her senses into sexual awareness was rapidly becoming a game that he truly enjoyed playing. In all of his experiences, he did not recall any female ever having been a virgin when she came to his bed. Nor had any been so instinctively responsive as Fiona. She melted into his arms, her curves fitting perfectly against him, her body pliant and willing, her mouth soft and open, allowing him to taste her, mewling so softly that he almost did not hear it…

He set his glass down. "I can delay sailing by an hour and go to the governor's house just before daybreak. Her window is on the second floor, and there is a rose trellis along the wall that should hold my weight. I can be there and gone before the rest of the household is even awake."

Andre looked at Marc and grinned. "Do you think

he wants to obtain information or to see the flame-haired mademoiselle in her sheer night-rail?"

Marc chuckled. "Maybe both?"

Christian ignored both of them. They left soon after, deciding to make a last visit to a special quadroon house on Rue Bourbon before sailing in the morning. Christian almost envied them. He did not have time to visit his mistress, Chantal. And he was not sure he wanted to. Lately, she had been chiding him for his lack of attention. And truthfully, since he had met Fiona Chantal's attractiveness had begun to diminish. Yet he could hardly despoil Fiona, much as he might want to.

He tossed and turned, trying to get a few hours' sleep before he rode over to Rue Toulouse, but that effort was useless. He finally got up, washed with the cold water in his basin, and put on clean clothes.

Streaks of red slashed across a lightening lavender sky, forewarning of heavy weather. He tied Jupiter to a post half a block away and made his way on foot to the governor's home. He skirted the stables, shrank back into the shadows as a guard passed by, and then breathed a sigh of relief as he reached the side of the house and began climbing the trellis. Having climbed rope ladders to lash down sails in heaving seas, he found this child's play. Still, Christian was amazed at how nervous he felt. He almost laughed when he reached her window. There was a brick ledge, probably for putting out a plant or two, but sturdy enough that he could lean on it and actually look into her window.

Then he frowned. Her bed was empty and she was nowhere in sight.

Chapter Seven

Fiona breathed a sigh of relief when she saw the *Dorada* still docked at the quay in the breaking dawn. Part of the relief was also that she had made it to the docks safely. Slipping out the servants' entrance had not been hard, nor had staying in the shadows to get by the guard. But New Orleans was a place that did not rest. The bordellos on Rue Bourbon were still lit, and she had to dodge more than one drunk on Rue Decatur near the wharfs. She tried to smooth down the rough homespun of the servant's dress she had purloined from the laundry, hoping it was not stained or soiled. Taking a deep breath, she tightened the sunbonnet that nearly covered her face and made sure her unruly hair was tucked under it. Then she made her way to the gangplank.

"I have a message for the captain," she said to the crew member who stood watch.

He glanced over her plain, loose, gray dress. "Where do you work, wench?"

Fiona bit her lip to not retort. She was posing as a servant, after all. "The governor's house, sirrah." She swept a glance through her lowered lashes, hoping the "sirrah' would flatter him, but he still looked suspicious.

"Why would the govn'r send a message to Captain Picard?"

"The message is not from him, sirrah. It is from…Mademoiselle Gordon."

The watchman grinned. "The red-haired bit-of-fluff he's been dallying with?"

Fiona felt her face flame, glad that the bonnet covered most of it. Did his whole crew know about them? And...*bit of fluff*? Was *that* how he thought of her? She had a good mind to turn and walk away. Fiona forced herself to be logical. Christian needed to know what danger he might be sailing toward. She managed a shrug.

"'Tis not my business to know. She said she had a...warning to give him."

"Warning? I can pass on the message then."

Fiona shook her head. "She said to make sure the captain heard it from my lips."

She glanced up at him again. He seemed to be trying to decide whether to take the risk of turning her away or arguing the point.

Finally, he sighed. "The captain is not here. Out for a bit of sport with his officers, probably. I guess you could wait in the salon."

She followed him below decks, silently fuming. Christian was out for a bit of sport? She knew what that meant. Rue Bourbon was full of *sport*. She had been a silly chit of a girl to think she meant anything to Christian. He probably thought her incredibly naïve.

Glancing around the well-appointed room with its gleaming teak paneling, polished brass portholes, and luxurious thick Oriental carpet just confirmed her thoughts. Christian was used to elegance...and, no doubt, quite elegant, knowledgeable, and *experienced* women as well. She really had been a fool. Her Irish temper began to simmer.

Spying the bar with its brass fiddles and crystal

decanters settled securely in bored holes, she narrowed her eyes. It was way too early for a drink, but perhaps a dram of good Irish whiskey would make it easier to face him, since he probably thought her a fool. That is, if Christian had any whiskey.

He did not. Fiona sighed, opened a brandy decanter, and poured a generous amount into a rounded glass. She took a sip. It was surprisingly smooth. Perhaps just a dab more to make it a real drink…after all, Christian still needed to be warned, but she would give him a piece of her mind as well. And then she would leave this ship and forget about him.

Her hair was not red for nothing. No one was going to call her a *bit of fluff.*

****

Christian looked over at his friends as they made ready to cast off. Marc looked none the worse for wear, but Andre looked rumpled and needed a shave. No doubt he had just left some doxy's warm bed. Christian wondered if perhaps he should have gone to Chantal's instead of trying to see Fiona once more before he left. The throbbing in his groin would at least have been satisfied.

Where in the hell could she have been at that hour? He had waited nearly thirty minutes, clinging to the trellis, one knee on the planter ledge, hoping she had made a trip to the garderobe and that she would return. No such luck.

The sun had risen and the tide was ebbing, the river flowing faster toward the delta with it. It was time to leave. Dock-handlers uncleated lines, throwing them to the crew, who aptly caught and started coiling them. The *Dorada* eased away from the wharf, Marc at the helm,

Andre consulting the compass, while the boatswain shouted orders to raise sail. Christian tried to ignore the smug, satisfied looks on his friends' faces.

"Why ith the boat moofing?"

Fiona's voice startled him. He swung around, nearly colliding with a sailor hauling on the mainsail sheet, and stared. She wore a servant's dress, but her bright hair had come undone and strands fluttered in the breeze like flames encircling her head. She had a strange smile plastered on her face and seemed to be looking past him. Then she blinked and lurched toward him, nearly tripping.

He was beside her in an instant, gripping her arm. "Steady there! What are you doing on board?" He motioned to the boatswain. "Prepare to put in at Esplanade wharf. Mademoiselle Gordon needs to go home."

"Nof!" she said and stumbled against him. "Noth until I sthp…speak myth mind."

Christian sniffed. "Have you been *drinking*?"

Fiona glared at him. Or at least she tried to. It came out more like she was trying to focus on where he stood. "Jus' a wee dram." She held her fingers up, trying to show him, and promptly swayed in the other direction.

Still holding her arm, he asked again, "What are you doing on board, and why are you drunk?"

"I am noth drunk." Fiona made an attempt to stand up straight and remove his hand, but he was not budging. "I am noth a bith of fluff either!"

"What are you talking about?"

She wagged her finger crookedly at him. "You th…thought to use me!"

Damnation! How had she found out he was relaying

information to Jean? She looked mad enough to spit.

"I wi…will noth be used for sporth!"

Christian frowned. "Sporth?"

"Sporth." Fiona sighed deeply as though he were an imbecile. "Eth-p-o-r-t. Sporth."

"Sport?" Christian felt an odd little tinge of relief flow through him and then a bit of guilt as her meaning sunk in. "You think I am using you for *sport*?"

"Yesh. It's what your watchman said."

Christian was suddenly aware of the interested eyes and ears of his crew. Andre was grinning like an elf, and even Marc was having a hard time trying to hide a smile. He vowed silently he would be having a conversation with whichever watchman it had been…and soon.

"Captain." The boatswain interrupted his dark thoughts. "Esplanade Wharf is coming up."

"Go on by," Christian replied, ignoring the man's raised eyebrow. "Whatever the reason, it appears that Mademoiselle Gordon is completely foxed. I cannot have her escorted home to the governor in this condition. We will proceed to Barataria. She can be escorted back from there once she is…once she is quite herself again."

He turned to Fiona, intending to be stern, but she blinked slowly and then slumped against him, oblivious to the world.

****

Fiona awoke some time later to a pounding head and a room that rocked back and forth, both drawing an immediate protest from her stomach. She groaned and closed her eyes, opening them slowly. The ceiling still was moving.

"Do you frequently partake of spirits before the sun rises?" Christian asked.

She turned her head slowly on the pillow to see him sitting in a wing chair not far away, a brass porthole letting sunlight stream in. She realized now the motion was the gentle rocking of the ship. He must have put back in to the wharf. Fiona sat up slowly, squinting her eyes against the light, hoping her stomach would ease its roiling. She started to shake her head but stopped quickly. "No, of course not. I came to warn you."

Christian raised a brow. "About what?"

"My uncle...he is sending Commodore Patterson with several ships to invade Grand Terre. He said he is not going to let any other ship get in his way. I thought—"

"When is he going to do this?" Christian asked sharply.

"Today, I think. That's why I came down to the docks." She swung her feet over the edge of the bed and planted them on the floor. It seemed to ease some of the dizziness. "I have to get back to the house before they realize I am gone."

"Too late for that, I am afraid," Christian said. "You are already at Grand Terre."

"What?"

"You passed out, Fiona. I could not have you carried back to the governor's home in that condition. I had planned to have someone from here escort you back. If you can walk, and if we hurry, Jean may still be able to do that."

"Jean? As in Jean Lafitte?" Fiona asked.

Christian nodded. "This is his home. He is usually quite hospitable to visitors, but time is of the essence if what you say is true."

"It is true," Fiona replied, getting up to walk

gingerly to the cabin door.

Christian took a firm hold of her arm, steadying her as they made their way from the private dock along a caliche path that wound through cypress trees dripping with Spanish moss and wind-bent oaks. She almost gasped when she saw the house in front of her. "It is so big… I thought pirates lived in tents when they were not on their boats."

"Pirates might," Christian answered, "but I would advise you to think of the Lafittes as privateers. They prefer the term."

Fiona almost gasped at the elegance of the inside as they were shown through double mahogany doors, and across a tiled foyer hung with gilt-framed oils depicting ships at sea, to a library that had two walls lined with leather-bound books. A lush Aubusson carpet cushioned their footsteps, and a gleaming, crystal chandelier shed light on a highly polished mahogany Chippendale desk whose curved, cabriole legs terminated in claw-and-ball feet. Two comfortable-looking overstuffed wing chairs faced the desk. Across the way was a brass bar with a glass countertop, several decanters standing on top of it.

"Would you like a drink?" Christian asked teasingly.

Fiona wrinkled her nose at him, but before she could answer, the door opened and a tall, dark-haired, dark-eyed man entered. He was dressed simply in a white linen shirt—sleeves rolled up and collar open—and buff-colored breeches, with Hessian boots. Even so, the cut and quality of the material bespoke wealth. He moved with both authority and the grace of a panther…or a man used to commanding the rolling decks of a ship at sea.

His eyes swept over her appearance, and Fiona tried

not to fidget. She knew she looked a sight in the wrinkled homespun dress and with her hair a mat of riotous curls sticking in every direction. Not to mention she probably still reeked of brandy.

He bowed slightly. "I assume I am making the acquaintance of Mademoiselle Fiona Gordon, niece to the lovely Mrs. Claiborne?" His deep baritone voice, with a trace of French accent, was well modulated. "I am Jean Lafitte. To what do I owe the pleasure of your…er, visit?"

Fiona tried not to stare. *This* was Jean Lafitte? He looked like an elegant gentleman who would fit right in with the rest of New Orleans' Society. He certainly did *not* look like a pirate. Not that she knew any pirates.

She had just finished telling him what she'd told Christian when a rapid knock sounded at the door and, without waiting for permission, a harried-looking, somewhat cross-eyed man stormed in.

"What is it, Pierre?" Jean asked mildly. "We have guests…"

Pierre nodded briefly to Christian and spared not a glance for Fiona. "The watch just reported the *Carolina* approaching, and she's got six warships with her."

"We have no quarrel with the United States," Jean said.

"We may know that," his brother replied, "but it looks as though they do not feel the same way. The crew is at attention, ready to attack. Shall I order our cannons manned?"

Jean shook his head. "We will not fire on American ships." He glanced at Fiona and then at Christian. "Take a pirogue and get her away from here. I do not plan on shedding blood, but neither do I want her in the middle of it."

"I can take the *Dorada* back up river," Christian answered.

"No. I do not want them having any reason to give chase. Leave her tied. I pray this is all a misunderstanding and the commodore can be reasoned with. But if they find out the governor's niece is here, all wagers are off. Now *go*."

Fiona started to protest. "Perhaps I can negotiate—"

"*No*." Christian cut her off, taking her arm with one hand and using the other at her waist to all but carry her from the room. "Jean is right. If you are found here, there will be hell to pay."

She had no choice but to follow him in a direction away from his ship, toward swamp land. Christian was uncharacteristically quiet along the narrow, uneven, dirt path, lifting her up when she tripped and hurrying her along. He helped her into the small boat and poled away from the makeshift dock.

It was then that she heard the first cannon shot.

Chapter Eight

Mon Dieu! What was happening? Christian clenched his jaw and forced himself not to turn around and go back. If the Americans had actually *attacked*... But why? Jean was still awaiting an answer to his offer to *help* the damn governor. Christian had hoped that Fiona had somehow misunderstood the message. That perhaps the *Carolina* was sent as a blustering show of force, although it was not needed. Another cannon fired, and Christian gripped the oars harder. He should be there with his comrades. But Jean had given him orders, and he always expected his men to follow through. It took every ounce of his willpower to continue rowing into the swamp.

Fiona looked at him, wide-eyed. "Will the pirates fight back?"

"You heard Captain Lafitte say they would not."

"They will surrender, then?"

Christian would have laughed, had the situation not been so serious. "Doubtful."

"Then what—"

"These swamps and bayous are filled with places men can hide and not be found, especially by men who do not know the area. I doubt your uncle will be successful in his attempt." He tried to keep the bitterness out of his voice.

She seemed to consider this. Then, in a small voice,

she askcd, "What will become of your ship?"

He did not want to think about the *Dorada* being abandoned. If Jean chose not to stay and fight but to retreat into one of the many hide holes, the ship would fall into the hands of the Navy. Would they take her? Or burn her to the waterline? His jaw clenched again. The *Dorada* was his first command.

"I do not know. It depends on why your uncle ordered this foolishness in the first place." Even as he spoke, the first big splats of rain began to fall from skies that had turned leaden. He should have known, with the red sky that morning.

Fiona looked up as the rain began to fall in earnest. "Maybe this will put an end to the cannon's firing? Powder does not explode when wet, does it?"

"True. Hopefully, the shots were merely warnings and negotiations are under way." He dared to hope that, anyway, and then he cursed. Fiona had crossed her arms, hugging herself, as her dress grew damp. He had not thought to take a cloak in their haste to leave unseen.

"You are shivering," he said, stripping off his sea jacket and handing it to her. "Put this on."

"You will get soaked," Fiona said.

"Take it. I have been wet before." He tried not to notice how the sodden dress clung to her body, outlining the roundness of her breasts and nipples, already tight with cold. "No sense in you catching a fever."

She hesitated a moment more and then complied, slipping her arms through the sleeves and wrapping the oversized garment around herself. Still, she shivered in the autumn air. With a sigh, he pulled on the right oar, changing the pirogue's direction and heading into a narrow bayou.

"Why are you changing course?" she asked after a short time.

"We are going to have to stop," he answered. "It is several hours of rowing before I reach a village where a horse can be had. You will be sick by then." He maneuvered the boat through a clump of reeds and bumped it against a gritty shore of a *chênière* where mangrove roots jutted out.

Fiona pulled his coat tighter and looked through rain-drenched hair. "We are stopping here?"

"*Oui*. There is a shanty not far in."

She looked dubious. "Out here?"

"Remember I told you there are hundreds of places men can hide? Trust me. I grew up learning these waterways. There is shelter here." He secured a line to one of the roots and stepped out into shallow water.

Fiona stood shakily, but before she could put a foot into the water, she was scooped up in his arms and being carried through the mangled-looking shrubby trees. "I can walk."

"No need to get your feet wet too," Christian replied, thinking how good she felt in his arms. Reluctantly he put her down when they reached the door of the makeshift hut. Checking the inside quickly to make sure no other creatures had decided to seek shelter also, he ushered her inside.

"I will have a fire going in no time," he said as he set about stacking the dry wood that was always kept stocked inside for just such emergencies. "With any luck, there might be beans and rice in the cabinet. People who use these shelters usually keep them supplied." He opened the tinder box, struck a flint, and soon had a small fire started. Satisfied that it would soon be blazing, he stripped off his wet shirt, draped it over a rough-hewn stool, and began to loosen the laces to his breeches.

Fiona stared at him. "What are you doing?"

"Undressing. I suggest you do the same."

"What?"

His hands stilled as he looked at her, trying very hard not to grin. "You need to remove your clothing so it can dry." Even in the dim light of the fire, he could see she was blushing furiously and wondered if that flush would cover her entire body. He would love to find out. But then he sighed. Taking advantage of the situation was not something he should do. Turning his back, he said, "There are blankets on the cot. You can wrap yourself in one of those."

She did not answer, but he could hear the slosh of wet clothing being removed. For the second time that morning, it took every ounce of his willpower not to turn around. He could only imagine what a lovely sight she would make as she removed the dress, the petticoat, and finally, the chemise, leaving her naked… His groin tightened.

"Here." Fiona thrust her wet clothing at him and he turned around. Even fantasizing about her had left him unprepared for the tantalizing picture she made with the blanket wrapped around her but leaving her arms and shoulders bare.

Merde. How could he be expected to be a gentleman when she looked like that?

****

Jean stood on the shore of Grand Terre watching the *Carolina* and gunboats approach. Behind them came three barges, crammed with soldiers. He glanced over to where two of his brigs and a polacca, as well as the schooner *Lady of the Gulf*, were moored near the entrance of the harbor. He could see the crews were preparing for battle.

"Set the smoke signals," he said to Pierre. "I want no ship's captain to fire on the American flag."

Pierre gave the orders, and soon a series of small fires burned along the edge of the water. Jean watched as each vessel responded, raising the American flag, as well as the Carthaginian one. He nodded to Marc, who stood beside him. "Set the stack ablaze as well. The *Lady* will hoist the white."

Marc looked at him in surprise even as he gave the order to light their emergency signal. "We are going to surrender?"

"We are going to try to find out what they want," he replied grimly.

"It does not look like an acceptance of your offer to help Claiborne, does it?" Andre asked sardonically.

"I rather think not," Jean replied, still watching the action on board the *Carolina*. A cannon fired a warning shot into the water as crew on the *Carolina* hoisted a white flag of their own. Only this one read "Pardon to Deserters" in bold letters. At the same time, soldiers poured off the barges, wading ashore, muskets and bayonets at the ready.

"If we fire on them now, we can stop this," Marc said.

Jean glanced around once more. His men waited on him. If he lifted his hand and brought it down, the battle would begin. He had strength in men and arms, and his other boats were being readied behind the island, but who would win if he fired on what he still considered to be his countrymen? He hesitated but a split second more.

"No. I will not fire on an America ship. We are Americans, whether the damn governor believes it or not. Pierre, the seventh and fifteenth flags, please. The *Lady* will put out to sea if she can. Marc, get to the ships behind Grand Terre. Take them into the bayous. Andre, let the rest of the men know we are abandoning camp. *Now*," he said as all three of them looked shocked. "They will not find us in the swamps. It will give us time to regroup and for me to get a message to Grymes and Livingston."

He looked once more at the *Carolina* before he turned and walked away.

Governor Claiborne had not heard the end of Jean Lafitte just yet.

****

Fiona busied herself looking for foodstuffs in the small shanty. Anything was better than looking at the massive amount of muscle and sinew Christian was displaying. He had wrapped a towel around his loins, but it was not covering very much. How could a man who looked like he was chiseled out of bronze move so gracefully?

She pulled her blanket up again. It kept shifting, and now the rough wool was causing strange sensations on the tightened tips of her breasts.

"I do not think anyone left any food," she said, closing the last small cabinet door.

"It does not matter," Christian replied. "As soon as the rain stops, we will be on our way. You will be home by nightfall."

Fiona wondered what her uncle would do when he realized she was missing. She had fully expected to be back before breakfast was served. Now she would have to think of some excuse… She sneezed.

Christian quickly removed the other blanket from the bed and laid it in front of the fire. "Come and sit. You need to get warm." He sank down to the floor, criss-crossing his legs and hiking what seemed like an awfully small towel even farther up his torso. If he moved just a little…

Fiona eyed the fire instead. It *did* feel warm. She *was* shivering. Although the weather was not cold for mid-September, the damp that prevailed in Louisiana could be felt to her bones. She sidled toward him, holding the blanket tightly.

Christian grinned and held out a hand. "I will not bite."

Gingerly, she placed her hand in his. Instantly a heat swept through her that had nothing to do with the fire in the hearth. Warning bells, like fog buoys, were sounding in her head. This was probably not a good idea. Definitely not a good idea with him practically naked and her wearing nothing but a loose blanket. Her aunt, for certain, would swoon…but Fiona's common sense was being overcome by the strange, invisible pull her body was feeling. It was as though fog really was rolling over her brain, obscuring everything except the steadiness of the man holding her hand. She lowered herself to the floor.

He made a sound that sounded almost like a growl and withdrew his hand from hers and stared into the fire. "I think I know why you felt the need to warn me this morning, and I even understand how you managed to beguile your way past my guard, but why," he asked as he turned back to her with a quizzical look, "were you out all night drinking?"

She stared at him. "I was not out drinking."

His brow lifted. "You were drunk."

Fiona remembered then why she had been angry and pulled the sagging blanket up again, but not before his eyes followed her movement and lingered on her neckline. "You called me a bit of fluff!"

His eyes shifted in surprise to her face. "I what?"

"Your watchman said you *dallied* with the red-headed *bit-of-fluff* niece of the governor." She felt her cheeks grow hot, and that was not because of the fire either. "I cannot believe you *told* your crew. I know you were sporting with your officers, but I—"

"Wait just a minute." Chrisitan placed his fingers against her lips, silencing her. "First of all, I am going to have that watchman flogged the next time I see him. Secondly, I never told anyone anything about you. Why would I?"

"Oh! So now I am so unimportant that I am not worth mentioning?"

Christian shook his head as though to clear it. "I have a feeling I am going to lose this argument no matter what I say. *Chèrie*, please believe me when I say that I like you. I enjoy your company. I have enjoyed our visits in the park. You are very intelligent. You are forthright and honest. I respect—" He stopped. "Why are you crying?"

Fiona brushed at her cheek. "It is nothing."

Christian sighed. "Only a very foolish man would claim to understand how a woman thinks, but one thing I know for certain. When a woman says 'nothing' she very much means the opposite." He reached over to remove a tear at the corner of her eye with his thumb pad. "So tell me why you are crying."

"I…I am not." Fiona tried not to sniffle. "It is just that I…I thought…you kissed me a little…Oh, God!" She hugged her knees and turned her face away. "I was so incredibly stupid to think you found me attractive. I should have known—"

She didn't get to finish because Christian caught her chin and in one swift movement had pulled her toward him, wrapping her in his arms, and his mouth came down over hers, hard and demanding.

It took her breath away. This was no gentle, teasing kiss like the others had been. His mouth angled over hers, his lips hungrily taking what he wanted, devouring her. His hands came alongside her face, pressing against her jaw, opening her mouth to him. And then he thrust his tongue inside, filling her as he tasted her, forcing her tongue to do battle with his.

Fiona, lightheaded as though she were a small, rudderless skiff drifting on the swells of the ocean, felt his hands slide down over her shoulders and around her back, and then he was using them to rub her against him, using a circular motion that brought first one breast in contact with his massive chest and then the other. Somehow, the blanket fell away, and she was vaguely aware of her tight, aching nipples brushing against his smooth, taut skin. The friction was nearly unbearable, and yet she wanted more… But she could not think. His incessant, deliciously torturous kisses drove her senseless. Nothing penetrated her mind except the need to be even closer to him. Her arms wound around his neck and she buried her fingers in hair.

With a groan, he slipped his hand between them to cup and knead her breast. Her heart skipped a beat as she felt herself riding the crest of a huge wave building in her body. Christian broke the kiss suddenly and dipped his head, his hot mouth closing on her nipple and drawing deeply. Fiona gasped as she crested the internal wave and dropped into sheer weightlessness.

But the feeling built again as he suckled the other breast, this time sluicing through her belly to throb harshly between her legs like surf crashing upon shore. A wetness formed there, like water seeping through sand as the tide receded…and then it came flowing back with full force as Christian rolled her onto her back, spread her thighs wide with his hands, and buried his face between them.

His velvet, warm tongue lapped softly at the wetness, sending tremors down her legs until her toes curled. He circled her tiny nub delicately, almost lazily, and Fiona felt herself floating once more and yet more pressure was building, like a surge before a storm, building…rising…

Christian covered the throbbing little bud he had been teasing and sucked hard. The tidal wave crashed over Fiona, and she thrashed violently.

She lay panting, the spasms still rising and falling. When she could breathe normally again, she realized Christian was still positioned between her legs, his dark eyes watching her.

"Do you still think I don't want you?" he asked.

Fiona smiled. "I don't think I have ever felt more like a woman." It was true. Her breasts felt heavy and full, her body boneless, and there was still a delightful throbbing between her legs. Where Christian still was. Fiona frowned suddenly, raising onto her elbows. "Am I not supposed to do anything to you?"

Christian grinned, his fingers tracing a path along

her inner thigh. "What would you like to do?"

Fiona furrowed her brows, considering. "I think I would like to…touch your…well, it would seem only fair if I—"

This time he laughed as he slipped over to lie beside her. "I do not think I have ever seen a woman have such a serious expression on her face during this kind of discussion," he said as he brushed the back of his hand along the side of her breast. "But this is not a game of tit-for-tat. You do not—*ever*—have to do something you do not want to do."

She looked into his eyes. "But I want to." Fiona reached tentatively for his large, thick appendage, ripened to a rosy apple color. She stroked a finger down its length, marveling at how satiny soft the skin was over what felt like a steel rod. The whole length quivered at her, and her eyes widened. "It moves on its own!"

"*Oui*. It moves quite well on its own," Christian said as he lay back, one hand stroking her thigh as he watched her.

Fascinated, she circled the head lightly with a fingertip and it jutted against her hand. She almost giggled and then closed her hand around the shaft, soliciting a groan from Christian. Instinctively, she began sliding her hand up and down, amazed at how his erection seemed to grow even larger. A small bead of moisture appeared on the very tip. Intrigued, she wondered what it would taste like and then she bent down, licking the droplet off.

Christian growled, low in his throat, and she glanced up at him, but his eyes were closed, his face strained.

"Do you not like that?" she asked, beginning to raise up, but his hand slid along her back to hold her gently down.

"I like it very much, *chèrie*," he managed to say in a hoarse whisper.

Emboldened, Fiona slipped a hand down to cup his heavy sac and then began to lick the length of his manhood in long, slow strokes as he had done to her. Christian growled again and his hand found her breast, rolling her nipple between his finger and thumb. The tingle shot through her like an arrow, piercing her belly and causing the little nub between her legs to swell and throb again. Whimpering, hardly realizing what she was doing, just knowing she needed more of him, her mouth closed over him and she suckled. He tasted slightly salty and very, very good. Greedily, she took more of him.

"*Mon Dieu*! You are driving me mad!" he panted as his hips rose, "but you must stop, *chèrie*, or I cannot hold out much longer."

The thought slowed her tongue and she lifted her head a little. "What are you holding out for?"

Chrisitian groaned again and tugged her toward him, encircling her with his arm, the other hand still fondling her breast. "If we do not stop now, you will no longer be a virgin. I cannot ask you to relinquish your maidenhood."

"Maybe I want to give it to you."

A slight moan escaped his lips as he brushed her hair back. "Do you know what that means?"

Her hand reached for his engorged member. "I have seen dogs mate. Do you want me to get on my hands and knees?"

Christian made a strangled noise that sounded suspiciously like a laugh but turned quickly into a small cough. "*Non.* There is a more pleasurable way to do it."

He hesitated. "You are certain you want to go through with this?"

Fiona touched his face. "I have never been so sure of anything in my life." She had hardly finished the sentence when she found herself on her back with Christian looming over her, an elbow braced on either side of her. She was caged, his body heat and scent enveloping all her senses, so she hardly felt his thighs spreading her legs wide, and the massive tip of him pressing against her wet core. He ran the shaft up and down her swollen folds, enticing the pulsating little bud until the sensation was all she could focus on, and then, with one smooth thrust, he impaled her.

The sharp sting of pain made Fiona gasp. Christian cradled her head, kissing her deeply. "I am sorry," he said. "It only hurts the first time, I promise." He lay still, allowing her muscles to stretch to accommodate him.

Fiona clung to him, her arms wrapped around his shoulders. Surprisingly, the pain began to fade. She wiggled a little, under him, getting used to his weight and the feel of his thick member inside her.

Slowly, he withdrew half way, and then equally as slow, he pushed in again. And then repeated it. Long, leisurely sensual strokes going in, filling her, jutting against her womb, then withdrawing. Fiona whimpered at the feeling of emptiness when he almost left her, but then he filled her again. She wanted more…there was a strange neediness building inside her. A desire, a craving…something that touched her very soul.

Again she felt as though she were a rudderless ship at sea, buffeted by winds that tossed her about, raising her to new heights of danger as the bow might ride the crest of a wave threatening to pitch-pole, only to plunge into deep troughs of tremulous swells that could, at any moment, swamp her and pull her completely under. But the waves were cresting more quickly now as Christian quickened his pace, the storm surge building inside her, threatening to explode…threatening what fragile hold she still held on consciousness. She felt something wet and hot pour into her as roller after roller of ferocious surf crashed onto the shore of her mind. Her body convulsed, and she felt like she flew into a thousand splinters.

She lay gasping for breath, Christian's sweat-slicked body still entwined with hers. "What happened?" she managed to ask.

"I have made you a woman," he whispered hoarsely and then tucked her into the crook of his arm as he slipped beside her. "Rest now, *mon amour*."

"Can we not do it again?" Fiona whispered contentedly.

Christian laughed. "I think I have awakened a vixen in you. *Oui*, in a little bit, *chèrie*, I will show you more pleasure."

Chapter Nine

"You do not have to come to the door with me," Fiona said for maybe the fifth time as the rented carriage stopped in front of the house on Rue Toulouse. "It might be better if you did not."

A muscle flexed in Christian's jaw as he handed her down from the carriage seat. "I have had enough of skulking about," he said. "Meeting you secretly in the park is no longer acceptable, now that we have made love."

A heated tingle shot through Fiona's body at the memory of that. She had always suspected that what passed between a man and a woman was quite pleasurable, but she had no earthly idea that her body could fly into sheer ecstasy over and over. Christian had brought her to the brink of madness only to ease up whatever delicious torture he was imposing and make her whimper for more and then soar again...and the blessed relief, when it came, made her see the constellations of the universe before she plunged down, like a bird with a broken wing, only to be caught on the updraft of another series of clever ministrations of Christian's hands and mouth to send her soaring once more.

But the hot rush of blood in her veins turned to icy water when she heard the rantings in the parlor when they entered the foyer. This was exactly why she had not wanted Christian to come in. As much as she wanted to lean out of the carriage and shout to the world that she loved Christian, she was afraid her uncle might still remember the duel, although she had not heard him mention it. Perhaps the pirate problem had made him forget. She hoped.

"The damn bastard got away *again*?" her uncle was nearly shouting.

"We followed them as far in as we dared, not knowing the depths of the channels," a familiar voice responded.

Her father. What in the world was he doing here?

"Fiona!" Her aunt saw them in the entranceway before anyone else did and hurried over. "We have been so worried! Where have you been all day?" She stopped talking and looked questioningly at Christian, a small frown forming. "Why are you here?"

Fiona took a deep breath. "This is Captain Picard."

Her uncle ceased talking in mid-sentence, and her father's eyes narrowed. Fiona had a sinking feeling that the duel was still fresh in her uncle's memory. Beside her, Christian straightened, his broad shoulders seemingly even wider and more muscular. He leveled a look at her father. "I do not believe we have met, sir."

"But perhaps we should have," her father replied as he walked toward them. "There had better be a good explanation why my daughter is with you."

"I...can explain," Fiona said, throwing a wild look at Cory, hovering in the corner. "Ah...I met Captain Picard at the Governor's Ball. Didn't I, Cory?"

Cory nodded. "I did too, Father. We...we had a conversation about horses."

"And so we met Captain Picard at the park—"

"You did *what*?" Her aunt's face went pale. "Oh, my dear, do *not* tell me you were arranging for a tryst—"

"No," Cory said quickly. "I had asked to see Captain Picard's horse. That's why we went."

Some color returned to Mrs. Claiborne's face, but she looked troubled. "Still, this is unseemly."

"It certainly is," Fiona's father said, glaring at Christian. "and it does not explain where she has been all day. Was she with you?"

Fiona opened her mouth to respond, but Christian held up his hand. "First of all," he said, looking Fiona's father directly in the eye, "Cory has been working with my Andalusian and exhibits a great deal of skill, but the truth of the matter is, I took an interest in your daughter and have enjoyed her companionship at the park."

Her aunt looked like she might swoon, but she reached out to grip the backrest of an armchair. "Oh, my dear! Was I not clear about how important appearances are? If you were seen without a chaperone, your reputation will be ruined!"

If only her aunt knew more than her reputation was already "ruined"—not that Fiona would trade what she had done for anything.

"That still does not explain today," her father said. "No carriage was missing, and it rained most of the day." He looked sternly at Fiona. "Where have you been and what have you been doing?"

Christian began to reply, but this time Fiona stopped him. "Captain Picard told me he was about to sail for Florida. Uncle William told us he had plans to invade that pirates' hideaway in Barataria and heaven help any ship that got in his way. I was concerned that Captain Picard might be fired upon, so I went to his ship to warn—"

"You went to the *docks*? By *yourself*?" Mrs. Claiborne sank into the armchair and began fanning herself with her hand. "What if you were seen?"

Fiona was beginning to get irritated over the emphasis on her reputation. It was not like she was the belle of New Orleans Society. Everyone thought her *odd* anyway. Everyone except Christian. "It was dawn. I am sure everyone connected with Society was still asleep," she said mulishly, "and besides, I dressed as a servant."

Her father's lip twitched at that, and then his face resumed its stern expression. "We will devise a suitable punishment for your misguided decision, but *where have you been all day*?"

"I was not aboard when she arrived, sir," Christian answered. "The watch showed her to the salon. She…fell asleep waiting for me. By the time she awakened, we were already near Grande Terre. It took some time to return." He glanced toward Mrs. Claiborne, still looking quite stunned, and then back to Fiona's father. "I can see where her reputation might have been compromised. I would like to do the honorable thing and—"

"Wait. No ships returned to port today," Governor Claiborne interrupted. "What is the name of yours?"

"The *Dorada*," Fiona responded, "and she is a splendid ship, Father. You should see her."

He looked grim. "I already have." He turned to the governor. "She was docked behind Grande Terre. When we raided Lafitte's library, we found his log. The *Dorada* is listed as one of his ships. The current bill of lading was for slaves to be picked up in Pensacola."

Fiona stared at her father, not believing what she had just heard. Then a buzzing began in her ears and the room began to spin. Someone helped her to the sofa. She thought it might be Christian. Fog drifted through her brain and, faintly, she heard her uncle shouting for footmen to restrain Christian, that he was under arrest for piracy.

Christian was one of Jean Lafitte's pirates? How could that be? The room spun faster, turning shades of gray, before everything went black.

****

Fiona stood with her head pressed against her bedroom window, watching the cold drizzle dribble down the windowpane. She sighed. What did it matter if it rained for weeks on end? She was forbidden to venture out *anywhere* without her aunt in tow.

Three days had passed since the fiasco of her return from Barataria. Christian had been arrested as an accessory to Jean Lafitte's illegal business activities and now sat in the calaboose along with the eighty men the commodore had managed to capture in the raid. Both Lafitte brothers had disappeared.

Christian was a pirate.

Fiona closed her eyes to keep the tears from sliding down her face. Every time that thought flitted through her mind—which it did nearly every waking minute—fresh agony washed over her. And then cold fury would follow.

How could she have been so incredibly naïve and stupid? Reflecting now, she understood why Christian had been so keen on meeting with her and asking all those personal questions about her uncle and father. She thought he had been interested in *her*. She should have known better. Men did not find overly tall, gangly women with orange hair attractive. Christian had been spying for the Lafittes. Gathering information. And she had fallen into the trap as neatly as a fox quarried a baby rabbit in its hole.

And yet… When he kissed her, she had felt such passion. When he fondled her breasts and told her she was beautiful, she had believed him. She had felt beautiful. Feminine. Womanly. For the first time in her life. And when he was *inside* her… Her body trembled and a hot sheen of mortification gushed over her.

Dear God. She had let him *inside* her…and worse, she had enjoyed every single minute of it, just like a lightskirt. And the other things she had done to him…embarrassment flooded her. He probably thought her no better than a dock doxy, wanton and loose. She had given him no cause to believe otherwise. If possible, she grew even more humiliated that she had actually begged for more. Fiona flung herself on the bed, cradling her face in the pillow so her sobs would not be heard.

Sometime later, she was staring unseeingly at the ceiling when someone knocked on her door.

"Enter," she said in a listless voice.

The parlor maid popped her head in, her usually cheerful, smiling face somber and tense. "Your father is here. Mrs. Claiborne asks that you come downstairs."

"I will need a few moments," Fiona said, and the maid ducked out. With another long sigh, she swung off the bed, smoothing some of the wrinkles in her skirt. Looking in the mirror, she pushed some wayward curls back behind her ears and dabbed a little cold water from the pitcher on her face. Her face was still puffy, her eyes rimmed in red. But then, what did it matter? Her father was probably only going to lecture her again.

He looked her up and down when she entered the

parlor a short time later, and a muscle clenched in his jaw. He nodded to her aunt.

"Sit down, Fiona," Mrs. Claiborne said. "We have some news to share with you."

In spite of herself, Fiona wondered if Christian had been released. Her emotions must have shown on her face because her father grimaced.

"Get any notion out of your head that you will see that rakehell again," he said, "and be glad the governor put him in jail where he is safe from me. The thought of him taking liberties with you… Well, it will not happen again."

"I understand, Father," she said quietly.

Her father cleared his throat and looked at her aunt again. "Go ahead and tell her."

Fiona recognized that tone. Her father only used it when he was about to give an order that would not sit well with her. The hair on her nape rose. "Tell me what?"

Mrs. Clariborne cleared her throat too, looking more flustered than Fiona had ever seen her. "Well, my dear," she began, "given that you came so perilously close to having your reputation completely ruined—thank God, no one seems to have found out, since we were discreet in looking for you—but it is time we put an end to this…this wanderlust you seem to have."

Fiona eyed her uneasily. "I am already confined to this house."

"Well, that is temporary. In a few months' time, as soon as preparations can be made, you will have a home of your own."

"I beg pardon?"

"Yes." Her aunt smiled a little too brightly. "You are to be wed. I assured your father that once you have a family—"

"I what?" Fiona interrupted, not caring that she was being rude.

"Fiona. Let your aunt continue," her father said in a stern voice.

"Once you have a husband and a home to run, you will be kept quite busy. When the children come, you will see how wonderful family life can be," her aunt said.

Fiona felt a hysterical bubble of laughter creep up her throat—and then it edged out. She began laughing, the pitch rising in intensity. She became aware that both her father and her aunt were staring at her in shock, but she could not stop. "It…is…too…funny," she managed to gasp out between more fits of giggles. She never *giggled*, but dear Lord, this was priceless.

"There is nothing funny about it," her father said. "The decision has been made."

Fiona hiccupped, the laughter stopping as quickly as it started. Anxiety overtook her. "What do you mean? Who would marry me?"

"The Farnworths have agreed that their son and you would suit," Mrs. Claiborne replied. "Such a lovely family, too. In banking. Not terribly wealthy, but they will do."

The Farnworths? Fiona drew her brows together. Who…vaguely, she recalled the young man who had approached her at the governor's ball…the one she had turned away because she had been watching Christian. She could not even remember what his name was, although she did remember that he had made a straight line to the charming Caroline. Proof, in her book, that someone had forced him to ask her to dance in the first place.

"This is ridiculous. I do not even know this…person. I do not want to marry."

"If you valued your freedom, you should have taken more care to protect it," her father responded. "My sister tells me you have not exactly made an effort to fit into society. We are damn lucky the Farnworths agreed to this match."

Only because they want to get into the governor's good graces. Fiona bit her lip. It would not pay to argue with her father right now. She knew him. Hopefully, she could wear him down if she acted docile at the moment. "You are sure this person wants to marry me?"

"His name is Charles. Yes, indeed. His mother said he absolutely beamed when the offer was made," her aunt said quickly. "We will plan a dinner for tomorrow night so you two young people can become acquainted." She turned to her brother. "Under my watchful eye, this time. I should have been more vigilant before."

Fiona heard little of the rest of the conversation about wedding plans and all the things that must get done. She was too busy plotting her own course.

The one thing she would *not* do was marry Charles.

Chapter Ten

Christian sat on the corner of a hard plank that served as a bed in the crowded cell and tried not to inhale the stench of unwashed bodies. His own probably did not smell too great either, after three days in the Cabildo. He ran a hand through his hair, recalling the conversation when he had first been brought in.

****

All eyes turned to him as he was pushed into a cell that already held at least a dozen of Lafitte's men.

"So they got you too?" Dominique said from a dark corner of the cell.

Christian squinted, his eyes adjusting to the dimness. "What in hell is going on?"

The men all started talking at once, but Dominique quieted them. "That raid cost Jean everything. Barataria is completely destroyed. Houses were looted and burned at the governor's orders. The commodore captured seven schooners, a cruiser, and a felucca and confiscated nearly a half-million dollars' worth of merchandise from our warehouses. And Claiborne dares to accuse us of piracy!"

"Why did you not run? Jean gave the order for everyone to leave."

Dominique shrugged. "Someone had to create a diversion so Jean and Pierre could be safely gone."

"I would not blame them if they were half the way

to Texas by now," one of the other men said.

Dominique gave him a reproachful look. "You should know Jean better than that by now. I do not doubt he has already sent word to Grymes to get us released. And Jean will regroup in the bayous. Governor Claiborne may have betrayed him, but the Lafittes feel strongly about America and this war."

****

Christian shook his head, trying to clear it, and leaned back against the wall. Governor Claiborne may have betrayed Jean by responding to his offer to help New Orleans with total destruction of Barataria, but what had Christian done to Fiona? He knew she felt betrayed; he had seen the look of comprehension and hurt in her eyes just before she fainted.

Damn. He had wanted to explain. *Oui*, he would admit that he had been sent to seek information and *oui*, he had sent that information on to Jean, but he wanted to make her understand the irony that they were all on the same side. More than that, he wanted—needed—to make her understand that his time in her company had been *real*...that he had meant every compliment he had given her and enjoyed every kiss that he had taken. That was *real*. And making love to her had been very, very *real*... He had never desired a woman as much as he did Fiona, and no woman had ever brought him as much pleasure as she did. Fiona had a natural instinct for pleasing a man and a surprising sense of adventure in following his lead, no matter what he had suggested over the course of those several hours. She had even been bold enough to tell him how good it felt when he'd spurted hot seed into her...

Mon Dieu! Christian shot up from the plank and began to pace in what small space there was to move about. *Sacrébleu!* He had taken no precautions! And how many times had he filled her? Three? Four? She could very well be carrying his child while he sat in the calaboose like a common prisoner.

"Prowling like a caged tiger is not going to help, *mon ami*," Dominque said, watching him. "What is the problem? Jean will get us out."

"I do not have time to wait for that," Christian replied. "I need to see Fiona."

Dominique shook his head. "Even if that were possible, do you think she would want to see you? Women do not take kindly to feeling used. She would probably be happy to have you rot in here."

Christian flinched. "That may be so, but I have to explain something to her. Time is of the essence. She might be… That is, she might need to visit one of the quadroon sisters for some…advice."

Dominique's eyes widened, and he drew Christian into the corner. "You think she might be with child?" he whispered.

He felt his face grow hot. "It is possible."

"*Merde*. Were you insane, not to—"

"Yes, I was," Christian interrupted him. "Damn it. I love her."

His friend emitted a low whistle and then patted his shoulder. "*Je vous plains*—I am sorry, *mon ami*—for you will be a dead man if you go to her."

Christian stared at the wall. That was something he did not need to be told.

****

Fiona smiled wanly as Charles carved and served her a portion of roast duck at yet another interminable dinner. Dear Lord, she was tired of sitting docilely prim and proper like she did not know how to slice a piece of meat for herself, let alone put it on her own plate. He sat down beside her, holding his back as stiff as his cravat was starched. Their conversation was just as stilted, even though Charles had been paying her court now for nearly two months. Fiona suspected he was no more enthusiastic about being betrothed to her—oddball that Society still thought she was, despite her aunt's ministrations—than she was to be considering marriage to him. Or anyone. After Christian…

She blinked her eyes, trying to stay the tears that still threatened to well up whenever she thought of Christian. He was still in jail, along with eighty or so other pirates captured in the raid, and her uncle showed no signs of releasing any of them despite the arguments that Mr. Grymes and Mr. Livingston made each time they called on the governor. They argued, as the fighting came closer to New Orleans, that Louisiana would need all able-bodied men and Lafitte's men knew the bayous, but her uncle turned a deaf ear. Even now, the threat of war droned in the conversation that floated around her.

"As cold and miserable as autumn has been, perhaps the British will fall back and wait for spring to actually attack," Mr. Farnworth said hopefully.

Her uncle almost snorted. "The conditions are not quite like Valley Forge," he said, "and the English are used to cold, damp, miserable weather. The last report I got from General Jackson was there were nearly fifteen thousand of them moving closer to Gulf waters. How long will it be before they realize we have only seven hundred federal troops and not quite that many local soldiers? That is, if the Creoles will actually consider fighting for the United States that they keep forgetting they are a part of."

"Well, dear, did you not tell me that General Jackson has agreed to come here?" Mrs. Claiborne asked.

Her husband nodded. "He's taken Mobile. I would expect he is on his way as we speak. Let us just hope that, when he gets here, he can convince the people of New Orleans to rally around him."

The conversation drifted onto other topics, but Fiona paid no heed, for an idea was forming. If she could get a chance to talk to General Jackson herself…

She hardly noticed when the dinner finally ended and the Farnworths gathered their things together to leave. Charles dutifully bent over her hand, his cool, dry lips barely grazing her knuckles. Fiona wanted to laugh at the way both his mother and her aunt watched them like hawks. Neither of them needed to fear that Charles would take liberties—he was far too prudish—nor that Fiona would let him. No passion stirred her at his infrequent touches. He was pleasant enough. Certainly, always a gentleman. She did not like—and did not dislike—Charles. She just felt absolutely nothing for him. Perhaps she should be grateful, for she would not again rush with total abandonment and wantonness into another man's arms. She had learned her lesson there.

But…the passing of October and November had lessened her anger. She now understood better why Christian had used her, even though she still felt the mortification of how utterly naïve she had been. The more she listened to her uncle spewing his version of how terrible Jean Lafitte was—and she had met the man—the more she began to root for the pirate…if he really *was* a pirate.

Perhaps, if she could speak to General Jackson, she

could somehow persuade him to see how valuable Jean Lafitte and his men could be. And perhaps…Christian would be set free.

Not that she ever intended to see him again.

****

Fiona almost got her wish a week later, in early December. Mrs. Claiborne flitted about, admonishing servants for imaginary specks of dust on the stair banister and sending the kitchen staff into a flurry, preparing all sorts of enticing morsels for the group of men that had been invited to meet with General Jackson. The French mayor was the first to arrive, followed closely by Mr. Livingston and Mr. Grymes. Fiona had offered to pour tea, much to her aunt's delight. She just hoped she would not spill it on anyone, but she had no other idea of how to get close enough to speak to the general.

Fiona almost dropped her tray of delicacies, though, when the general finally arrived and was ushered into the parlor. She had heard he was a tall man, but she had not expected him to be so gaunt. His face was thin and haggard, his long, gray hair mussed. And his clothing! She heard her aunt gasp and almost snickered. He wore an old leather cap, a blue cape that was torn in several places, and a uniform that was becoming ragged. His boots were not only *not* polished, they were still caked with mud. Fiona had visions of the servants beating the carpets frantically tomorrow, rain or no rain.

Yet somehow, when he began to speak, his voice was deep and strong, his eyes vibrant and penetrating, and Fiona found herself mesmerized. On his way to New Orleans, he had gathered four thousand troops: regular soldiers, men from Tennessee and Kentucky, the Mississippi Dragoons. He had ousted the British from two forts in Florida that the Spaniards had given over, and he had run the Indians at Mobile inland. This was a man who could get things done! She would simply have to find a way to talk to him.

And then her heart sank, as the butler announced two more guests. Fiona turned to see commodore and her father walk in. Her father arched an eyebrow in surprise to see her pouring tea. He knew her too well not to suspect she was up to something. Any attempt she made now to secure the general's attention would be foiled. She could have thrown the whole tray of crumpets across the room at this interruption of her plans.

Well, she would wait. She would find out where the general was staying and, if need be, she would secure Cory's help to sneak out of the house one more time. What did it matter if they got caught after the fact? The Farnworths would probably cancel any wedding plans, which would only save her from figuring out how to avoid getting married.

She was bored nearly mindless with this existence. A little adventure might be just what she and Cory both needed.

****

As it turned out, an escapade was not necessary. A few nights later, the Livingstons gave a large dinner for the general. Fiona's uncle had told them that, over the past few days, General Jackson had ridden to the various makeshift camps of Ft. St. Philip on the Mississippi River and Ft. Petite Coquilles on the Rigolet, to inspect the troops. Even the pitiful numbers of trained men and the inadequate supply of arms and ammunition did not deter him. Somehow, miraculously, he managed to rally them by using a word of praise to the untrained, a suggestion here and there where needed, and assurance to the officers that he would fight with them.

Still, Mrs. Claiborne worried over how the rough Indian-fighter known as "Old Hickory" would be received by the cultured Creoles.

Fiona was astonished at the change in the general's looks. Although still gaunt, he appeared in a perfectly tailored, spotless uniform, every inch a composed and elegant gentleman. He moved with perfect ease as Mr. Livingston introduced him to the ladies, bowing slightly and genuinely smiling at each of them. The effect was that most of them fluttered their eyelashes and batted their fans at him.

"I do not think you need worry about his effect on Society," Fiona said to her aunt as she watched the procession.

"It would seem not," Mrs. Claiborne answered. "I had no idea he could be so charming. He almost reminds me of that interesting Mr. Clement I met once."

The evening passed with tormenting slowness as course after course was presented and dawdled over. Fiona fidgeted in her chair, wishing people would just eat instead of go through all the niceties of stilted conversation and the elaborately slow sipping of separate wine selections for each course. Finally, desserts were finished and the party moved to the ballroom where a string quartet played.

It was one of those rare times when Fiona wished she were a graceful dancer. One coquettish debutante after another giggled when General Jackson would bow gravely and ask for a dance. Caroline positively glowed when he asked her twice. Fiona noticed Charles watching the girl overtly.

Fiona tapped her foot impatiently, hardly listening to Charles prattling on about some business endeavor he was involved in with Caroline's father. They were going to have to talk soon about this farce that both of them were ready to reject.

A reel finished and General Jackson stepped out onto the veranda. This was her chance! "Charles," she said, interrupting him, "would you mind getting me some punch?"

He looked surprised but nodded. "Of course. I will be back shortly."

He had hardly turned away before Fiona headed toward the veranda. She forced herself to walk sedately, lest she draw attention to herself. Approaching a single man by herself in the dim light from the French doors was already beyond propriety.

"General Jackson, may I have a word with you?"

Turning at the sound of her voice, he looked down at her. "Miss Gordon, I believe?"

"Yes." Fiona was amazed that he remembered the brief introduction earlier. "I…I do not have much time, but I need to tell you something."

He frowned slightly. "Perhaps we should step inside."

"No."

"No? This is not an invitation to a tryst, is it?"

Fiona colored, glad that he could not see her blush in the dim light. "No, of course not. I mean…that is, you are…well, that is not…" She took a deep breath. "I wanted to tell you that there are a thousand men who know the swamps and bayous between here and the Gulf like they do their own hands. They want to help."

"Indeed? Why have I not met them?"

"They have had to stay hidden. They are…wanted."

The general studied her. "Are you speaking of the pirates that the governor outlawed?"

"Yes. But they are not outlaws."

"No?" he asked.

"No. Or, at least I do not think so. Mr. Lafitte is as much a gentleman as you are."

Both of his brows raised. "You have *met* Jean Lafitte?" When she nodded, an odd little twitch lifted a corner of his mouth for a second. "I can assume your uncle does not know about that?"

Fiona nodded again and then felt her face heat at the implication. "It is not what you think… I do not have time to explain, but I was at Barataria when the *Carolina* arrived to destroy it. I heard Mr. Lafitte give the command that no one was to fire on an American ship."

The corner of his mouth twitched again. "You are an unusual young lady."

"So I have been told," Fiona answered, "but the point is that Jean Lafitte wants to help defend New Orleans from the British, and right now there are a number of his men rotting in the Cabildo as we speak. Hundreds more in the swamps will come out of hiding if given the chance. They are Americans, wanting to help save New Orleans. How can you turn that down?"

"Fiona?" Charles called from near the door. "Are you out there?"

"I am coming," she answered and gave General Jackson a swift look. "My uncle hates the pirates for some reason. I do not know why, but can you afford to turn them away? Can you really afford that?"

She turned and hurried away, leaving the general staring thoughtfully after her.

Chapter Eleven

Jean looked down at the letter in his hand, scarcely able to believe that Governor Claiborne had attached his signature to it. He handed it to Andre and motioned for him to stay back. Taking a deep breath, Jean climbed the stairs to the meeting room above the Exchange on Rue Chartres. The governor had given his oath in granting Jean safe passage to and from this meeting that General Jackson had asked for. If this were a trap, Andre and Marc would have the authentic letter proving the governor was a liar.

There were no guards when Jean opened the door and went inside. Governor Claiborne looked none too pleased, but Grymes and Livingston were both smiling. The tall, almost emaciated man whose skin looked thin as parchment and almost as yellow, studied him with penetrating eyes. Jean masked his surprise. Swamp fever had not been kind to the general.

General Jackson rose and came around the table to extend his hand. His grip was surprisingly firm, as was his voice when he thanked Jean for attending and then motioned him to sit.

Jean looked at the governor. "I am glad to be here, but I am wondering why you have had a change of heart?"

Claiborne looked distinctly uncomfortable. "It seems my wife's niece decided to approach the general before I knew anything about it."

Again, Jean hid his surprise, wondering what had really transpired between Christian and the outspoken Yankee woman. She hardly seemed the type Christian usually pursued, but...

"The young lady mentioned that there might be as many as a thousand men hidden in the swamps who could be valuable to us," General Jackson said. "Is it true that your men would be willing to aid us?"

"*Oui*. I already offered our services once, but the reply I received was not...hospitable," Jean replied and watched a slow flush creep over Claiborne's face.

"They are willing to swear allegiance to America?" the general asked.

Jean turned to look him directly in the eye. "They *are* Americans. I *am* American. I believe that Grymes and Livingston can both vouch for me when I say I already declined to help the British."

Claiborne sat up straighter. "What? The British approached you?"

"Yes," Livingston interrupted and then preceded to explain. When he finished, the governor was looking somewhat mollified.

"We would be honored to have your men join us," General Jackson said.

"With two conditions," Jean replied. "I want pardons for all of us, and I want my men in prison released."

General Jackson looked at the governor.

A muscle ticked in Claiborne's jaw. "Done," he muttered.

"Good." Jean leaned back in his chair. "Do you by any chance need more weapons?"

"We recovered some weapons, along with the ships," the governor told the general before Jackson could reply. "Of course, they will be put at your disposal."

The general nodded and looked at Jean. "Are there more?"

Jean allowed himself a grin. "*Oui*. Commodore Patterson and Colonel Ross did not find one rather important warehouse. I have a variety of weapons, including guns, powder kegs of ammunition…and seven thousand five hundred pistol flints that I presume will come in handy?"

The general's grin matched Jean's as Claiborne gaped. Jackson extended his hand. "I believe we are in accord, Mr. Lafitte."

Jean shook his hand. "I will call my men in. Now then," he said as he settled back once more. "The Baratarians are excellent spies, as well. Would you like to know what the British fleet is doing?"

****

"I have to trust that the general is doing the right thing in releasing Lafitte's men," the governor said to Mr. Livingston that night at the dinner table. "I still think they are pirates, and not one of them is welcome in this house. I believe I made myself quite clear on that point."

"I believe Jean understood your point," Mr. Livingston said in a neutral tone.

Fiona kept her eyes on her dinner plate and tried not to fidget. Christian was free! In that moment she forgot she had intended never to see him again. She *had* to…just to make sure he was well. Covertly, she slanted a look at Cory. If they could just get to the park tomorrow…

"I am beginning to recognize that look, Fiona," her uncle said grimly. "You can forget any wild scheme you are planning. Your father left strict instructions that you do not leave this house without your aunt as chaperone, and I agree with him."

"I was just thinking—"

"Women are not supposed to think!" he exploded. "If you had not taken it upon yourself to corner General Jackson on the veranda, those pirates that I worked so hard to capture would still be in the calaboose!"

Fiona threw down her napkin and stood up so quickly her chair nearly tipped over. "Do you think New Orleans stands a chance—*any* chance—of defeating thousands of trained British soldiers without help from locals who know the bayous and swamps? The Creoles do not think this is their war! What—"

"That is quite enough," the governor thundered. "You are excused from this table!"

She glared at him, ignoring her aunt's gasp and the startled look from Mr. Livingston. "Fine! But you are being totally unfair to those men." Turning, she ran from the room.

Several hours later, she was thoroughly regretting losing her temper. How stupid could she be? She knew…she *knew* better than to fight her battles like that. Her father was much more forgiving when she did not confront him head-on. Her father would be furious at her rude, inexcusable behavior…and in front of a guest, as well. She was doomed. She really was.

So she was surprised the next morning when a light knock came on her door and her aunt entered.

"It is a lovely day for December. I thought you might enjoy a carriage ride?"

Fiona stared at her. "I am going to be allowed outside?"

Her aunt nodded. "Although he was not as volatile as you, Mr. Livingston quite agreed that you had a point." She turned back to the door. "I will leave you to get ready and meet you downstairs." She paused. "I had my own little conversation with the governor as well." Then she smiled. "I believe my husband now understands that women can, indeed, *think*."

****

Fiona was astounded at the sight that greeted them as the landau rolled down Rue Toulouse and turned left on Rue Decatur. As usual, New Orleanians filled the square and the nearby market, but today they were not strolling or shopping. Most of the well-dressed gentleman and ladies were simply gaping.

A steady stream of boats, all shapes and sizes, was making its way up the river to dock at the wharves. Men of every nationality—American, Creole, Slavic, free men of color as well as mulatto and quadroon—stepped off the boats and made their way to the Exchange where Jackson was signing up recruits as fast as they could enlist.

"Baratarians!" Cory said excitedly.

Fiona peered out the curtained window, realizing now why her aunt had insisted on the enclosed coach. Unlike Christian and his friends or even Jean Lafitte himself, these men had rough looks to them. Many had deeply lined faces from too much time spent outdoors and almost all had long hair, bushy beards, and mustaches. Some wore kerchiefs knotted around their heads, while others sported gold hoop earrings or chains of gold visible on chests that were only partially covered.

And all of them carried weapons—guns, knives, wicked-looking long swords, dueling rapiers, and the short-bladed but lethal cutlasses.

Her aunt's eyes rounded. "Dear Lord. These are the men who are going to protect us?"

"You could hardly ask for any more dangerous-looking men," Cory said enthusiastically. "One look and those fancy redcoats will turn tail and run."

"Perhaps." Her aunt fanned herself quickly. "But I think we have seen quite enough." She took her parasol and tapped the roof of the coach. "We will go to the park now," she said when the driver leaned down.

The flowers in the park were gone, although patches of green grass remained in places. Fiona tried not to be too obvious as she surveyed the people strolling or riding. The dratted curtains kept her from getting a full view of everything, and she hoped that Cory was smart enough to look for Christian from his side of the coach.

"Do you suppose we could stop the coach and walk a bit?" Fiona asked. "I have not had enough exercise in days."

Her aunt shook her head. "William was quite firm that we remain inside the coach."

Fiona sighed. She should be grateful she was out of doors at all. She pulled back the curtain again—and then gasped. Christian was leaving the park on Jupiter! Why had she not seen him earlier? He looked magnificent in buff-colored breeches that hugged his muscular thighs and a black riding coat perfectly tailored for his broad shoulders. She moved forward on the seat, intending to wave, but her aunt pulled her back.

"Do not forget your manners, my dear. It is totally improper to be so wanton with your affections."

Fiona sank back against the leather squab with a sigh. So close…and Christian did not even know she was here.

Her aunt was eyeing her, and she tried to keep her face impassive, but she wanted to scream. So close…

"It would do you well to remember that you are betrothed to another man," her aunt said softly.

Fiona stared numbly at her. Betrothed to another man. To Charles Farnworth, who only had eyes for Caroline. Could no one else see that?

She wanted to laugh at the irony, but she was afraid she would start crying instead.

****

The Christmas ball at the Grymeses' home was well underway when Jean Lafitte arrived with his lieutenants and captains. Fiona's eyes swept over the group quickly, looking for Christian. He was not there. She could hardly contain her disappointment. Since so many lethal men now roamed the *Vieux Carré*, the governor had forbidden any of his household outside the premises unless escorted by a dozen footmen, and Fiona had not had the opportunity to go to the park again.

Mr. Grymes called for a receiving line to form so he could present Jean Lafitte and his men formally to Society. Fiona knew her uncle was probably seething, but he could hardly set the rules for another man's home. And General Jackson—who had thoroughly charmed the ladies as well as gained the respect of the men—walked by Mr. Lafitte's side, adding another indignity that her uncle would have to accept. Nonetheless, he took his place at the beginning of the line.

As Fiona took her place beside her aunt, farther back, she had to admit the group looked nothing like the pirates from the bayous. Jean Lafitte cut quite a dashing figure in black pantaloons, black satin waistcoat, and a black superfine topcoat that set off his raven hair and dark eyes. The striking contrast of a snowy white cravat only accentuated the very white teeth in his tanned face.

"Madame Claiborne," Jean said, as he bowed over her hand and actually kissed her knuckles rather than the air over them. "It is so good to see you again."

Her aunt blushed and then her eyes widened as he straightened and smiled at her. "Mr. Clement?" she whispered.

He inclined his head. "At your service always."

Fiona frowned. Her aunt *knew* Jean Lafitte? But why did she call him by another name? Oh, Lord, if her uncle ever found out! And then, Jean was in front of her.

He took her hand in his, probably breaking any number of Society rules, but he seemed not to care. "I want to thank you especially, Mademoiselle Gordon, for having the courage to intervene as you did. My men will always be indebted to you."

"New Orleans needs every able-bodied man to defend her," Fiona responded, sensing from her aunt's disapproving look that ladies did not discuss wartime needs. "I saw no reason for eighty such men to rot in a cell—"

"Fiona!" her aunt gasped.

"She is quite right, Madame," Jean said and then leaned toward Fiona before he moved along the line. "Christian will be here," he whispered.

A feeling of total elation swept through her. He was coming! She hardly heard the rest of the compliments from Lafitte's men as they proceeded past her. Christian was actually going to be here soon!

An hour later, as the band was beginning its last set, he still had not arrived. She had scoured the room numerous times, telling herself she might have missed him and knowing she would recognize his tall, broad-shouldered form anywhere in any crowd.

"My fault," Charles said gallantly as she tripped and then stepped on his toes while he led her down the line of dancers. "I do think you are improving."

Fiona gritted her teeth. Her aunt and Mrs. Farnworth had been pressuring her to learn to dance, since she was now betrothed. She had at first resisted, finding excuses for not attending dance lessons. However, since she was bored to pieces staying inside the house, she finally relented and agreed. She pitied the poor dance instructor, a rather portly gentleman of some years, who tried not to wince each time she stumbled—or merely plodded—through the intricate steps of a quadrille or cotillion.

She was too tall and gangly to ever be graceful like the petite Caroline, who flitted through these moves like a faerie wraith, her tiny feet skimming across the polished floor.

Fiona was just glad not to slip, slide, and land on her bottom. She gave a quiet prayer of thanks when the music finally stopped.

"There. We have done our duty to 'dance,' " Fiona said. "Please ask some of the other ladies to dance so you can enjoy part of the evening. I plan to fetch some punch and find a chair." She probably should have been insulted at Charles' perfunctory refusal to leave her alone and then, at her repeat, his quick acquiescence to find the charming Caroline, but she really did not care.

And then she breathed a true sigh of relief, for the musicians began the new risqué dance called a waltz. She had never tried it, but she was quite sure it was even more difficult to move within someone's actual embrace.

"You have learned to dance while I was locked away," a deep voice said from behind her.

Fiona whirled, bumping into Christian's powerful chest. She inhaled his warm male scent, along with the fragrance of soap and leather, and looked into his eyes, feeling as though she were falling into bottomless wells of darkness. So mesmerizing...

Christian caught her arm to steady her, and shards of heat pierced her skin, igniting nerve endings everywhere. Before she could respond, he slid his hand down to capture hers and slipped his other arm around her waist and stepped out into the circling throng of dancers.

"What are you doing?" she gasped.

"Dancing. It's called a waltz, I think."

"But I cannot dance!"

He laughed. "You already are." Pulling her closer, he added. "Just relax and follow me."

How could she relax when she was being held so close her breasts brushed against his jacket and her skirts whished across his thighs as he turned her with him in the dance? Totally improper, she was sure, but her body was too much on fire for her to care.

The dance ended much too quickly, and he reluctantly released her. To her own amazement, she had not tripped or stumbled even once. She had actually felt light on her feet and...feminine. She wanted to press her hardened nipples against his chest again.

As though he read her thoughts, Christian caught her hand and led her silently out to the veranda, finding the darkest corner available. A fleeting thought went through

Fiona's mind that she should definitely *not* be doing this…

And then Christian was kissing her. His warm, firm lips angled across her mouth, planting light kisses at the corners, then sucking in her lower lip before taking her mouth fully again. His tongue probed and she opened eagerly for him, wanting to feel him filling her while her lower body thrummed with its own want of being filled. Her tongue battled his, wanting to taste and explore him as completely as he was her.

"I have missed you so much," he whispered in her ear before gently nibbling her lobe and continuing down her neck. His hand slipped up to caress the underside of her breast.

Fiona moaned and turned into his hand, allowing him to cup her, and then felt his hand fall away as he abruptly stepped back.

"Why—" The sound of her uncle's thunderous footsteps stopped her cold.

"Get back into the ballroom this very minute," he hissed in a whisper that others would not hear. "I will not have this disgrace!" He turned to Christian. "I made it abundantly clear to Mr. Lafitte that you were not to bother my niece again. She is engaged to be married to a pillar of New Orleans Society and I will not have her name tarnished by the likes of this. You have ten seconds to be gone or I will have you hauled back to the calaboose."

Even in the dim light, Fiona could see the whiteness of Christian's face as he paled from the news. He turned to her. "You are betrothed?"

She felt her own blood drain from her face. She wanted to tell him that she intended to talk to Charles.

That pursuing a loveless marriage was not what she wanted. But she could not say that with her uncle standing there threatening the man she *did* love.

He had to leave *now*. She swallowed hard and nodded her head. "Yes."

The look he gave her nearly shredded her heart. Hurt, betrayal. Something else. But he gave her no answer, just simply turned and walked away.

Chapter Twelve

The look on Christian's face haunted Fiona for days. She wanted desperately to see him and to explain, but General Jackson had put New Orleans under martial law. Soldiers were on guard everywhere and, while supposedly they were there to defend *all* Orleanians, women stayed off the streets out of self-preservation.

Besides which, her uncle made sure she knew Christian had been sent to *Isle Dernière*, the last of the larger islands stretching out into the Gulf. Jean's other men were stationed at Grande Terre and Grand Isle, while Lafitte had been placed in charge of the Temple, his old auction center.

Still, with all the efforts, there were too many waterways and inlets that could not be protected by Jackson's minimal forces, and the British moved closer and closer to New Orleans.

They were having a small dinner with the Farnworths one evening when Mr. Grymes was announced.

"I am sorry to interrupt," he said as he sat down and was offered dessert, "but word just arrived from General Jackson that the British tried to land on Chandeleur Island."

Governor Claiborne put down his napkin. "They would have to go through Lake Borgne for that, and it is too shallow for their frigates."

"Quite true. They came in on forty-five small open boats." He paused, looking distinctly uncomfortable.

"What is it?" Claiborne asked.

"We lost five gunboats that tried to defend the island."

Fiona heard her uncle curse under his breath, and she held hers. The lake was mere miles from the city. If the British were to reach the mainland…

"Does the general have orders for us?" her uncle asked.

Grymes nodded. "Every able-bodied man that owns a weapon is being called to muster. Now that we know what direction they are coming from, the trained soldiers will be needed to move to meet them and the citizens of New Orleans must defend the city if the line is breached." He turned to Charles. "The young men are the strongest. Report to Ft. St. John in the morning for training."

Charles swallowed hard. "Yes, sir."

"I must go," Grymes said. "Livingston and I have a lot of people to inform about this latest move. Good night."

For moments after his departure, everyone was quiet, contemplating the news. Fiona glanced at Charles. Although a bit pale, he seemed calm. He was leaving tomorrow. She was running out of time to talk to him. She put her hand on his arm and smiled sweetly at her aunt.

"Given the circumstances, I would like to have a few moments in private to speak to Charles?"

He looked more surprised than her aunt did, but Mrs. Claiborne recovered quickly. "Of course, dear. Use the parlor. We will be right here."

106

As if she needed a warning that chaperones were nearby! But Fiona was not going to argue the point, and she was careful to leave the door slightly ajar to ensure the propriety that everyone seemed to feel so important.

She moved two small chairs closer to the fireplace and motioned for Charles to have one of them. He gave a glance to the horsehair sofa and then sighed as he sat where she indicated.

"I take it you are not about to swear undying devotion to me while I am in training?" he asked.

Fiona blinked at him. Was he being humorous? Her brows knit. "No, I was not."

"No one can fault you for honesty," he replied.

She lifted her chin. "True. And I do want to be honest with you. I think you should know that I do not wish to marry you."

He nodded. "I cannot say I am surprised. You have not even allowed me to give you a chaste kiss on your cheek."

Had she been that obvious in her non-interest? For a moment, she felt a twinge of guilt. Then she smiled brightly at him. "Think of it this way. If we are no longer betrothed, you are free to pursue Caroline."

A strange look of desire flitted across his face so fast Fiona almost did not see it. Almost. And she could not fault him for it. Just mentioning Christian made her feel the same way. Then Charles turned passive.

"In case you may not have noticed, Miss Frazier is surrounded by a bevy of beaus. She rarely allows a second dance with anyone at a ball."

"Well, then, when this war is over, you must try harder to win her attentions."

Charles looked pensive, and then he shook his head.

107

"When this war is over, we will wed, just as planned."

Fiona could not believe her ears. "What? Why? You certainly do not profess to love me any more than I do you!"

He shrugged. "Love hardly matters when duty calls."

Duty? It was his *duty* to marry her? It was hardly a compliment, but then, what did she expect? She was no prize southern beauty, but her pride still stung. "At least you do not lie about it," she said stiffly.

He glanced at her quickly and then looked into the fire. "I will be honest about something else, as well. My father's ambitions lie in Washington if it gets rebuilt. He wants to be a congressman. Governor Claiborne is his steppingstone for that." He sounded resigned. "So, even if Miss Frazier would have me—and I would like nothing better than to run a plantation—it does not suit my father's plans, and I am his only son. I am expected to help him succeed." His expression softened somewhat as he looked at Fiona. "But I swear that I will respect and honor you and you need never fear my wrath."

"But—"

"I think you young folks have had quite enough time alone together." Mrs. Farnworth burst through the door with a big smile. "Your father is ready to leave." She turned to Fiona with an even brighter smile. "I am so glad you and Charles are taking to each other so nicely. And since we will now have to wait until this horrible, silly war is over, we can plan a much bigger and more elaborate wedding." She turned to Fiona's aunt. "You see, there is a silver lining in this cloud that besieges us."

A short time later, Fiona leaned against the closed door of her bedroom, the sudden silence from Mrs.

Farnworth's chirpy voice making her ears ring. Or maybe she was feeling dizzy. She certainly did not feel well. Instead of sorting everything out neatly and being through with Charles, everyone now thought she truly cared for him. Somehow, she had only become more entwined in this crazy scheme to marry him.

God's Blood! What was she going to do?

****

Christian hoisted another beam onto the barricade they were making near the beach at Last Island and wiped the sweat from his brow. Even though the December winds were brisk, he had been working tirelessly from dawn to dusk every day, doing as much heavy labor as possible. It was only when he was near complete exhaustion at night that his mind would let his body rest.

Fiona was engaged to be married. *Merde*. It was the last thing he had expected to hear when he attended the ball. He had purposely arrived late, to avoid a scene with the governor in the receiving line.

Mon Dieu! She had felt wonderful in his arms while they danced. The soft, rounded mounds of her breasts pressed to him…when he tightened his arm a bit, he could even feel the stiff peaks of her nipples through his frock coat. And that piece of folly—holding her much too close—was what, no doubt, had attracted the attention of the governor and led to the interruption of the pleasurable taking of her mouth in kisses that hardened him instantly. But even that interruption did not change the facts.

Fiona was engaged to be married.

With a low, menacing growl that made the man working next to him step back, he bent down and hoisted yet another timber on the barricade and then another and another. He worked like a man crazed. The grueling labor was the only thing keeping him from going back to the city and ripping Fiona's fiancé apart limb by limb.

How could she have consented to marry? Then he shook his head at his own foolish thought. Marriage choices were often made without consent. Was that what happened? Why? Then he froze, half bent over. What if Fiona carried his child? It was possible; he had foolishly thrown caution to the wind in his urgent need to have her. Claiborne and her father would want any pregnancy to be legitimate, even if it meant the groom was not the father.

He was damned if he would let any other man raise his child. With renewed effort, he threw another log on the defense wall, hardly noticing its weight. He would take care of this matter as soon as they ran the bloody British off.

Fiona was *his*.

Chapter Thirteen

Without much enthusiasm, Fiona helped as her aunt supervised the hanging of garland and holly in the parlor one morning. Two days until Christmas and she felt a lingering emptiness.

"I know you probably miss the snow and the smell of pine trees," her aunt said as she handed her an end of garland, "but give Christmas in the South a chance, dear."

She could not tell her aunt that her listlessness had nothing to do with the weather. Christian had left nearly two weeks ago without her being able to see him. Charles had also been gone, so she'd had no chance of trying to persuade him to break the engagement. She simply could not marry someone she felt absolutely nothing for…especially after she had seen how his face lit up at the thought of Caroline Frazier. Maybe she could convince her aunt to help, if her aunt knew the whole truth.

"I would like to talk with you about something."

"Of course. Just as soon as we finish here, we can—" Mrs. Claiborne stopped at the sound of male voices at the front door. "Oh, dear. I wonder what is wrong now?"

They both hurried to the foyer in time to see a group of military men surrounding General Jackson, who introduced them to the governor.

"The British have invaded our plantation with seven

thousand men," a major said in a grim voice.

"That is only nine miles from here!" Claiborne exclaimed as he ushered them into the library.

Fiona glanced at her aunt, and they moved quickly to join the men. The governor seemed too shocked to even notice them, but Fiona fully intended to stay if he tried to order them away. Christian was out there someplace.

The governor poured brandy, but Jackson waved it away, preferring to pace back and forth in front of the fireplace. Fiona knew he was still suffering the aftereffects of swamp fever, but she was always amazed at how he seemed to suddenly become stronger and taller when faced with an emergency.

No one spoke for several minutes, and then General Jackson began barking orders.

"Take the Tennesseans and close in on Villeré Plantation, he told one general and then turned to another. " I want you in charge of a contingent at Bayou Bienvenu.." He looked at a colonel. "Your plantation adjoins Villeré?"

"Yes, sir. As does Lacoste Plantation on the other side."

"Good. From your location, you will be able to attack the redcoats' right flank.." He turned to a man whose golden skin spoke of mixed blood. "Major d'Aquin, your free men of color and the Choctaws still stand ready to join us?"

"Absolutely, sir."

"Your men will take the left flank then, at Lacoste."

"Yes, sir."

"Commodore, have the *Carolina* weigh anchor and move near the British encampment. Await orders before firing. Lieutenant Beluche, I want you and Dominique to head the artillery. Also, have your Baratarians line the river's edge in case of English scouts slipping in." Jackson looked at the governor. "And I would like you to head the corps on Gentilly Road."

"Of course."

The general took a deep breath. "I suggest we waste no time getting our troops ready. We attack tonight. Dismissed."

As Fiona watched the men hurry away, she wondered if Christian would be called in closer to the city now that the fight for New Orleans was about to begin. She closed her eyes.

Please keep him safe, Lord.

****

For the better part of the day, ever since General Jackson sent word out that the British had taken over Villeré Plantation, men—ranging from boys with peach-fuzz chins to white-haired gentlemen with determined looks on their faces—had steadily streamed through the streets of the *Vieux Carré* to enlist in General Jackson's army. Farmers and field hands, carrying hoes or pickaxes, joined the group as did men of color.

By three o'clock that afternoon, women and children lined the streets, jostling for position to send their men off to war with shouts of "Good Luck!" and "*Bonne Chance!*" along with some more flavorful epithets to describe the British and what should be done for them. The women of Society did not even flinch to hear such language when Fiona knew most of them would have swooned had those words been said in their parlors.

"We probably should not be out here," Fiona's aunt

said as one particularly crude sentiment was made.

"I want Cory to see me when he goes by," Fiona replied and then added, "and Charles too," since Mrs. Farnworth was standing beside her. "It is the very least I can do, since I cannot join them."

Mrs. Farnworth gasped. "Good gracious! You cannot possibly mean that you would want to actually engage in battle?"

Fiona opened her mouth to reply, but her aunt's rather sharp elbow found her ribs just then. She wanted to remind them she knew how to load and fire a musket, but that was a skill not appreciated. "I just want to be able to help."

"And we shall, when our men return," her aunt replied. "Surely this battle will be finished by morning."

Fiona had her doubts, but said nothing as the first group of volunteers, mainly young men practically dancing in the street at the prospect of fighting, went by.

Tall, lean Kentuckians in coonskin caps marched past, followed by the flatboat men who had poled them down the rivers. Tennesseans, dressed in brown homespun, their famously lethal rifles held high, came next.

Shouts went up as Jean Lafitte's Baratarians filled the streets, their various sword and knife blades gleaming in the sun. A lot of them were still bearded and wild-looking, but their swarthy faces did not seem so menacing now. *These* were the men who had supplied the powder and flints for the regular army. *These* were the men who knew the swamps and bayous as well as any gator or snake. *These* were the men who would be guiding the Orleanians past the bogs and quicksand. A deafening roar rose from the crowds as Dominique You and René Beluche rode past, horses pulling their heavy cannon behind them. The pirates were now heroes.

Fiona looked at the colorful mix of French and Spanish flags waving alongside the Stars-and-Stripes. Snatches of "*La Marseillaise*" could be heard along with "Yankee Doodle Dandy."

"Look," she said, "here comes Uncle William."

As the governor's contingent walked by, Cory and Charles in the unit, the crowd hushed and then, slowly, they all began to applaud, French, Creole, and Americans alike.

Tears sprang to her aunt's eyes. "William will be so proud to hear the people are finally behind him."

A Frenchwoman standing nearby glanced at her. "*Oui*, Madame Claiborne. *Les Britanniques* have insulted all of us by claiming Monsieur Villeré's plantation. They have insulted all of New Orleans. We will stand together to defend her, *non*?"

In response, her aunt smiled and reached for the other woman's hand. Together, they turned back to watch the men march off to war.

****

Christian wiped the residue of gunpowder off his hands, secured the leather powder pouch on his belt, and carefully dried the gun's pan. He squinted. Fog was settling in, pale strands like wraiths seeping up from the river, spreading over the banks, its spiraling tendrils clinging to the trunks of cypress. He knew the *Carolina*'s cannon stood ready to fire again as she had for the past two hours, but Jackson had called a halt when the British retreated into the woods.

He crept back from the edge of the river and joined the other Baratarians who had been brought up from the islands. They made their way to the makeshift camp Jackson called headquarters. Dominique and Beluche were already there, although Jean had been asked to stay at the Temple, just in case the British decided to come around that way. Christian knew he would regret missing a good battle.

Even Jackson was smiling a little as he sipped the strong chicory coffee. "This smells good. Do I want to know if you smuggled it in?"

Dominique grinned at him. "Better not to ask."

"Do you think they will attack again before dawn?" Christian asked as he accepted a cup of coffee from Beluche and sat down.

"Not likely," the general said, "although we have set a watch. Our plan worked well. The *Carolina* kept them focused with her cannon fire, and Dominique's artillery hammered the levee. Your commanders were able to close in from the land sides."

Christian raised an eyebrow. "Do you think it's over, then?"

Jackson shook his head. "I met the British general once. He will not concede defeat so quickly. Not with nearly twelve thousand men at his disposal." He set his tin cup down. "We will get some rest and then, before dawn, we move back to the Rodriguez Canal."

"Retreat?" one of the younger officers asked in surprise.

Christian looked at the man sharply. It was to Jackson's credit that he did not take the man to task for questioning him, but the general merely shook his head. "We can defend ourselves better there. The redcoats suffered losses tonight, but we are still outnumbered six-to-one and our ammunition is limited."

But for the next two days, all was quiet. Christian wanted nothing more than to ride into New Orleans, make sure Fiona was all right and find out if she carried his child, but he could hardly ask for permission to leave when both sides were playing a waiting game.

The *Louisiana* joined the *Carolina* on Christmas Day, anchoring across the river from her. Jean arrived on the twenty-sixth with alarming news that the British had landed more troops at Chef Menteur and were in the process of erecting a battery from which to fire at the *Carolina*.

Christian listened as Jackson issued emergency orders to have the levee cut at Jumonville Plantation, below the British camp, hoping the river would rush in and force the British into retreat.

Hours later, a message came back that the deed had been done, but the river level did not seem high enough to cause major flooding. Jackson cursed roundly. To make matters worse, a wind was rising, thanks to a weather front, and the *Carolina* would have trouble weighing anchor and moving upstream against strong headwinds.

Christian awoke to cannon booming and a splay of red flares lighting the pre-dawn sky. Shoving into his boots, he grabbed his musket, reaching for his powder pouch as he raced toward the river.

The bow of the *Carolina* was on fire, making the feat of raising anchor impossible even without strong winds that were spreading the flames rapidly toward the main mast with its canvas sails. Even though a few brave gunners stayed aboard to return fire, the rest of the crew was scrambling down the gangplank, splashing into cold water, wading to shore.

Jackson rode his horse bareback along the shore, bellowing orders to tow the *Louisiana* down river.

Christian joined Marc and Andre, peering into the leaping shadows on the far bank. He raised his musket.

"Hold your fire," Marc said. "Jackson does not want us hitting any of our own men who swam over there."

"The redcoats are not shooting anyway," Andre added. "They are safe behind that battery with their cannon."

"Where the hell is Dominique with our artillery?" Christian asked. Before either of them could answer, a resounding boom from their side rent the air, followed by another.

"I would say they have arrived," Marc answered grimly.

The British returned fire, striking the *Carolina* once more. The hull cracked, the tall foremast pitching forward as the deck crumbled. The remaining crew dove into the water at the sound of wood splintering. With a heart-rending groan, the *Carolina* began to sink. Christian watched in silence as what was left of the proud ship burned to the waterline.

Jackson emerged from the darkness as suddenly and silently as an owl taking flight. "Inform your men. The British smell victory and will attack at dawn. We will meet them at the Rodriguez Canal."

Christian looked uneasily at Marc and Andre, but they were already turned away. The Canal location brought the British two miles closer to the city…and to Fiona.

Jackson looked at him. "They won't get by us, Captain Picard."

Christian nodded. He hoped the general was right,

because the women of New Orleans had been left defenseless.

****

Fiona paced the length of the library, looking out one window at the brown, dried grass of the garden and out another window at the gray, dreary, mist-covered street. How much longer was this war going to continue?

"You are going to wear a dreadful path in the carpet," Mrs. Claiborne said as she looked up from where she and Mrs. Farnworth were tatting lace on to linen handkerchiefs. "Why don't you join me?"

Fiona looked at the sofa. "I am too edgy to sit. We have been cooped up inside this house for weeks."

"Well, it certainly is not safe to be out and about. You know that."

She turned back to the window to contemplate the drizzly day. When the men had marched off, everyone thought they would be back in time for Christmas. Then New Year's Day came and went, along with news in bits and pieces from the messengers the governor sent back, that the British commander had brought several thousand reinforcements. The good news was that more than two thousand Kentuckians had also arrived to help General Jackson. The bad news was that both armies were even closer to the city. When the wind was right, cannon could be heard by those still inside the city.

She wondered where Christian was and if he was safe. She had asked the messenger once if he had seen Christian, but his expression became closed. All he would say is that Lafitte's men were in the middle of the fighting.

So, each day, Fiona prayed that Christian was still alive. And each night, she lay awake remembering the taste of his tongue, the warm firmness of his lips, how his callused hands gently caressed her body arousing her flesh and—God help her—how his thick, hard erection had felt *inside* of her. She wanted him desperately, and she wept. Even if she could persuade the surly messenger to deliver a message to Christian, what could she say? Charles had not agreed to dissolve the betrothal.

"I know you miss Charles," Mrs. Farnworth said. "I miss my husband dreadfully even though I know he is fighting right beside the governor." She patted Mrs. Claiborne's hand and smiled.

Fiona felt a slight twinge of guilt that she had not thought about Charles at all. Pensively, she looked at Mrs. Farnworth, wondering if she would understand how Fiona felt. Maybe—

But her aunt was already speaking. "We must not worry, Beatrice. You know the missive that arrived yesterday said the English attack at the Piernas Canal was false, as are others. I feel confident that General Jackson has the British on the run."

"With the help of Jean Lafitte and his men," Fiona said, "we should not forget that without the—"

"Madame Claiborne," the elderly butler interrupted without knocking, his voice raised in pitch and his eyes wide. "A messenger has arrived from Chalmette."

Fiona hurried over to him as her aunt rose quickly to join her. Chalmette was directly on the river. "What has happened?"

A thoroughly soaked young man, his uniform filthy and his boots encrusted in mud, appeared beside the butler. "Trouble, ma'am. The redcoats have dug out Canal Villeré—"

Fiona froze. The canal was a direct route to the

Mississippi…and Chalmette. If the British ships managed to slip through—

"General Jackson is certain the British will attack in earnest in the morning. You are to gather the women in the most secure home. The governor felt Madame Porée's home would be a good choice."

"Of course," Mrs. Claiborne said. "Beatrice, please notify the ladies on your street and have each of them notify others. Have them bring food, blankets…anything that can be gathered quickly. We do not know how long we will have to stay sheltered."

"Tell them to bring knives, as well," Fiona interjected, "and any other weapons the men may have left behind."

Mrs. Farnworth looked at her in shock. "General Jackson will stop the British from setting foot inside New Orleans.'

"I hope so," Fiona answered, "but we do not have to be defenseless, either."

It wasn't until she looked around the crowded parlor and dining rooms of Madame Poreé's home, several hours later, that she realized how truly defenseless they would be. At least a hundred women and children were there. A few of the women were stoic, sitting quietly by the tightly barred windows with butcher knives in their laps, and others quietly prayed, the beads of their rosaries clicking as they murmured in French, Spanish, and English. Far too many, though, were clearly terror-stricken…crying, clutching their children, thus frightening them into tantrums. A few women even swooned, although no one seemed to be particularly sympathetic to those who did.

"Beauty and Bounty! Beauty and Bounty!" one of

the ladies moaned dramatically. "That is what my husband said the British were threatening!"

A new chorus of wails went up. "We will be raped if the redcoats break through!"

"Our homes destroyed!"

"New Orleans ransacked!"

"We must have protection," one of the belles said, wide-eyed. "We are saving ourselves for our husbands. We cannot be ruined!" Her remarks were met with hysterical shrieks from the other girls. To Fiona's surprise, Caroline did not add to the hue and cry. In fact, she looked decidedly composed.

Fiona shook her head and headed for the kitchen. The few menfolk who had accompanied them—mainly aging servants—had long ago taken refuge by the warm fires of the cook's hearth. They looked almost as frightened as the women, although they sat in nearly total silence. Having instructed the maids to brew large amounts of chamomile tea to settle the women's nerves, she moved down the hall to the library. A small fire was banked in the hearth, the glowing embers giving off a faint heat. But, thankfully, it was quiet.

Fiona curled into one of the big armchairs and rested her head against the high back, wondering where Christian was. She had heard the Baratarians had been called up from the outer islands because General Jackson needed all available manpower. Would Christian be in the front lines tomorrow? She prayed he would not be shot…or worse. The memory of his touch…the taste of his kiss…the way his dark eyes looked so intently into hers while he made love to her… Fiona fisted a hand against her mouth, biting into the soft pad of her thumb to keep from crying. There was so much she wanted to tell Christian, so much that needed to be said. She did not want him going into battle without knowing she loved him.

The battle would be waged not five miles from the *Vieux Carré*...she contemplated slipping out the servants' entrance and trying to find him. Her hand reached out to clutch her *Sgian Dubh*—the small, two-edged blade of last resort many Scots and Irishmen carried. Her father had given it to her years ago, and she was comforted by the feel of the soft leather on the handle. She knew how to use it, although she had not practiced since moving to New Orleans. Still...she would be armed...

Then she placed the knife down. Even her Irish tenacity knew it would be sheer recklessness to venture out. She had no idea where Christian was, and she certainly could not defend herself against a group of men—from either side—who might be desperate for a female. Any female.

With a sigh, she stood and slipped the knife into its sheath inside her garter and then smoothed her skirts. This was one time she would have to adhere to propriety...and there were hysterical women who needed to be calmed down. It was going to be a long, long night.

Taking another deep breath, she opened the door and walked toward the parlor.

Chapter Fourteen

Dawn had sent the first pale streaks against a dark sky when Christian strapped on his sword and loaded powder into his musket. As he walked toward one of the five small batteries where Dominique was in command of cannon, he noted the Tennesseans were carefully wiping their rifles as they joined the Kentuckians and Baratarians already in place behind the ridged-earth barricades reinforced with boards and cotton bales.

For most of the night, they had heard the sound of British hammers from their camp barely six hundred yards away, the sound somewhat muffled by the dense fog. A scout had returned saying the English were building scaling ladders, to which General Jackson had given a wry smile. "Tomorrow, gentleman, we fight," he'd said.

Christian climbed the short ladder to join Dominque on the makeshift battlement. "I haven't seen Jean," he said.

Dominique shook his head. "The general sent him across the river to aid in blocking any passes in the canals the British may have found. Said Jean was of more value to him over there."

They didn't have time for more conversation, as a British rocket suddenly lit up the lightening sky. Beluche's cannon immediately returned fire from the next battery, and Dominique quietly gave the same order to his cannon man.

A loud cheer went up from the British as the cotton bales of the crude barricades went up in flames. Men rushed out to drag them away even as the Tennesseans aimed their deadly rifles.

As if on cue, the lingering fog lifted, and Christian caught his breath. The British were marching toward them, at least sixty men abreast, in slow, measured steps, the morning sun setting off their bright red coats.

"What the hell—?" Dominque said. "Do they think they are in a parade?"

"I believe they are adhering to courteous European rules of warfare," Christian said dryly.

Dominique grinned. "Bloody hell, then. We'll show them how the Yanks fight."

Cannon thundered. Rifles cracked. Muskets popped. British soldiers began to drop, their stately column swerving away from the main battery but, nonetheless, continuing to march forward. Christian could see the officers riding behind the foot soldiers, waving swords and no doubt shouting encouragement, although it could not be heard over the roar of what now was continuous fire from the Americans.

"Sheer suicide," Christian muttered under his breath as he took aim and pulled the trigger and then his eyes widened and he slowly lowered his gun. The big, black horse that the British general rode, itself a throwback to the destriers of knights, was riderless.

"The general is down!"

Christian heard the shout even as the line of redcoats began to waver and then falter. Almost in unison, they turned and ran, no longer concerned about proper lines or orders from the officers who were desperately trying to rally them. The Tennesseans and Kentuckians gave pursuit, screaming strange battle cries that curdled Christian's blood even as he watched the bright-coated English disappear into the trees.

Only the dead and dying remained on the field.

New Orleans—and Fiona—were safe.

At least, for now.

****

Dawn brought the firing of cannon, rattling the glass panes of Madame Poreé's house. Several of the belles shrieked, while the older women, their faces pale from the strain of a sleepless night, moved their lips silently in prayer.

"The guns sound closer than last night," Caroline said quietly.

Fiona looked at her. Of all the belles, Caroline was the one Fiona would have wagered would act the most helpless, yet she had calmly poured tea last night and even soothed Mrs. Farnworth's near-hysterics.

"The fog has lifted. It muffled the sound before," Fiona said. "That's why the cannon sound closer."

The frightened servants put food out on the sideboard, but no one seemed hungry. The shelling was continuous, and Fiona wished she could decipher which were the American guns.

Then, suddenly, there was silence.

The women waited with bated breath, scarcely daring to blink. Slowly, they looked at one another.

"Is it over?" one of the matrons murmured.

There was no answer. The women just sat in silence, waiting. Finally, after some moments of no gunshots or cannon, Fiona's aunt ventured, "I believe it is finished."

From the tightened, pinched looks on the older

faces, Fiona realized no one wanted to ask the unspoken question of who won. Were the British even now advancing into the streets of New Orleans to carry out their threat of "Beauty and Bounty"? Would they ransack the city and set fire to it? Fiona glanced at the shuttered windows. How long would it take the British to smash them or ram through the door to find a room full of women? She smoothed her skirt, feeling the comforting handle of her knife, and lifted her chin. She might ultimately be overpowered, but not before she had done significant damage to an attacker. Searching the faces of the matrons, she saw the same determined looks on their faces and almost smiled as she noticed Caroline had a small paring knife on the table beside her.

Still, Fiona's nerves were on edge as the time seemed to creep by. She glanced at the grandfather clock. Half-past ten o'clock. The guns had stopped nearly an hour ago. A tiny bubble of hysterical laughter rose in her throat. If her father had been here, he would not believe nearly a hundred women gathered in one spot could be so quiet. Even the belles were subdued, their sobbing now diminished to silent shaking.

And then, as the chime of the clock rang eleven, a horse's hooves clattered down the cobblestone street. Heads snapped up as ears strained. Then came the cry.

"Victory! Victory is ours!"

Fiona flew to the front window, throwing open the shutter and leaning out as a grinning soldier on a prancing horse looked up at her.

"It is really over?"

"The redcoats turned tail and ran, ma'am. The pirates—uh, privateers—are chasing them through the swamps. They won't get far with Jean Lafitte after

127

them!" He whooped and then he sobered. "But we have wounded, ma'am. Can the womenfolk come to tend to them?"

"Of course," Mrs. Claiborne said from over Fiona's shoulder. "We will gather supplies immediately."

It took just over an hour for the women to arrive at Chalmette, and Fiona gasped at the sight. The battlefield was awash in a sea of red-coated bodies, the brown grass and churned mud bathed in a sickening stench of pooled blood. Intermingled in that seemingly unending river of red were patches of brown shirts and blue uniforms. The air vibrated with the moans and groans of hundreds of dying men.

Fiona heard retching behind her, but she did not need to turn around to see how many were becoming ill at the sight and smell. She did not blame any of them, for she was having to swallow hard to keep her own bile from rising.

Someone brushed her arm. Turning, she was surprised to see Caroline. Although her face was pale, the girl's jaw was set. "Men are dying. We waste time standing here."

Hastily concealing her astonishment, Fiona nodded. "Why don't you start over there?" She pointed to her right. "And the rest of us can fan out every few yards."

Their voices seemed to bring the rest of the women out of their stupor. Medical supply baskets in hand, they began to move slowly forward, kneeling to give comforting pats to those less injured, stopping to quickly bandage limbs that bled while signaling to the able-bodied men—including Charles and Cory, thankfully—who moved toward them with blankets that served as stretchers for the wounded to be carried to the carts that had arrived from the forts. At the moment, it did not matter whether the men wore red or blue. Saving lives was why they were here. Far too often, Fiona had to close the eyes of an unseeing man starring at the sky.

The work was backbreaking and exhausting, but no one complained. Fiona hiked up her skirt, securing it around her waist with a piece of rope to allow her to plough through the mud more easily. Her calves were exposed and she would no doubt get quite a lecture from her aunt when they were finished, but she did not care. So far, she had not found Christian among the wounded, but she was determined not to leave until she had walked the entire field.

Finishing a quick bandage tie, she stood, placing her hands on the small of her back to stretch and then gaped at the sight of Caroline, not far away, with her skirts hiked up as well. Blood and mud smeared the fine muslin, and her silky blonde hair hung in matted strands as she pushed it away from her face, but she appeared to give it no mind. Perhaps she had misjudged the girl. Fiona glanced around and then, in spite of the situation, began to grin. About half the women had followed her example and there were probably more exposed legs on the battlefield than in any brothel in New Orleans. And not one woman seemed to care that there were soldiers working beside them.

They continued their work until the sun was low in the sky. Her aunt had just declared they would need to return home soon when a keening wail shattered the air.

Fiona shaded her eyes with her hand. Mrs. Farnworth was kneeling beside a still form, Charles at her side.

Fiona and Mrs. Claiborne hurried toward them, but

Caroline was closer. By the time they arrived, she had embraced Mrs. Farnworth and was crooning softly in French. The woman seemed to quiet under her touch. Charles put a hand on Caroline's shoulder, and she looked up at him. "Take care of your father's body," she said. "I will stay with your mother." She turned Mrs. Farnworth away from the sight of her husband's body being removed, murmuring again in French. The older lady clung to her.

Charles brushed past Fiona, hardly noticing her, as he escorted his father's body to the waiting cart. Fiona and her aunt followed along behind his mother and Caroline. There was no question now about the need to return to the city and take care of arrangements.

Fiona scanned the field once more. They had not found any Baratarians wounded. Had they fought at Chalmette or across the river? The soldier this morning had said Captain Lafitte's men had chased the British into the woods.

Had Christian been a part of that?

She could only pray that he was alive and well.

****

Sporadic fighting continued. Upon the governor's return, Fiona learned five English ships remained in the river, firing on Fort St. Philip but not advancing. What bothered her more was the fighting at Barataria. Reports came to her uncle that Jean Lafitte was holding off the remnants of the British forces at the Temple. Its *chênière* of tall oaks and mounds of shells made it a natural fort. On the tenth of January, the commodore sent six newly arrived boats to Lake Borgne to assist the Baratarians, but still no word came about Christian.

"It does you no good to fret, dear," her aunt said one

evening nearly a week later when Fiona could not sit still and paced restlessly in the parlor.

"I want to see Christian," Fiona replied. "I do not understand why I cannot send a message."

Mrs. Claiborne looked up from the embroidery she was working on. "You are still betrothed to Charles. It would not be proper."

That stopped Fiona, and she stared at her aunt. "Are you jesting? Ever since Mr. Farnworth's funeral, Caroline spends her time with Charles and his mother."

"No doubt they are both in need of comfort. Caroline has always been a kind girl, although I know you did not care for her much."

"That has changed," Fiona answered as she sank into a chair. "She—and the other girls as well—proved they are more than just fluff balls."

Mrs. Claiborne smiled. "Yes, and the matrons have seen that you—your rather strong personality—can be an asset. You have been accepted by Society, my dear. Marrying Charles will firmly establish you, especially now that he will head his father's bank."

"Charles wants to marry Caroline."

Her aunt frowned. "Has he taken advantage of her?"

Fiona grimaced. "No, I am sure he has not. But he *told* me how he feels…the only reason his parents agreed to our match was because his father wanted to be a congressman. His father is no longer here. Charles does not want to marry me any more than I want to marry him."

Mrs. Claiborne regarded her for a long moment and then resumed her stitching. "I will need to talk with Beatrice then, but I daresay your uncle and your father will both be disappointed."

"I think my father would want me to be happy."

"Of course. But Captain Lafitte's men have shady pasts, in spite of—"

"They are heroes!" Fiona interrupted, leaping to her feet to pace again. "And President Madison has pardoned all of them. What more can we ask for?"

Her aunt sighed and laid down her hoop. "I thought I recognized Captain Picard the night you brought him here. There is scandal associated with him."

Fiona halted. "Do you mean that duel he fought? He explained the lady was a business friend who had no father or brothers to protect her honor. That makes him a knight in shining armor, in my book."

"The 'lady' in question—Chantal Neville, I think William said her name was—is a quadroon friend of Madeleine Rigaud…and Madame Rigaud was one of Captain Lafitte's favorite mistresses. Before they were declared pirates and a price placed on their heads, these men cut quite rakish figures in the evening hours, almost always in the company of beautiful quadroons who accepted lavish gifts. So what do you suppose Captain Picard's relationship really was with his lady *friend*?"

Fiona's heart leapt up her throat and then plummeted deep into her belly. Her face flamed, yet her blood felt like ice in her veins. Christian had led her to believe this was a woman who ran a business… She had been naïve enough to think he meant a legitimate business. The woman had been his mistress! That was why he defended her…because he cared about her. Did he still care? Her aunt had said, "…*is* a friend…"

Fiona swallowed hard. "Does she…does she still live here?"

Her aunt looked at her with sympathy. "I believe a

cottage was provided for her on Rue Burgundy."

Hot tears sprang to Fiona's eyes. Before they could spill over, she turned and fled the room.

Chapter Fifteen

It was finally over. For the past two weeks there had been skirmishes. Jean had driven the British down river, after Chalmette, and on the seventh, the new general who had taken over the British forces asked General Jackson for a prisoner exchange, indicating the English were ready to retreat. The soldiers Jackson had left at the Villeré and LaCoste plantations had been withdrawn, as had smaller forces left in place at Lake Borgne and other parts of Barataria to be sure no British ship returned.

Christian grinned at Marc and Andre as they marched along behind Jean and the Kentuckians and Tennesseans en route to the parade on Rue Chartres.

"It will feel good to have a hot bath and a real bed tonight," Marc said.

"*Moi*? I want to dine on *Boeuf à la Bourguignonne avec Gratin dauphinois*…along with a fine claret," Andre replied with a grin, "and a willing woman."

A willing woman. Christian could not wait to see Fiona again. Thoughts of the sweet taste of her mouth, the feel of her tight nipples crushed against his chest, her soft, lush body writhing beneath his as he thrust into that deliciously hot, tight sheath made his groin tighten painfully. He would make her see that marriage to Charles was *très folie*.

"Well?" Marc asked.

Christian blinked. "What did you say?"

Andre laughed. "I think *notre ami* is already thinking of a particular woman, *non*?"

Christian was spared answering as the contingent of men ahead of them turned the corner of Rue Sainte Ann onto Rue Chartres and a huge cheer went up.

Crowds lined the streets and leaned over wrought-iron balconies…there were even people standing on rooftops shouting. Flags draped across houses and shops. Pine branches and flowers twined around poles. The roar was deafening as the crowd followed the soldiers to the *Place d'Armes* where an arch of triumph, decorated with more flowers and boughs, had been built for the troops to pass through. Two girls representing Liberty and Justice stood on either side. A double line of young ladies, dressed in white gowns and blue veils, representing various states and territories, formed a pathway to the steps of the cathedral where the clergy stood, dressed just as festively. A band played the newly written "Star Spangled Banner." Mayor Girod shouted in both English and French for silence so the speeches could begin, but it was not until Beluche fired the cannon that had accompanied them that the crowd's noise moderated.

Christian heard little of the speeches and paid even less attention to Jackson being crowned with a laurel wreath. He was pretty sure Old Hickory was more annoyed than pleased. Christian searched the crowds for Fiona. He had not seen her among the crowds along the parade route. Was that good or bad?

The ceremony was almost over when he finally caught a glimpse of bright orange hair. She was standing near the church's steps, accompanied by her aunt and Charles and his mother. The governor helped Mrs.

Farnworth up the stairs to receive an award. Vaguely, Christian recalled that her husband had been killed during the big battle, but his eyes were on Fiona. Dressed in a watered-silk gown of turquoise that made him think of warm Caribbean waters, it was clear from the tight fit to her slender waist and flat stomach that she was not with child. A feeling of disappointment flashed through him. If he had sired a baby, his argument over marrying her would be so much easier.

Then he frowned. Charles had taken her elbow and was escorting her up the stairs to join his mother…and Fiona was smiling at him. Christian pushed back a manic urge to rush up on that stage and pull her away from the man. In desperation, he waved at her.

Fiona's head slowly turned and her eyes met his across the sea of people. Her smile faded and then she looked away.

His heart jolted. Her rejection of him could not have been plainer if she had spoken the words.

Why the hell was she angry with him?

****

The crowded ballroom on the second floor of the Exchange was stifling, the floral scent of thousands of blossoms almost overwhelming. Fiona would have preferred staying home so she would not have to see Christian, but she realized that not only was this a victory ball, it was a healing of sorts. People of every description were in attendance—shopkeepers, plantation overseers, blacksmiths, as well as the rugged Kentuckians and Tennesseans—mingled with the Creole and French society on an equal footing. The men had fought together and the women had rallied to care for the wounded after the battle. And, on a personal healing level, Fiona knew she had been accepted, quirks and all, by these people.

From her secluded spot behind a potted palm, Fiona swept her gaze across the immense room, telling herself she really did *not* want to see Christian. She spotted Jean Lafitte, tall and darkly elegant in a cutaway black frockcoat and black trousers, talking and laughing with her aunt. Her uncle, standing beside them, was not glowering for once. It seemed another miracle had happened.

Marc and Andre stood near the group as well, talking with Cory, but there was no sign of Christian. Perhaps he had not come. Fiona sighed, telling herself it was relief she was feeling.

She watched as Charles twirled a smiling Caroline around the floor. She truly *did* feel relief that her betrothal was over and thankful that her aunt had talked to Mrs. Farnworth. Once that lady knew her son loved Caroline and that she seemed to feel the same way about him, Mrs. Farnworth had no problems with breaking the engagement. In fact, she had even applauded Fiona for being so honorable about it all. Not that, in Fiona's mind, there had been anything honorable about the whole idea anyway.

A reel ended, and the crowd cleared a spot for General Jackson to dance with Mrs. Jackson, who had arrived in New Orleans a few days prior. The band struck up "Possum Up De Gum Tree" and Fiona grinned, watching the tall, lanky general hopping around the circle with his short, plump wife bobbing along beside him. An odder-looking couple she had never seen, yet they looked happy together.

"Hiding again?" Christian said from behind her.

Fiona managed not to jump at the sound of his voice,

but her heart pounded and her pulse raced as though she had been gamboling around the dance floor too. She turned slowly, hoping to keep her expression neutral.

"I did not know you were here."

"I just arrived. I had a bit of business to tend to."

Business. Her temper began to simmer. She was not quite the naïve fool she had been before. "Were you visiting Chantal?" she asked before she could stop herself, then clasped a hand over her mouth.

Christian lifted an eyebrow as he took hold of her arm with one hand, placed the other firmly on her back, and guided her toward the balcony. "We are going to talk."

"I am not going anywhere with you," Fiona answered.

"Yes, you are, *ma chèrie*."

"I am not your cherry!" Fiona tried to dig her heels in, but her satin slippers just slid along the polished wood floor.

His mouth quirked up. "I can see I will need to teach you a few French phrases." He opened the door and drew her outside into the cool air.

She shivered, although she didn't think it was from the cold. Immediately, he took off his frockcoat and draped it around her shoulders, bringing the collar together under her chin. His warm, male scent enveloped her.

"Now, what is this about Chantal?"

Her tingling stopped. Fiona straightened her shoulders, trying to remove his coat, but his fingers held it—and her—firmly in place.

"Your mistress. The one you said was a business acquaintance who had no one to defend her honor.

Honor? What is honorable about being a…a…woman who accepts pay for…for…doing what we did—"

"Stop right there, *chèrie*. What you and I did was make love." He ran the pad of his thumb along her chin gently. "Do not ever compare it to anything else."

Fiona tried to ignore the pleasing sensation. "Do you deny she was your mistress?"

Christian looked into her eyes. "No. I have not been a monk. Taking a mistress is a convenient thing to do. It eliminates the risk of becoming diseased by a brothel woman and keeps a man from getting caught in the parson's noose."

"That is hardly flattering to hear," Fiona retorted.

He tilted his head. "Chantal knew exactly what the arrangement was. I would provide her with a house, clothing, jewelry, an allowance. In return, I would be allowed exclusive visitation." Christian held up a hand as Fiona began to speak. "The time period was a year. After that, we would either renew the contract or I would deposit a sum of money into an account for her to live comfortably on until she could make other arrangements." He shrugged. "It is the way life is in New Orleans."

"There really is no need to explain," Fiona said as stiffly as she could, "since you are obviously still seeing her."

He cradled her face in his hands. "I am *not* seeing her. I had Grymes deposit a cheque in the bank for her the day after I made love to you. I have not seen her since I was released from the calaboose."

A small shiver went through her at the gentle possessiveness of his touch. "What other business could you possibly have during evening hours?"

Christian grinned suddenly. "I was looking for just the right gift for you."

Fiona felt her eyes go round. "Gift?"

"*Oui*." Christian reached into his coat pocket and brought out a small box. "I hope you will accept it."

Her hands trembled as she took the box and opened it. Then she gasped. Nestled in a soft bed of black velvet lay a gold ring in which diamonds surrounding a square-cut emerald winked rainbows of colors while the emerald flashed green fire in the dim light. "It is beautiful," Fiona breathed, "but I cannot possibly accept such an expensive gift."

"You can if you consider it an engagement ring," Christian answered.

Startled, Fiona searched his face for any trace of a jest, but he was perfectly serious, his dark eyes intent on her. "You…want to marry me?"

"*Oui*. I have loved you since I made love to you. It nearly killed me when you said you were betrothed to Charles Farnworth. And at the cathedral, when you stood next to him…I wanted to strangle the man with my bare hands. I was going to call him out—"

"You were going to risk a duel for me?"

"*Certainement*." Christian smiled at her. "But then Cory found me and gave me the news that you were no longer betrothed. I decided not to take any chances that the governor or your father would choose another suitor. If it suits you, I want to purchase land and set up a horse-breeding business with your brother and you."

"You want me to be your business partner?" Fiona began to bristle. "Is this ring a first payment for replacing Chantal?"

A look of painful hurt crossed his face. "I guess I

deserved that," he said, "but I do not want you *ever* to compare yourself to her. Never. I want you to be my wife." He took the ring out of the box and slipped it onto her finger. "Will you marry me, Fiona?"

Not sure she could trust her voice at the moment, she nodded slowly.

"Is that a yes?"

"Yes," she whispered, "Oh, yes. I have loved you—"

She did not get to finish, for his mouth was on hers, claiming her. His lips were soft and warm, but his kiss demanding. He thrust his velvety tongue inside her, tasting her fully. Fiona clung to him, her nipples pebbling to hard buds, as he crushed her to his chest. Her tongue battled with his as their kiss deepened, and she grew hungry with need. Instinctively, she pressed her hips against his flat belly, felt the hardness of his arousal, and felt herself grow damp. She mewled softly and Christian growled. With an effort, he drew back, leaving them both gasping for air.

"Banns are supposed to be read," he said, his hands sliding over her shoulders and down her arms, "but I do not think I can wait to make you my wife."

"I have no wish to wait either," Fiona said. "If we boarded one of your ships, Captain LaFitte could marry us, could he not?"

Christian grinned. "I believe maritime law allows that."

She smiled back mischievously. "Then let's go find your captain."

They re-entered the ballroom and found Jean with her father, the governor, General Jackson, and several others. As they approached, Jean spoke to the group.

"The real Battle of New Orleans has been won, and not against the British." He gestured to the people on the dance floor. "New Orleans is united. No more French or Spanish or Creole." He acknowledged Christian and Fiona with a smile. "No more pirates, either. Just Americans."

Fiona smiled back. Her own battle with New Orleans was over too. Now she would become a part of it with her husband.

Treasure of Campeche: Chapter One

Ilsa Drescher's neck ached and she lifted her blonde mane to rub the stiffness out. She'd been sitting in a cramped position, half-buried in a sand dune, peering carefully through blades of pampas grass, for more than two hours. Far past the foam-crested rollers, a schooner lay at anchor, riding the increasing swells of the Gulf of Mexico. She bore no name nor flew a flag, but Ilsa didn't need to see the Jolly Roger to know it was a pirate ship. Spanish galleons carrying gold from Mexico made the high seas a lucrative business, especially in a place as isolated as south Texas.

The men who dinghied to the sandbar to explore the shipwreck that had carried her parents and other ill-fated German settlers wore no uniforms, their bare upper torsos bronze in the sunlight that also caught the glint of gold ear-loops. If Ilsa's parents had survived, she would be in for a sound scolding for even looking at half-naked men, but her parents were gone, swept out to sea by last week's storm that grounded the ship.

One man in particular caught her eye. Taller than most, his long, sun-bleached hair blew back from a chiseled face with high cheekbones and a strong jaw. Fascinated, Ilsa watched as his broad shoulders strained and biceps bulged, hauling on one of the ropes attached to the top gunwale of the listing caravel. The other men grunted in rhythm as they heaved on the lines.

"It's no use," one of them grumbled. "We'll never right her."

"We're trying to stabilize her," the tall man answered in a rich baritone tinged with a French accent. "I'll not risk the lives of my men slipping under an unsteady wreck." Even as he spoke, the ship seemed to shudder and then settled more heavily onto her port side. The hole in the hull gaped black in the low tide.

"There." With a nod, he flicked the rope from the gunwale and waded thigh deep into the water. His body sliced through a breaker with dolphin grace as he made the first dive.

Ilsa held her breath for what seemed an eternity before he resurfaced with a small wooden trunk. She gasped, recognizing it as her mother's.

"Nothin' but clothes," one of the pirates complained as he watched his leader rummage through the trunk.

"Not quite." The captain removed a smaller case, which he opened, and held up a locket. "This is good quality. Perhaps there's more."

His men needed no further encouragement. Eagerly, each of them dove beneath the waves. Ilsa clenched her fists. That necklace was her father's gift to her mother! She had a good mind to march out there and snatch it from the pirate's clasp.

Before she could move, however, someone grabbed her from behind and pulled her up from her burrow. A large hand clamped over her mouth stifled her scream. She looked up into the savage face of a giant Carancahua Indian scout. *Mein Gott*! The Spanish monks who'd given her and the few other survivors refuge had warned her of wandering off. Why hadn't she listened?

The pirate's head whipped around at the muffled

sound. Surprise registered on his face as she was dragged from the sand, clawing at the Indian. He called out something in a language that made the Indian pause, and then headed her way.

Ilsa ceased her struggling to stare at him. He was unarmed and hadn't called to his men to assist him. He must be mad to approach a savage like this!

He spoke to the Indian again in the same language and gestured toward her and then held up the necklace. The Indian grunted and held out one hand. The pirate shook his head, smiling, and indicated that Ilsa be released first.

She suddenly found herself sprawled at the pirate's feet. Without taking his eyes from the Indian, he bent slightly and wrapped an arm around her waist, lifting her to her feet as easily as though she were a sack of feathers. For a moment she was pressed against his side and heat seared through her.

"Walk—slowly—toward the dinghies," he said as he released her.

Ilsa hesitated, her eyes on her mother's locket. "That's my—"

"*Now.*"

She could tell he was a man who was used to instant obedience, yet she still lingered as the Indian fumbled with the clasp to open the pendant. It was the only thing she had left of her mother's!

The pirate's eyes turned dark and stormy. "Would you prefer to have us both killed, *Mademoiselle*?"

The clasp popped open, and the Indian stared at the miniature inside the locket and then he looked at Ilsa and back to the trinket. Horrified, he hissed something at her and threw the locket down, a long knife appearing suddenly in his other hand as he took a menacing step forward.

"Could you use some assistance, *frère?*" a voice behind them inquired mildly.

"I could, Andre," the pirate answered, keeping his gaze fixed on the Indian and not turning. "Is Louis with you?"

"Right here," another man answered as he handed him his sword. "Shall we make quick work of this? There's plundering to be done, and the boatswain warns the glass is falling."

The pirate gave a quick glance at the clouds darkening the horizon. The Indian pointed at the clouds and made a gesture toward Ilsa. He muttered something low, then turned and walked away.

Ilsa bent and scooped up the necklace, only to find the pirate's warm, strong hand covering hers.

"Let me see that."

A tingle coursed up her arm and to the pit of her stomach at his touch. How strange. She'd never felt the like. Reluctantly, she released her prize.

He studied the picture inside. "Is this you?"

Ilsa shook her head. "My mother. We look alike. She…she died in the wreck."

His gaze penetrated her, his eyes a clear, rich hazel now that the anger had ebbed. "I'm sorry. Did your father survive?"

Holding back tears, Ilsa shook her head. "Only a handful did. There's a small mission not far inland. The monks have given us refuge for a few days before we head north." She took a deep breath and held out her hand. "If you'll give me that, I had better get back."

A corner of his mouth lifted in a half-smile as he

tucked the necklace into a pocket of his wet breeches. "Since you don't do well at following orders, *Mademoiselle*, I'll keep it until we're safely back on my ship."

She tried not to dwell on how those wet pants clung to him and outlined his muscular thighs. The very few men—boys really—that her overly-protective father had allowed to court her hadn't looked like this. She had the strangest urge to want to feel the muscles of his broad chest and shoulders. The priest would surely have her doing penance if he knew. She swallowed, her throat suddenly dry. "Once you're on board and I'm on shore, how will you return it?"

"Because," he said as the quirk became a full-fledged grin, "you're coming with us."

"I most certainly am not! I may have lost my parents. I'm not about to lose my virtue too." Her mother—equally protective—had been quite firm that a girl should be a virgin when she married.

He raised a dark eyebrow. "I'll take care of your virtue."

She felt her cheeks warm. "I'm sure you will." She was two-and-twenty years old; she'd heard stories of what pirates did to women. One of her mother's fears, once they'd reached the warm Caribbean waters, was being boarded by pirates.

"Women are bad luck on board," Louis interrupted. "Let her go."

"I'm afraid I can't do that," he answered. "That Indian thinks she is a devil-spirit because of her picture. He'll be back, with others of his tribe, to kill her. The monks wouldn't stand a chance in defense." He turned to her. "You wouldn't want to be responsible for a massacre, would you, *Mademoiselle*?"

With a sinking feeling, she knew he was right. The missionaries had only begun to gain the trust of the Carancahua. She straightened her shoulders and looked into his eyes. "My name is Ilsa Drescher. If I am to be your…guest… I will be protected?"

His eyes glinted with amusement. "*Certainement.* You have my word."

She raised her chin. "You're a pirate!"

He grinned again, his white teeth flashing in his tanned face as he bowed low. "Privateer. Marc Rochelle, captain for Jean Lafitte, at your service."

****

Ilsa was still dumbfounded as they boarded the ship and she was shown to a stateroom. Pirates were dangerous men—witness the one who leered at her when she was lifted over the rail a short while ago, her drenched skirts riding up way too high on her legs—but Jean Lafitte was notorious. When the caravel docked in New Orleans, she'd heard plenty of stories about him… His former fortress at Barataria housed a thousand barbarous pirates and who knew how many wanton women. The place he irreverently called the Temple had been a source for illegal auctions of smuggled goods. He brazenly walked openly on the streets of New Orleans and attended Society's balls, often with a beautiful woman draped on his arm. Every trap set for him he managed to escape. Pardoned by President Madison for helping win the Battle of New Orleans, three years later the pirate and his brothers took up smuggling again, moving their base from the Barataria swamps to a place called Campeche, along the Texas coast. Marc Rochelle worked for Jean Lafitte?

Ilsa clasped her hands together and viewed her surroundings. The cabin was paneled in expensive teak, the red-gold of the wood gleaming from the gamboled oil lamps swaying with the increased pitching of the ship. A teak table was bolted to the wall, the chairs on either side heavily upholstered in satin brocade. The boat lurched suddenly and sent her sprawling on the full-sized bed. Surprised to discover a feather mattress, she fingered the soft angora wool comforter that served as a spread. Jean Lafitte's captain obviously had good taste.

Her thoughts riveted back to her current situation as the schooner heeled over sharply. Waves pounded against the hull as the ship began to pitch in earnest. To her ears, each slap sounded as loud as a musket crack. The wind whistled a sharp keening through the rigging as someone shouted orders to take in sail. She shuddered at the thought of any man climbing the wobbly rope ladders to venture onto wooden yards to haul in the canvas, no doubt soggy and water laden. Heavy footsteps thudded overhead on the deck. The boat listed again, and she clung to the side of the mattress. Perhaps it was the best place to stay. She closed her eyes, the constant yawing of the ship making her dizzy, and then brushed away a tear as the realization that she was penniless and destitute hit her. *Gott in Himmel,* she hated being dependent on a man, let alone a pirate! Could Marc protect her from a mob of lawless men?

As if she had conjured him, the door flew open and Marc stepped inside. His dark glance swept over her as she lay on the bed and he gave her a lopsided smile.

"Waiting for me?" he asked.

She blushed and struggled to sit up, which wasn't easy due to the softness of the mattress and the pronounced heel of the schooner. "Certainly not. I got tired of being thrown about the cabin. What are you doing in this room?"

His eyes gleamed mischievously. "This happens to be my quarters, *Mademoiselle*."

Ilsa jumped up as if it suddenly bitten. "Then I can't stay here."

He raised an eyebrow. "And where would you like to go?"

"There must be another room…somewhere…"

Marc shook his head. "All taken. We have a full crew."

"Then I'll stay on the deck."

"You will stay off the deck. Even as we speak, the man who ogled you is being flogged for his impertinence."

Ilsa winced. "Is that really necessary? He didn't actually say anything or…or touch me."

He frowned. "My men know my rules. I will not tolerate insubordination. You will stay in this room. Do I make myself clear?"

She really hated being given orders. "And if I don't?"

His expression changed, and he stepped closer. So close she could feel his body heat and inhale his warm scent of soap and spice, mingled with the briny scent of the sea. He bent his head, his mouth just inches from hers.

"Then I shall put you over my knee and give you a very personal flogging myself."

Ilsa forced herself to look into his eyes even though her breathing was ragged. "You wouldn't dare!"

His brow lifted. "I would." Marc straightened and

moved to the door. "With as fast as the barometer has fallen, this storm's going to be bad. We're running close-hauled out to sea, and I'll need every man on deck paying attention to his work. You'll be safe here as long as you don't venture out."

"And when you return, sir? How safe will I be then?"

He turned around. "I told you I would protect your virtue. Privateers have very few rules they follow, but one thing we value is our word. You have mine." He studied her. "In return, I expect you to obey me."

Ilsa nearly sputtered. The stubborn streak her father had always said she inherited from him rose to the surface. "You don't own me."

A muscle twitched in his jaw. "*Mademoiselle*, when we get to Campeche, you may wish I did." Giving her a stiff bow, he left.

Ilsa stared at the closed door. Dear *Gott*, what was she going to do in a nest of bloodthirsty, lust-driven pirates? Would she be safe at all?

Chapter Two

The sun shone on a flat sea the next morning, and only a cat's paw breeze ruffled the sails, but as they glided toward the Aranzázun Pass, Marc saw the wrecked ship was gone.

"The storm and tides must have lifted it enough to set it adrift," he said to Louis as he scanned the horizon. "That means we head home."

"The woman?" Andre asked. "Wouldn't it be better if we went ashore and paid a visit to the padre? If the Carancahuas have already been there and found her gone, we can leave her. The men already blame her for the storm that rose so quickly. And now we've lost the booty from the wreck as well."

Marc grimaced. Sailors, even pirates, were a highly superstitious lot. They depended on their ships to withstand the trials and dangers that the high seas tossed at them. The *Giselle* was no different. She had weathered many a storm to bring them back to port safely, and she had remained intact through numerous rammings when capturing Spanish galleons. She was also a stern taskmaster. Sailors who fell overboard were thought to have invoked the wrath of the ship's spirit. As a result, the men swore their allegiance to their vessel as they would to a woman…and not one they were willing to make jealous by the presence of another female on board.

Damn his luck for being on the shore yesterday.

Damn the girl for being out there anyway. Why had the monks not kept closer tabs on her? He sighed. They probably had tried, but Ilsa, in the short time he'd known her, had already proved to be a willful, independent-thinking vixen. She had even disobeyed his orders—his *orders*...something not one of his men would dare to do—and ventured out onto the deck once the wind dropped. Louis had found her, thank God, before any of the other men had seen her. Marc patted the key in his pocket. At least, he'd had the sense to lock the cabin after that escapade. He almost grinned, remembering how she had hissed and her eyes shot blue flames of fire at him for that. He wondered how spirited she would be lying beneath him in bed. Then he pushed the thought away. She was, no doubt, an innocent ingénue, protected by loving parents until now.

"I've told her I'm taking her to Campeche," he said. "Jean can make arrangements to have her sent to New Orleans or wherever she wants to go."

Louis shook his head. "Have you forgotten Lt. Kearney's visit last year, requesting us to leave? President Madison thinks we've abandoned Campeche."

Merde. He *had* forgotten that. It was unlikely that Lafitte would take the chance of reminding Governor Claiborne in Louisiana that Jean had ignored the "request" to vacate Campeche by escorting the girl back to civilization, especially when the forbidden slave-running trade was still lucrative. Probably the only reason Kearney and the *Enterprise* had not been back was that their part of Texas was annexed back to Spain in 1819. Lafitte would take no chances, either, of having it found out that he was working for the Mexican revolutionaries or that Spaniards thought he was working for Spain. Sometimes, the complications of espionage and privateering made Marc long for a regular, normal life on dry land.

"It's too dangerous taking her inland here," he said.

"More dangerous than men with mutiny on their minds?"

Marc shot his second-in-command a sharp look. "What have you heard?"

Louis shrugged. "Mumblings. Jacques suggested she be thrown overboard."

Marc clenched his jaw. "Perhaps the flogging he got for leering at the lady wasn't enough. I don't approve keel-hauling, but I'll not have any man undermine my authority at sea. Especially not new crew."

"We could chain him below decks, but..." Louis hesitated.

"But what?"

"It might incite more men. He's already been flogged for ogling the girl, something that goes unnoticed at Campeche—"

"She is not a whore!" Marc interrupted.

Louis nodded. "Even so, if Jacques is punished further, she may very well be blamed for causing it."

Marc turned to scan the shoreline. It looked deserted. "We may not like what we find if we go in," he said.

"If they've been massacred, we'll have no choice but to take the girl with us. Even the most superstitious man could see that." Louis squinted his eyes to search the shore too. "It would be better to leave her with her people if they're alive."

"Her parents aren't alive."

"*Mon ami*. Are you forgetting Ashantee? She will

not be happy having you bring a beautiful woman home."

Marc groaned inwardly. His quadroon mistress had become far too possessive recently, even though he had made it clear from the beginning that was all she would ever be. "I provide very well for her. She has no reason to complain."

Andre joined them at that moment. "I thought you knew women better than that," he said.

"I'm not taking Ilsa back to be my mistress!" As much as he might like to sample her luscious body, he had given his word. "She is not that kind of woman."

"*Touché*. That is the point, I think, that Ashantee will not miss."

Marc forced his voice to sound nonchalant. "You know the kind of life we lead. I have no room—or time— for *l'amour*."

Andre grinned. "Did I use that term?"

Sometimes Marc wished they weren't such good friends. Then he could smash his fist into Andre Dubois' laughing face. Louis, at least, was somber. The last thing Marc needed was for some woman—and he had to admit that Ilsa was beautiful…and maybe he did admire her stubborn streak just a little—but he definitely did *not* need her to be complicating his life. Or causing Ashantee to withhold her favors because she was angry with him. He gritted his teeth.

"Give the command to drop the anchor. We're going in."

"*Oui, capitaine*." Still grinning, Andre moved away. Louis shook his head and followed him.

Marc glared after them. A blonde, blue-eyed *fräulein* was not going to complicate his life. He simply wouldn't allow it.

****

Ilsa jerked on the brass handle of the door and then cursed roundly when it didn't budge. She paced the small area, fuming. The *hund* had locked her inside the cabin last night. All she had wanted was some fresh air when the seas settled and the boat stopped pitching and rolling. Was she his prisoner? She stopped in mid-pace. "Captive" was a word that came to mind. Pirates plundered for loot. They profited from illegal slave trade. What if Captain Rochelle planned to sell her? *"You don't own me,"* she'd said and he'd answered that she might wish he did when they got to Campeche. She lifted her head, suddenly aware that the boat did not seem to be moving. Peering out the porthole, she studied the shoreline. It remained stationary. They had apparently dropped anchor. *Mein Gott.* What if they just intended to throw her overboard? She'd heard the sailors muttering about what bad luck a woman was on board.

Ilsa swung around as the door opened and Marc stepped through, carrying a tray. The mouthwatering smell of cinnamon porridge reminded her she hadn't eaten since yesterday morning. Did pirates serve a last meal to their victims?

Marc set the tray down on the small table and gestured for her to sit. "There's been a change in plans," he said.

Her stomach felt as though she had swallowed a lump of coal. A *hot* lump of coal. Suddenly her knees felt weak and she sank into the chair.

"Do you feel ill, *Mademoiselle*?" he inquired as he moved closer. "Are you given to *malaise de mer*?"

She might have laughed at the thought of being

seasick, since she'd made the journey across the Atlantic without so much as a stomachache, but the thought of being tossed overboard stuck in her mind. Marc's closeness made her all too aware of how big he was and how powerful his arms and shoulders. She remembered how easily he had picked her up and climbed the rope ladder. He could just as easily toss her over the side of the ship to pacify his men.

But she would not let him see her fear. Her father had taught her some survival skills. She could swim if they didn't truss her up like a turkey first. Perhaps it would be better not to resist.

"Is this my last meal?"

He blinked. "I'm sure the monks will feed you, although perhaps you may have to do penance first."

Ilsa frowned. *Monks*? "You're taking me ashore?"

"*Oui*. I've sent Andre to scout out the mission first. If the Indians have already been there and not found you, it should be safe to return to your people." Reaching into the pocket of his breeches, he pulled out her mother's necklace and placed it in the palm of her hand, closing her fingers over it. "This is yours, *non*?"

The warmth of his hand sent a pleasant shiver through her. Ilsa wondered again about her reaction to him. He was dangerous and she should move as far away as she could get in this small room, yet her body felt an irresistible urge to move closer. She should be grateful— she *was* grateful, she was—that he was returning her to her people. The settlers had been selected to be a part of Stephen Austin's grant from Spain to settle in the fertile land between the Brazos and Colorado Rivers. Had their ship not been blown off course, they would have made landfall farther north and her parents would still be alive.

She had a duty to work that land in their memories. And being set ashore was so much better than being taken to a pirates' den where who knew how many criminals lived and what indecent, immoral things took place? Marc had made it clear he would not be responsible for her once they got to Campeche. The men didn't want her on the ship, either. So this was a much better idea. *Much* better. Yes. She should be happy at this turn of events.

Suddenly, she realized she was holding onto his hand, and Marc wore an amused expression. She jerked her hand away, nearly dropping the necklace. "Thank you for being so kind."

"*Il n'y pas de quoi,*" he said with a small bow and then added, "You are welcome." His expression changed as he heard boots stomping toward the cabin. He turned as Andre pushed open the door. "*Qu'est-ce que c'est?*" he asked sharply.

Ilsa didn't need to understand French to know there was a problem. Andre's mouth set in a thin line and he glanced over at her before answering.

"They're gone."

"Gone?"

"It seems the *padre* was only too eager to give the Germans some supplies and send them on their way once the Carancahua chief indicated that one monk a day would make a *plat savoureux* if they stayed."

Marc narrowed his eyes. "*Bâtards!*"

Ilsa frowned. She knew *plat* mean "dish"… Then she felt the blood drain from her face. "*Savoureux*" sounded like "savory." The Carancahuas were rumored to be cannibals. Could it be true?

"I can see we do not have to translate for you, *Mademoiselle,*" Marc said grimly.

Andre looked even more grim. "The glass is falling again. Boatswain says another squall is on the way."

Marc cursed softly and then turned to Ilsa. "It seems like you will be a guest at Campeche after all."

She might be a guest, but she would not be a welcome one. The sailors were going to blame the storm on *her* for being on board. From his tone, she knew Marc didn't welcome being forced to protect her from that superstitious lot, and she hated having to depend on his protection. But what awaited at Campeche? What would the infamous Jean Lafitte do with her?

Chapter Three

Marc widened his stance on the rolling stern deck and observed his crew. The harsh bands of wind-driven rain had mostly stopped and the men were soaked to the bone, as was he. Being wet didn't account for their surliness, though. He'd seen the dark looks slanted his way when someone didn't think he'd see. A few signs of the cross by the more religious in the height of the gale that had broken one of the spars hadn't gone unnoticed either. Nor had the more typical Creole gestures to ward off evil. Near hurricane-type storms were unusual in late spring and the sailors blamed Ilsa. He'd even heard mutterings of "witch" more than once. He smiled. Perhaps she was a *sorcière*, at that. He couldn't seem to keep his mind off what it would be like to taste the lush fullness of her lips.

He turned his head slightly as Louis joined him. "How goes it on the bow?"

"The bowsprit took a bit of damage."

"Is the figurehead intact?" Marc asked. The last thing he needed was for the wooden, bare-breasted woman that rode beneath the sprit to have sustained damage. Some of the men's beliefs in voodoo were strong, thanks to their many years in the swamps near New Orleans. The crew would see it as a direct omen that the *Giselle* was jealous of her female passenger.

"Intact," Louis said. "It was the first thing I checked

after Jacques hinted it had been damaged."

Marc heaved a sigh of relief. "We should make port in twenty-four hours. If we can keep the men from mutiny until then, I'll have our passenger safely on land." He would deal with Jacques also if there were any more problems.

Louis scanned the sky. The dark clouds that had unleashed so much fury were just a small line on the horizon. Even though the swells were still running, the wind had dropped. "We'll be dead calm in an hour or two," he said, "and we can't use the foresails with the broken spar."

Marc groaned. "That means being out to sea at least forty-eight hours, even with the men rowing." There wasn't a single pirate from Lafitte's band who liked to row. They'd want to enter the bay close-hauled, sails as full of wind as the ship's stores were with booty. On this trip, they'd even lost the spoils of the wrecked caravel. Ilsa would no doubt be blamed for that, too. He had to keep her safe. He'd given his word.

As if reading his mind, Louis asked, "What will you be telling the men about the little *fräulein*?"

"Andre has already told the crew the Germans are gone. We've no choice but to take her with us."

"It might set better with them if they thought she was your captive, then."

Marc considered. They had captured men before. Survivors from boarded galleons who'd then been shipped off as slaves, but none of them had been a woman. Still, if the crew thought she would bring a good price—one that would be split among them as other loot was—it might ensure she'd be left alone and unharmed. He could always give them coin from his own reserve in lieu of actually selling her. Slowly, he nodded. "Spread the word, then."

Louis nodded and left. Marc's gaze swept the deck once more, and he noted with satisfaction that Andre was keeping close to Jacques, ensuring no threat of a mutinous uprising from that quarter. Turning, Marc made his way to the stern and the captain's quarters below deck. As he unlocked the door, he wondered what kind of mutiny he could expect from the little blonde vixen within.

****

Ilsa jumped off the bed as the handle to the cabin door turned. She didn't want to be found lolling on the bed again. If whoever was there were someone besides Marc... She shuddered and then sighed with relief when his big frame filled the doorway, his shirt plastered to his skin in a sinful way.

"You're dripping wet," she said.

"*Oui.*" A corner of his mouth lifted in a sardonic smile. "In case you have not noticed, Mademoiselle, we've had some stormy weather." He began unbuttoning his shirt.

"What...what are you doing?"

He arched an eyebrow. "I'm planning to change into some dry clothes." He stripped off the shirt and walked over to the chest of drawers, one hand undoing his wet breeches.

"You're going to change...here?" Ilsa hated the way her voice pitched high on the last word, but his hulking, half-naked presence—the chest with its hard, rippling ridges...the muscular shoulders and arms—nearly overwhelmed her. He filled the small room completely with his maleness. Her eyes fixated on his trousers and the bulge clearly outlined by the wet cloth. She'd never seen a man naked from the waist down.

"This is my cabin." His mouth quirked again. "You are quite welcome to watch, if you like."

She felt her face heat, realizing that he had noticed where she had been staring. She turned away quickly and moved to the door. "I'll just step out for some fresh air—"

"No, you won't." In two strides he was beside her, his hand grasping her arm. "It's not safe for you out there."

She didn't think it was very safe for her in *here* either, for her body had begun to tingle everywhere. Her breasts suddenly felt heavy and achy. Ilsa fought an urge to press herself up against him and rub her peaked nipples across his hard chest. She felt her face flush again. She licked suddenly dry lips. Where were these thoughts coming from?

His eyes darkened and smoldered as he put a finger under her chin and lifted her face toward him. "*Chèrie*," he said softly, "your mouth is begging to be kissed."

Before she could stop him, his arms encircled her waist and he pulled her close, his mouth covering hers. His lips were warm and firm, the pressure gentle. He angled his head, as he coaxed a response from her. His tongue lightly traced the outline of her lips, persuading them to open. Ilsa made a soft mewling sound deep in her throat as his velvet tongue began a slow, easy exploration of her mouth. She slid her hands over his shoulders, loving the hard, rippled feel of his muscles and the surprisingly silky texture of his hair. She hardly noticed that his hand slipped up to cup her breast until she felt his thumb flick over hardened nipple. She gasped even as he suddenly pushed back from her.

His eyes were still dark with desire as he grabbed his shirt from where he'd tossed it and flung open the door. "Forgive me, *chèrie*. That was not supposed to happen." Without bothering to put the shirt on, he moved down the gangway, leaving Ilsa staring breathlessly after him.

Chapter Four

"Did *la petite belle* keep you up last night?" Andre asked with a grin as Marc stood by the rail midship the next morning as they neared the coastline of Campeche.

He truly would have liked to throttle his friend. Ilsa had kept him awake all right, even though he'd used Louis' quarters to sleep while Louis stood his watch. All Marc did was toss and turn, remembering the sweet taste of her mouth, how perfectly the soft curves of her body had fitted against him, and how her rounded breast had filled his hand. He couldn't ignore the fact that she had responded to him as well. That her arms had gone around his neck and her fingers threaded his hair...or that contented purr that came from her and made his erection painfully hard. He rubbed his unshaven chin. "Why do you ask?" he growled as Andre looked over the rumpled clothes he wore, still encrusted with the dried saltwater from yesterday's storm.

"You look a bit disheveled," Andre said diplomatically, although he couldn't quite wipe the smile from his face.

Marc ignored the smirk. He'd showered in Louis' quarters, but he was going to have to return to his cabin for a change of clothes. He recalled Ilsa's fascination with his undressing yesterday, and his groin tightened at the thought of slowly stripping for the little temptress, even as his mind pushed the thought firmly away. He had absolutely no business taking advantage of such innocence, and he certainly didn't have a place in his life for a woman who would expect an honorable relationship.

"Come with me," he said abruptly to Andre and started toward his cabin. When they reached it he added, "Take Ilsa for a short walk."

One black eyebrow arched high on Andre's forehead. "Ah," he said understandingly, "you have had a small *raisonnement* and do not wish to face *la belle* alone?"

Marc gritted his teeth. "We have not had an argument. Ilsa simply requested to take some fresh air." The look he gave Andre would have quelled a lesser man, but Andre just gave him an incorrigible grin.

"*Naturellement*," he said. "I shall be delighted to escort *la belle* wherever she wishes to go."

"*Non*. She is to go only as far as the companionway to the stern deck. Return in ten minutes." Without giving Andre a chance to retort, he pushed the door open.

Ilsa spun around, a wet cloth from the water basin in her hand. Her bodice was unlaced, the dress pushed down around her shoulders, exposing the creamy cleavage of her full breasts. She gasped and her face went scarlet as she saw Andre behind him. "*Verflucht!*" she said and Marc suspected she had just cursed him. She jerked her sleeves back up, covering herself, her eyes sparking blue fire.

"You might knock first!"

"No *débat*, eh?" Andre murmured, his green eyes gleaming mischievously as he gave a lavish bow to Ilsa. "Forgive me, *Mademoiselle*, for intruding. *Le Capitaine* wishes for me to escort you on a brief walk." He glanced at Marc obliquely and then back to her. "If you should wish to go."

Ilsa tied the laces of her gown and raised her chin. "I should very much like to go on deck," she said and swept past Marc without looking at him. Andre chuckled and then shut the door before Marc could push him through it.

Marc glared at the closed door. So now the little vixen was angry at him! What had he done to deserve that? She had not resisted his kiss, and he had barely brushed against her covered breast before he had stopped himself last night. He certainly hadn't done anything to ruin her. He shook his head as he quickly changed into clean clothes. Ladies always had expectations of men. It was one more reason he needed to leave her alone.

He joined Andre and Ilsa on deck. The men were lowering sail as the schooner approached the small harbor. The tide was in, allowing them to pass over the sandbar, and the pier began to fill with Campeche's residents. A group of women waited on shore to welcome the men home. Marc saw Ashantee among them, her long, dark hair blowing in the wind, her golden skin kissed by the sun. He smiled as the boat bumped gently against the dock and lines were thrown. At least, his mistress knew where she stood with him. She would give him no trouble.

Chapter Five

Ilsa tried not to stare as she was escorted down the gangplank with Andre on one side and Marc on the other. She had expected a crude, makeshift camp of hovels, but this… Campeche was a complete village.

Straight ahead of her was an impressive two-story red-brick building. Cannons mounted from its roof pointed directly toward the inner harbor they had just entered. To one side were barracks and, past them, large warehouses. Far to the other side were an empty cattle pen and a stable. The dirt streets surrounding the brick building were filled with shops, saloons, and a boardinghouse. Small cottages stood scattered here and there.

Ilsa was jostled suddenly as a buxom brunette with the golden skin of a quadroon pushed past her and flung her slender arms around Marc's neck. "I have missed you, *chéri!*" she purred in a low-throated voice and then gave him an open-mouthed kiss.

Heat seared Ilsa's face as she quickly looked down at the ground. She should have known that Marc would have a *mätresse*. How foolish she had been to think their kiss might have meant anything to him. Hadn't he said it should never have happened? She felt her face grow even warmer as she remembered how she had responded like a wanton to him, running her hands over his bare back, opening her mouth and savoring his tongue, pressing herself closer, welcoming his hand on her breast. *Du lieber Gott*! No man had ever done any of those things to her before. No man had ever made her entire body tremble and turn her knees to melted butter. Ilsa took a deep breath and raised her chin. She had hidden her feelings well earlier; she would continue to do so.

"Andre, who is this person you've brought with you? A captive?" the quadroon asked as she linked her arm with Marc's and scrutinized Ilsa, taking in her rumpled, water-stained dress and muddied shoes. "She's going to need some cleaning up—and more meat on her bones—if you expect to get a good price for her."

Ilsa stared at her, feeling the blood drain from her face. They really *were* planning to sell her? *Gott in Himmel*! Why had she thought Marc would protect her?

"She's not a captive, Ashantee," Marc said as he disengaged himself from his mistress. "Ilsa's ship wrecked off the Aránzazn coast."

Ashantee's unusually colored gray eyes narrowed speculatively. "Why did she not stay with her people?"

"Her parents died. The others…deserted her."

"Why?" Again, she swept her gaze over Ilsa. "Is she diseased? She's awfully pale."

Marc's eyes crinkled at the corners as he tried not to smile. "She's healthy, as far as I know."

Ilsa felt herself blush. Was he making a reference to her overly enthusiastic reaction to him last night?

"Then why not sell her?" Ashantee asked. "I think Jim Bowie is about to run some slaves north. He could fetch a good price for her once they cross the Sabine—"

"I told you. She's not a captive and she's not for sale." Marc replied. "She'll stay at the boardinghouse for now as my—our—guest."

For a moment, Ashantee's eyes hardened and Ilsa felt as though twin blades of steel pierced her. The woman obviously did not like her, but Ilsa was too relieved to care. Then, the subtle threat disappeared from the *mâtresse's* face as she looked up at Marc and smiled. She ran her fingers along his bicep possessively.

"*Certainement*," she murmured demurely, "you know best." She smiled at Ilsa and reached over to brush Ilsa's hair back in a friendly gesture. Ilsa suddenly yelped in pain. "*Merde! Pardon!* My ring got caught in your hair," Ashantee said as she removed a few strands from it. "I should be more careful. Forgive me." She turned back to Marc. "But come, let me welcome you home properly."

"I'm afraid it will have to wait," Marc answered, "I have urgent business I need to discuss with Jean first." He nodded at Andre. "Would you escort Ilsa—Miss Drescher—to the boardinghouse? Tell Mrs. Campbell I will foot the bill." He turned and strode away.

Ashantee gave Ilsa a warning look before she swept up her skirts and flounced away.

****

"You seem to be somewhat distracted, *mon ami*," Jean said as he splashed cognac into a snifter and handed it to Marc in the oak-paneled study of the brick building he called Maison Rouge. He raised his own glass in a salute. "You brought the *Giselle* and her crew home, safe and sound, from the storm. That is more important than losing the caravel's bounty."

Marc accepted the glass and studied the gold-and-red pattern in the Oriental carpet that covered the hardwood floor. Jean would not miss whatever small amount of goods they could have salvaged from the caravel. Other ships carried far more expensive goods than what would have been on the German settlers' boat. He thought about the gold locket that meant so much to Ilsa.

Jean Lafitte tilted his head to study Marc. "It is the woman, *n'est-ce pas*?"

Marc took a swallow of the smooth French brandy. Why he had told Ashantee he had urgent business that couldn't wait, he didn't know. She always was ready to accommodate him, and this was the first trip he could remember returning from that he didn't go first to her bed. But her kiss had not stirred him. Instead, he remembered Ilsa's soft lips under his, her mouth opening to allow him entrance…and the fact that she had been standing there watching him. She truly must be an *enchantresse*.

"The crew blamed her for the storm and our lack of booty," he said.

Jean shrugged. "Superstition. What surprises me is that the Carancahua gave her up so easily."

"They're superstitious too." He had told Jean of the picture inside the locket and how Ilsa's people had taken a hasty leave.

"So what do you plan to do with her?"

"*Moi*?"

"*Oui*," Jean replied and swirled his cognac. "You captured her. She is yours."

Somehow, he didn't think Ilsa would see it that way. Her eyes would spark blue flames at him if he even mentioned it. "I've told her she is not a captive," he said.

"No doubt a wise decision on your part. I was told you were seen leaving her cabin in a state of half-dress." Jean grinned. "Women capitulate much more easily if they think it was their choice."

Marc groaned. Whoever had seen him leave certainly had been quick to spread the rumor. *Merde*. Nothing had happened except a kiss. From her cold treatment of him the next morning, she obviously blamed him for taking advantage of her. He cursed silently again. "Could we arrange for her passage to New Orleans? She could find suitable work there." Even as he said it, a voice inside his head protested her leaving, but he pushed the thought aside. There was no place for the little temptress here at Campeche.

Jean shook his head. "The only ship I have leaving is a slaver. I can't risk her going to the authorities with that news."

Swallowing the last of his brandy, Marc put the glass down. "Perhaps I could arrange an escort to take her to the land her people are settling."

"Too far. You'd be gone too long." He sighed. "Bowie spotted the brig *Enterprise* on his last run. I can't take the chance of not having you here if Lieutenant Kearney returns."

When he returns, Marc thought, but kept silent. The privateers were living on borrowed time, and Jean knew it. The United States had made quite clear that they wanted no more interference with Spanish ships. Jean had quite convincingly persuaded Lt. Kearney on his last visit to give him some time to disperse the people at Campeche, but that had been nearly a year ago. "I don't think it would be wise to keep her here."

"*Oui*, but we have no choice. I do not envy you, *mon ami*, when Ashantee learns of your indiscretion." Jean raised his glass in mock salute. "One should always keep *la maîtresse* away from *l'amour du coeur, non?*"

Marc groaned inwardly. Ilsa was not the love of his heart, but he knew Ashantee's fiery temper. More than likely, he would be sleeping alone tonight.

Oddly, the thought didn't bother him that much.

Chapter Six

Ilsa looked out the window of the second floor room of the boardinghouse and watched as several women in colorful skirts and lowcut blouses linked arms with some of the pirates from the *Giselle* and moved off toward a row of cottages not far from the barracks. She didn't need to be told who—or what—they were. She didn't see Marc's tall, broad frame among the men, and she squinted, trying to see if Ashantee was perhaps with another man, but the raven-haired beauty was not in the group.

Letting the curtain fall back, Ilsa nibbled her lip. The woman had made it abundantly clear that she was involved with Marc. Was it exclusive? Did he care for her? Ilsa had a vague idea that a *mätresse* knew how to please a man. The memory of Marc's warm, firm lips on her own and the daring thrill of his hand brushing her breast sent searing heat pulsating through her body, followed by a pain as sharp as a dagger point as she remembered that Marc had kissed Ashantee right in front of her. That's how little "their" kiss had meant. It was nothing compared to an experienced *kurtisane* who no doubt knew what to do to his body everywhere. How she longed to know what those skills were! Had Marc laughed secretly at how *dumm* Ilsa was?

Another thought struck her, simultaneously sending both fire and ice through her veins. Her stomach felt queasy while her nipples began to throb. Marc was paying for her room. What would he expect in return?

Gott. She had to get some fresh air. She grabbed a shawl that Mrs. Campbell had lent her and headed down the stairs. Once she got to the street, she turned in the opposite direction from the group of cottages. She wandered along the shops, marveling at the vast array of merchandise displayed. Everything from silks and linens to spices, trinkets, and utensils. She picked up a black lace fan, admiring the intricate detail, and then quickly put it back as it dawned on her that everything here was smuggled goods. She frowned. All of this merchandise was taken by pirates. Men who sold their captured victims as slaves and burned ships…

"Why such a scowl, *Mademoiselle*?"

Ilsa jumped at the sound of Marc's rich baritone behind her and then felt her stomach flutter as he reached around her shoulder, his breath warm on her cheek.

"You should have this," he said as he picked up the fan and held it out to her. "It would make a nice contrast to your hair."

Ilsa clasped her hands behind her and shook her head. "I couldn't."

He gave her a quizzical look. "Why not?"

She couldn't very well tell him that she wouldn't take stolen goods. That it was…criminal. Everyone who lived here was a part of this way of living. She shook her head again. "It wouldn't be proper for me to accept a gift from you."

His mouth quirked up. "Do you think I would expect something in return?"

Ilsa felt her face flame. The thought had flitted through her mind, scandalous as it was. Her traitorous body wanted Marc's touch, his embrace. Yet…she would not be like those women she had seen disappearing into the cottages. Her chin came up.

"I don't wish to become beholden to you. I intend to repay whatever expenses I'm incurring."

He arched an eyebrow. "How do you expect to do that?"

Her face heated again, but she kept her gaze steady. "I shall get some sort of job while I am here."

The quirk turned into a grin. "There's really only one kind of—job—women do here. I don't think you'd be interested in…um, being a *participante*."

"There must be something—honorable—that I can do! Perhaps work in one of these stalls?"

Marc shook his head. "These goods have been split among the men. They usually barter with each other for what they want. Of course, Jean keeps the expensive treasure of Campeche securely hidden. These stalls are mainly for the traders that put into port, or General Long's troops. Both groups are too rough for a woman who isn't… Well, it's not women's work." He turned and said something in rapid French to the stall owner. The man nodded and disappeared, only to reappear almost instantly with a swath of material. Marc took it from him and shook it out.

Ilsa gasped at the gown of blue watered-silk with delicate, black lace trim along the scooped neckline and the edge of the short, puff sleeves. The empire waistline flowed in smooth lines. A dress fit for a queen.

"It's yours," Marc said and placed it in her hands.

"I can't—"

"Yes, you can. Jean asked that I bring you to dinner at Maison Rouge, and he will expect you to be dressed in proper fashion." He put the fan on top of the dress. "Don't forget this."

"I don't want to be indebted," Ilsa said stubbornly.

"I told you not to worry about that. It can be discussed later," he said. "Now let me walk you back to the boardinghouse before one of the—ladies—that do work here decides she wants that dress."

He offered his arm and Ilsa took it, her body warring with her mind. Just how much later were they going to "discuss" her debt? And how would she pay it? A tingle of anticipation shot through her.

Chapter Seven

Marc opened the door to the room in Maison Rouge that he used when in port and caught the musky scent of Ashantee's perfume. As his eyes adjusted to the dimness of the interior, he saw her near the armoire, one of its doors open.

"Looking for something?" he asked.

Ashantee spun around, one hand to her mouth and then quickly recovered. "Ah, *mon cher*," she said in a sultry voice as she glided toward him, "the last time I was here…" She swept a glance toward the bed and back to Marc. "I left without my barrette."

He crossed his arms over his chest. "And you think it might be in my wardrobe?"

She gave a graceful shrug, causing the wide neckline of her blouse to slip and expose the soft top of her breast. "I would think you put it somewhere safe."

"I haven't seen it."

"Ah. Well." She put her hands on his forearms and gave a gentle tug. "Since I am here, let me welcome you home properly."

"I don't have time right now."

"Why not?" Her fingers trailed down to undo his breeches.

He stayed her hand. "I said, not right now."

She stepped back, lower lip thrust out in a pout. "It is that woman you brought back, isn't it?"

"Ilsa has nothing to do with this. I have things to do."

Ashantee's eyes narrowed. "She's a little scrawny for your taste, *non*? Does she have some special skill as a *putain*?"

Anger flared through Marc. "She is not a whore. Her parents were killed in a shipwreck. I merely saw her safely here."

"So you had to be *Le Protecteur*?" she asked, her voice dripping with sarcasm. "I am sure the *fräulein* was most appreciative."

He felt a muscle tick near his jaw. "Are you jealous?"

"*Non*! I know well how to pleasure you. *Jalousie*?" She laughed, but it sounded brittle. "I have no reason—"

"That's right," Marc interrupted. "You have no reason to be jealous. I have never told you that I love you. When you agreed to be my mistress, you knew how it would be. No commitment. No forever. All I promised was that I would take care of you financially when the time came for you to leave."

"You are cruel, *monsieur*!" Tears welled up in her gray eyes.

Marc sighed. He knew they were crocodile tears, but as a gentleman, he could not ignore them. "I have no intention of being cruel, Ashantee. If you truly wish to please me, I would ask that you befriend Ilsa. Campeche must seem a strange place to her. Make her feel welcome. Get to know her."

Ashantee dabbed at her eyes with the handkerchief he offered and gave him a speculative look. "Perhaps I have misjudged the situation," she said demurely and handed back the square of linen. She moved to the door and opened it, turning back before she left. "You are right. Getting to know the German girl will be a good idea."

Marc frowned as he watched her go. It wasn't like Ashantee to acquiesce so easily, nor did he care for the glint that had fleetingly passed through her eyes. He sighed again, hoping that a catfight wasn't in the offing.

****

"Would you care for more wine, *madamoiselle*? It is a fine claret," Jean said as he held a crystal glass up to the chandelier light in the dining room of Maison Rouge. "The new use of corks and bottles has produced a deeper red than in the past. Ruby. Much like your lips."

Ilsa smiled as she accepted the glass from him. Jean Lafitte certainly wasn't what she had expected of a pirate. *Privateer*, she remembered him emphasizing when they had been introduced. He was tall, with a leaner build than Marc, his black hair slightly streaked with gray at the temples, his dark eyes attentive, his smile quick and easy. A thoroughly charming gentleman who would have been at ease in any European court.

"Marc told me what happened," Jean said as he set the decanter down. "My condolences on the loss of your parents." He glanced at Marc and then back to her. "You are welcome to stay here as my guest, of course."

She caught Marc's small frown and wondered if he wished she were gone. He probably would rather be with his *maïtresse* instead of sitting here at dinner with her. Ilsa swallowed past the sudden lump in her throat. She had no right to want Marc to kiss her again, nor any reason to believe he might want to. The only reason she had this gown was because Jean Lafitte expected his guests to be dressed properly. She could see that now, since he was dressed in a black frockcoat with red satin waistcoat and a snowy cravat at his throat. Even Marc wore a dark, tailored coat and crisp linen shirt, although he had left the collar open and she could see just a bit of his muscular chest. She looked away quickly when he glanced her way, not wanting him to think she was flirting or that she longed to be cradled in his arms. He hadn't escorted her to the boardinghouse on their arrival…he'd had Andre do it. No doubt Marc wanted to be with Ashantee. The woman was beautiful and…and *experienced*. What would it feel like to be made a woman in every sense of the word?

Her thoughts were interrupted as a servant entered. "James Bowie says he needs to speak with you, Captain."

Jean looked faintly annoyed. "I am entertaining a guest. He knows that."

"Yes, Boss, he do," the servant replied, "but a ship's gone down." The man glanced at Ilsa and then back to Jean. "The slaver you were expecting."

"Damnation!" Jean stood, his eyes suddenly glowing coals of fire. "Get the small boats manned."

"Already done." A man in buckskin breeches and jacket said from the door. "I didn't think you'd want me to wait to issue the orders."

"Good work, Bowie," Jean said as he stripped off his frock and waist coats. "*Mademoiselle*, please enjoy the cuisine," he said with a slight bow. "It is a shame we cannot join you."

Then he and Marc were running through the door and down the hall.

****

Ilsa watched from the shelter of a scrub oak the next morning as Jean Lafitte's men brought wet, bedraggled, and half-naked slaves ashore. Some were clearly exhausted and struggled to walk, while others tried to assist them. Whips cracked in the air above their heads, urging them on. Jacques seemed to take particular pleasure in prodding one young female slave, even though she was keeping up with the rest. They were herded into an empty cow pen near the stables and their legs shackled.

"How many did we lose?" Jean Lafitte asked as he neared the pen.

"About half," the man named Jim Bowie answered. "Damn shame."

"Arrgh, that's several thousand dollars of flesh lying in Davy Jones locker," another man added.

"Did the captain survive?" Jean asked.

"Aye. Campbell came in on the last boat."

"Send him to me. I want a full report," Lafitte said and turned back to the house.

Ilsa stared after him. He had hardly looked at the slaves, who were cold and no doubt hungry. It was hard to compare the gentleman from last night's dinner to this uncaring, hard man.

"You shouldn't be out here," Marc said from behind her.

She turned and inhaled sharply. He was thoroughly soaked, his clothes clinging like second skin and outlining the hard ridges of his belly and the muscular curves of his thighs. Ilsa forced herself to gaze away from that powerful body and looked into his eyes. "What happened to you?"

He shook his head, spraying droplets of water from

his slicked-back hair. "I went diving for any survivors that might still have been shackled to the oar-wells."

She closed her eyes. "What a horrible way to die." She quickly opened them as she heard a man scream and then gasped as one of the pirates started beating a young male who was trying to resist.

Putting a hand on her shoulder, Marc gently turned her around. "Come. You don't need to be seeing this."

"Why are they being beaten? They nearly died. They should be fed instead."

Marc inclined his head. "They'll be fed bread and beans to keep up their strength."

"Ah, the *fräulein* is worried?" Ashantee sidled up to Marc, placing herself between them. She smiled at Ilsa. "No need to worry, *mon ami*. The Boss always keeps his slaves fed until market day. He wants them to fetch a good price."

"I think it's disgusting that those poor people are going to be sold like animals," Ilsa replied.

Ashantee gave a delicate shrug. "It is life in America."

Ilsa looked at Marc. "Can't they at least be fed something besides bread and beans? From the food that was on the table last night, I know Mr. Lafitte has bountiful stores."

Ashantee laughed before Marc could answer. "She is precious, *non*? To care so much?"

Another slave screamed and Ilsa felt tears welling up in her eyes. Marc cursed. "*Excusez-moi*, ladies," he said. "I had best go stop that."

Ilsa watched as he took long strides across the yard. He yanked the man off the slave by his collar and blocked the blow as the other swung around to fight. Ilsa could hear the thud as Marc's fist landed in the man's stomach and he fell to the ground moaning in pain. "Enough," he said and looked around. "Anyone else want to disagree with me?" He got some black looks, but the other men slunk away.

"Well, at least he's done the right thing," Ilsa said and turned to Ashantee, but the woman was gone. She caught a glimpse of the quadroon's brightly colored skirt at the door of a shop that held herbs before she disappeared inside. Ilsa turned to go back to the boardinghouse and saw Jacques heading her way. She quickened her pace, not wanting to confront him, but he stopped by the herb shop and looked behind him before going through the door.

Ilsa breathed a sigh of relief and hurried on.

Chapter Eight

Ilsa wandered idly past the shops the next morning, in the opposite direction from those poor, captured slaves. Marc had joined Lafitte and others in salvaging what they could of the wrecked slave ship, and she was at odds as to what to do. She had to do *something* to take her mind off those people who had drowned…and those who had lived, only to be sold.

Yesterday, Ashantee had suggested that if she were so concerned about the slaves, maybe she work in the kitchen. Ilsa didn't know if the quadroon was serious or not, but it wasn't a bad idea. She decided to return to the boardinghouse and ask Mrs. Campbell about it.

The older woman appraised her as she explained that she needed to keep busy, that she wasn't used to having idle hands. "Maybe I can cook," she finished.

"Cook?"

"Yes, I often cooked *kartoffel klösse und fleischpastete* at home."

Mrs. Campbell blinked. "What on earth is that?"

"Potatoes and meat pie," Ilsa replied and swallowed a sudden lump in her throat as she remembered the aroma of the fresh, warm *brot* her mother always baked to go along with the dinner. She suddenly missed the food of her homeland. The rest of the German settlers should have reached their new homes by now. Was someone preparing a *sauerbraten* to celebrate?

"Interesting," Mrs. Campbell said, "but perhaps you could start with something a little less substantial? Dessert maybe? Our cook always complains that its extra work for him, although he does an excellent job."

Ilsa felt herself brighten. "*Apfeltorte*—apple torte—is a favorite of mine!"

"I think you may be in luck, then. Captain Lafitte keeps a fresh supply of fruit on hand."

Ilsa did not want to know where he would get fresh fruit on what was a sandy island with scrub trees. She was only too aware of the wealth of fruit that grew in Mexico and was probably aboard Spanish galleons the pirates captured. She pushed the thought away, just grateful for something to do as she followed Mrs. Campbell to the kitchens and was introduced to the cook.

She had just finished patting the dough into a tin pan when Ashantee entered. The quadroon smiled at her. "I was told you were in here cooking."

Ilsa forced herself to smile back. She wasn't at all sure Ashantee actually liked her, but the woman was trying to be friendly. "I'm making a special dessert for tonight," she said and started laying apple slices over the dough."

Ashantee came closer and raised the bowl that held a sweet, creamy mixture. "What do you do with this?" she asked.

"It goes over the apples," Ilsa answered.

Ashantee gave it a delicate sniff. "Hmmm. Perhaps you could add some nutmeg to it?"

"What is nutmeg?"

The other woman laughed lightly. "It is a spice from the Indies, somewhat like clove, with a hint of mint and pepper. I'll get some for you."

She returned a short time later with a pouch. Ilsa held it up to her nose. "It smells wonderful," she said and sprinkled the contents over the apples.

Ashantee nodded. "The men like spice in their foods. I'm sure you'll be well complimented."

And she was. More than one pirate returned and asked for a second helping when the evening meal was served. To her disappointment, the torte was all gone by the time Marc and Jean returned from their salvage.

"The men speak highly of your dessert," Marc said as he filled a plate and joined her at the table where she had taken a late dinner. "Perhaps you'll make it again soon?"

"I'd be delighted to," Ilsa said with a smile that faded as Ashantee approached them.

"Ah, you have returned," the quadroon said to Marc as she placed her hand on his shoulder possessively and leaned over to kiss him. "I have missed you."

A strange look crossed his face, but he moved over to allow Ashantee room to flounce down beside him on the bench. The woman leaned against him, her ample breast pressed into his arm, and ran her hand seductively along his cheek.

Ilsa gathered her utensils and stood. "Excuse me," she said and turned away before either of them could see the disappointment on her face. She had no right to be disappointed. Marc had done what any gentleman would do. He had escorted her to safety and given her a place to stay. Why would she expect more than that? It was obvious, even to her, that Ashantee was his woman. How could Ilsa expect him to give up a skilled, experienced woman who knew what to do to pleasure a man? To give her up for a virgin? She bit her lip as she hurried toward the kitchen. She was a complete *dummkopf* for even thinking he might be interested.

Ilsa blinked back tears. She would not cry. She set her plate on the kitchen table, thankful the cook's back was turned, and left through the back door to make her way to the boardinghouse.

She would not cry. Not over a fairy tale that wouldn't come true.

****

The dining room was strangely deserted the next morning when Ilsa made her down from her room. Mrs. Campbell moved around with a frown on her face.

"Where is everyone?" Ilsa asked. "Usually, this place is full."

The woman's frown deepened. "It seems a lot of men got sick last night."

"Sick?"

"My husband said he thought at first the men were drunk, giggling like girls and acting like fools talking to themselves, but then the vomiting started, along with the cramping and flushed skin that turned cold."

The door opened just then and an unsmiling Louis came toward Ilsa. *"Le capitaine* wishes to speak to you, *mademoiselle*. You are to come with me."

Ilsa put down her napkin and stood. "Of course. What does he wish to talk to me about?"

"You will see."

Perhaps Jean Lafitte had found a way to send her back to civilization. She nearly trotted to keep up with Louis's long strides. The idea should be elating, but instead, she felt a touch of melancholy. She would never see Marc again. Then she remembered how brazenly familiar Ashantee had been with him at dinner. There was no future for Ilsa with Marc. She knew that.

Both Marc and Ashantee were seated in Jean's study when Louis opened the door for her to enter. Jean turned from gazing at the small fire in the hearth. "*S'il vous plaît*, have a seat," he said.

Ilsa looked around the room. Something was wrong. Ashantee avoided looking at her and Marc's eyes were troubled. She sat. "What is it?"

"You made dessert for the men last night?" Jean asked.

She nodded. "Yes. *Apfel*—apple—torte."

"How did you make it?" he asked.

She knotted her brows. "A simple pie dough. Sliced apples—oh. Was I not supposed to use your stores, *mein Herr*? I am sorry—"

Lafitte waved his hand. "I don't care about the apples. What else did you put into that dessert?"

"A mixture of egg, sugar, and cream."

"Anything else?" His dark eyes bore into hers.

"Nutmeg. It was a lovely spice I'd never tasted before."

He raised an eyebrow. "You helped yourself to my spices as well?"

"I got them for her," Ashantee said in a small voice, "but I told her to use only a little."

Confused, Ilsa stared at her. Ashantee had said no such thing. Had she? No. She hadn't. She had stood there and watched while Ilsa poured the contents of the bag over the tortes. Was she deliberately lying? Ilsa frowned. More than likely, she was afraid *Kapitän* Lafitte would be angry with her for taking the spice. Well, Ilsa wouldn't argue and get her into trouble.

"I'm sorry if I shouldn't have used the spices," Ilsa

said. "I'll be glad to work to repay you whatever they cost."

Jean began pacing. "The spices are meant to be used. I just need to decide if what you did was deliberate or not."

"I don't think I understand," Ilsa said.

"In large doses, nutmeg can cause delirium," Marc answered her from his chair, his eyes watchful. "Followed by becoming ill and falling into a stupor."

"Men can die on their own vomit," Jean said as he paused to face Ilsa. "Was that your intent?"

She felt herself blanch. "*Mein Gott*! No! Why would I want to do that?"

"That is exactly the question I would like to have answered," Jean replied.

Ilsa looked at Marc. "Please. You have to believe me. I would never try to sicken anyone, let alone kill someone! I didn't know—" She felt the sting of tears welling up in her eyes and she blinked them back.

A muscle twitched in Marc's jaw. "Perhaps you should refrain from using spices that you are not familiar with."

Ilsa twisted her hands together in her lap. "I am truly sorry. I was only trying to be useful. It won't happen again. *Ich schwören*—I swear—I meant no harm."

"There, *mon ami*," Ashantee soothed as she moved over and took Ilsa by the arm. "Let me take you back to your room. It was a simple mistake that can be forgiven, *oui*?"

She looked at Jean and he waved them both out.

Ilsa felt herself tremble as she allowed herself to be led out. Jean—and worse, Marc—were now suspicious of her. Over a simple mistake. Why hadn't Ashantee warned her about the nutmeg?

She glanced at the quadroon who smiled at her brightly. Just whose "mistake" was it, really?

****

Jean poured Louis and Marc a brandy after the women left and took a healthy swallow before he spoke. "I'm not sure it was just nutmeg that made the men sick."

Marc stopped with his glass half way to his mouth. "What do you mean?"

Jean shook his head. "According to the surgeon, the symptoms of euphoria followed by vomiting are typical if the kernels are pressed and the oil used. He's heard of men who see and hear things that aren't there. But the severe cramping? Most of the men reported they felt like they'd been spliced open with a knife. That's *not* typical."

"The woman's bad luck," Louis said.

"Don't be superstitious," Marc replied. "Nothing happened to us coming back."

"*Non*? Have you forgotten the storms, *camarade*? Two of them with hurricane squalls this early in the season?"

"Coincidence. Freak storms happen."

Louis narrowed his eyes. "And the wreck? The one we wanted to salvage? It was gone the next morning. Did the *fräulein* have something to do with that?"

"How could she have, *homme*? She was on aboard the *Giselle*."

He shrugged a shoulder. "Perhaps she has powers—"

"Are you letting the old New Orleans voodoo nonsense go to your head?" Marc tried to hold on to his temper. "Ilsa—"

"There's some here who believe in voodoo." Louis shrugged again. "Jacques claims she's a witch that lured us to shore that day."

"*Merde*! I would think you had better sense than to listen to Jacques! I had him flogged for taking improprieties with her. *Certainement*, he will want to blame her."

"Perhaps," Louis answered, "but the men fell sick after they ate apples. Is that fruit not a witch's favorite? I believe I can quote stories of poisoned apples from as far back as King Arthur's time, if you wish for some substance to the rumor."

"Rubbish." Marc tossed his brandy back and set the glass on the desk. How anyone could believe that Ilsa would deliberately plot to harm anyone… She was too kind and gentle-hearted to even consider something like that. And she was alone in the world. A tremendous urge to protect her nearly overwhelmed him. He had never before felt this incredible need to keep a woman safe. A seething rage began to build inside him, and he clenched his fists. "Ilsa is innocent. Do I have to call you out about this?"

"There will be no dueling," Jean said and turned to Louis. "I want those rumors squelched. If you can prove that Jacques is instigating this, I'll have him put out to sea. In any case, I do not need disharmony among the men. Not with Kearney and the *Enterprise* out there." He looked at Marc. "You're prepared to vouch for this woman?"

He had never been so sure of anything in his life. Against his own judgment, he realized that he cared for her. Ilsa was all that was good. "*Oui.*"

Jean studied his face and then nodded. "I will hold

you to that. Now then. To prove to the men that I put no stock in rumors, I will assign the *mademoiselle* to prepare my meal and yours. She will be seen each night serving me food and wine."

"*Capitaine*. Do you think that is wise—" Louis began, but Jean held up a hand.

"It may not be wise, Louis, but it will be effective. I will not have mutiny at Campeche. Now go and tell Andre so he can alert the rest of the officers."

Jean turned back to Marc after Louis had gone. "And you, *mon ami*. I shall give you the delight of informing the *mademoiselle*." He poured another brandy and gave a mock toast. "Perhaps she'll be grateful enough to warm your bed, *non*?"

Marc felt his face heat and hoped he wasn't as red as an untried boy. Lafitte had an uncanny ability to sense things. Lust for Ilsa—for taking her in his arms and pressing her sweet curves against him while he tasted those full, lush lips again—was something Marc had firmly tried to put out of his mind.

But *mon Dieu*. What a reward that would be.

Chapter Nine

It was well into the afternoon when Ilsa approached the kitchen. She met no one in the hall since the kitchen was at the back of the house separated with a brick wall to prevent the spread of a fire should it occur. The cooks took time to rest after the noon meal was served. Since Ilsa had been working in the kitchen for over a week, she had been counting on that.

She had overheard *Kapitän* Lafitte telling Andre to prepare the slaves for delivery to the Bowie brothers' other ship due to arrive in a day or two. Before they left, Ilsa was going to make sure the slaves had at least one decent meal instead of beans and bread.

Quickly she moved about, removing leftover capon from platters, along with a half-wheel of cheese, and placing them in a clean linen cloth she had appropriated from the laundry closet. She hesitated over a spicy rice mixture flavored with almonds and raisins, but decided it was too messy. Then she grinned as she removed a tin cover from a plate. *"Gâteau au chocolat"* Jean's chef had proudly called it. The moist cake with its sticky, dark syrup would be just the thing for those poor slaves to enjoy. She put the cover back on and picked up the whole thing.

There was a door from the kitchen that lead directly outside. Once through the door, she skirted the bins of firewood and peeked around the corner. The back yard appeared empty. Staying close to the wall of the house, she made her way toward the pens where the slaves were held. With one last glance at the yard, she walked quickly across the small road and behind the rows of shops. Clinging to the shadows, she managed to make her way to the slave enclosure.

An older ebony-skinned man saw her. "You not be here," he said in broken English.

Ilsa motioned for him to come over as she set the food down and slid it beneath the fence. "I wanted you to have this," she whispered.

The man's black eyes widened, but before he could move, he was pushed aside by younger men who had seen either Ilsa or the food. Whooping, they rushed over. More roars of approval came as they eagerly tore into the food and stuffed it into their mouths.

"Hush yourselves," the older man hissed to them, but it was too late.

Ilsa felt herself being roughly lifted. She stifled a cry as a huge pirate with fetid breath pinned her arms behind her. He yanked them harder. "That'll teach you for feeding them devils."

She swallowed a groan, fearing her arms would break. "I only—"

"You only gave good food to animals," the man growled. "Weren't your food either. That's stealin'." He looked over to where a crowd was gathering and smiled smugly. "Know what Lafitte does with thieves here?"

"Ooh, *mon ami*," Ashantee said as she moved to the front of the group. "What have you done?"

"She's stole good food that's meant for us," the man answered as he tightened his grip once more. "That's what she's done."

195

"Let her go." Marc came striding down the road toward them.

"You ain't the Boss," the man replied, although he stopped tugging at Ilsa's arms. "She stole food to feed them darkies."

Marc glanced at where the slaves stood, some with food in their hands, others trying to eat it as fast as they could. He turned back to the man holding Ilsa. "I said to let her go. Jean has rowed out to intercept the *Enterprise*. I am second in command." He smiled coldly. "Do you not remember what *le capitaine* does to men who hurt women here?"

Ilsa felt her arms suddenly free as the burly pirate backed away. "Ain't hurtin' her," he mumbled.

Marc's hazel eyes darkened. "Perhaps we should ask the lady."

She saw the man's face blanch and remembered the flogging Jacques had taken on the ship. She didn't want to be the cause for another man to be beaten. "I'm not hurt."

"Are you sure?" Marc asked as he moved closer and laid a hand on her shoulder.

Ashantee joined them and linked her arm with Ilsa's, effectively brushing Marc's hand away. "Do not worry. I will take care of her. There is a special ointment that can be prepared. She will not even be sore tomorrow." She gave a little tug and Ilsa tried not to wince. "Come with me, *mon ami*."

Somehow, Ashantee didn't seem like "a friend" as she kept saying she was, but Ilsa wanted no more trouble. "I'll be fine," she said to Marc and allowed Ashantee to lead her away.

She ordered a tray for dinner, preferring not to have

to face Marc, or Jean if he had returned, at the dining table. She had only done what she thought was right. What would it matter if those poor people had some food that tasted good? These pirates ate as grandly as aristocrats. Why should they begrudge such simple things as capon and cheese to people who were about to be sold?

Sighing, she pushed her tray aside and got ready for bed. Perhaps a good night's sleep would help her come up with a plan to persuade *Kapitän* Lafitte to feed these people better.

She was awakened several hours later by a loud banging on her door, and then it burst open as she swung her feet to the floor. Marc stood illuminated in the light from the hallway. He was clearly angry. Clutching her robe, she stared at him. "Why are you here?"

"The question is, have you been here all night?" he asked in a clipped tone.

"What…? Yes. I have," she answered. "Why?"

"The slaves have escaped," he said as he stepped into the room, his eyes never leaving her face.

"How could they escape?"

"You tell me. The gate was unlocked, the tethers had been removed. The guard was hit on the head from behind and saw nothing."

Ilsa gasped. "You think I released them?"

"It doesn't matter what I think," Marc answered, "but there are men out there ready for a lynching. Andre and Louis are holding them off. I suggest you get dressed."

"Where are we going?" she asked.

Marc leaned over the bed where she sat, his face inches from hers. "That, *mademoiselle*, is the least of

197

your worries."

****

Ilsa tucked strands of loose hair behind her ears as she stumbled along behind Marc toward a dinghy tied to the dock near the *Giselle*. He had hadn't given her time to plait it, and her dress was only partially hooked. At least she had on shoes.

In spite of the danger she was in, her body still held a warm tingle from their escape through the second-story window. Marc had swung himself onto the ledge and then ordered her to put her arms around his neck and wrap her legs around his waist as he climbed down the trellis. Her face heated and her knees went suddenly weak at the memory of something very hard and thick jutting against her most private area.

Marc caught her arm. "Watch your step," he said and then held the dinghy against the dock for her to climb in. Releasing the line, he nimbly stepped in and sat down on the seat opposite her. Dipping the oars into the water, he silently began to row them toward the mainland. "Thank God there's no moon," he muttered.

"What?"

"Shhh. If we're lucky, we won't be seen. Or followed."

Ilsa didn't say anything more, nor did she complain when Marc poled the boat through marsh thick with cattails and sawgrass.

"It's not a dock," he said when he'd secured the painter to a clump of reeds, "but she'll be hidden here and not found."

He stepped over the rail, and Ilsa heard his boots splash in the water. She bit her tongue not to ask about water moccasins or alligators or anything else that might live in swamplike conditions. Then, Marc's strong arms were around her waist, lifting and holding her tightly against him as he sloshed his way onto the shore. He set her down on the sand and took her hand.

"This way," he said and moved toward a line of misshapen mesquite trees.

Some of the low branches caught at her hair and more than once prickly cactus tore at her dress, but Marc kept going deeper inside the straggle of trees and bushy undergrowth. Ilsa fervently prayed that rattlesnakes slept at night. When he stopped suddenly, she ran into him.

"It's still here," he said as she rubbed her nose, "and even better, not occupied."

Ilsa peered into the darkness past his shoulder. In the moonless night, she could barely make out the shape of some sort of shack. How he'd ever found it, she didn't know.

"Does someone live here?" she asked.

Marc shook his head. "Jean had it built as a shelter for the men he sent to guard Campeche from a land invasion when we first arrived. I don't think it's been used in a year or two." He walked toward the door and opened it. "It's not exactly luxury, but it will have to do. Wait here until I see if there are any vermin that have adopted it as home."

Ilsa shivered at the thought as she watched Marc reach for an oil lamp hanging just inside the door. Within minutes, a pale yellow glow illuminated the room. "All clear," he announced after poking into every corner and moving the small cot.

Ilsa put a tentative foot inside the threshold. The room was snug and surprisingly clean, probably due to the wooden shutters on the windows that bolted from the inside. A small hearth was built into one wall and a table with two chairs took up a corner.

"There should be a trunk by the bed," Marc said as he sat down and pulled off his boots. "See if there are some dry clothes in it." He stood and began to loosen the lacings to his breeches.

"Wha…what are you doing?" Ilsa tried to keep focused on his face, but her traitorous eyes were fascinated with where his hands were.

His full mouth curved up at one corner. "Didn't we have this conversation aboard the *Giselle*?" he asked. "I'm going to change out of these wet pants."

Ilsa felt her face heat and hoped it wouldn't show in the dim light. Turning quickly, she knelt and opened the trunk. A familiar, comforting scent of cedar rose from it. Rummaging, she found only blankets and towels. Disappointed, she turned back. "I don't see—*oh!*"

Marc had stripped both the pants and his shirt, although he still wore his drawers, if that's what men called them. In the weak light, his muscular body looked like a bronze statue. His broad shoulders sloped and sculpted into large biceps, his chiseled chest and hard belly ridges indented more by the shadows of light flickering from the lamp. Powerful thighs and well-developed calves completed his perfection. And something was moving beneath the white cloth that hugged low on his hips.

"If you keep looking at me like that, I may not be responsible for what happens," Marc said.

Ilsa felt her face flame again and averted her eyes. "There aren't any clothes. Just blankets and towels." She pulled one out and handed it to him. "You can wear this, I guess. It shouldn't take your clothes long to dry, once we have a fire."

"I can't take a chance on building a fire," Marc answered. "If any of the men have come ashore, they'll see it or smell it. In fact, I'm going to extinguish this lamp as soon as we've made a pallet with the blankets here on the floor."

Ilsa glanced at the bed. "That's very gentlemanly of you to take the floor."

Marc grinned. "You can have the bed if you want it, but who knows what's living inside the stuffing after all this time."

Ilsa suppressed a shudder. "I didn't think of that."

Marc spread the blanket on the floor and then held his hand out for the rest. "At least these are clean," he said as he finished the makeshift bed. "Do you want to undress in the dark or just have me turn my back?"

"Undress?"

"*Oui*. Despite my best intentions, your gown is soaked at the hem and your shoes are damp. Without a fire, the night will get cool. I won't have you catching swamp fever because of wet clothes."

Ilsa's shudder this time had nothing to do with either the cold or what critters resided in old ticking. The idea of lying beside an almost-naked Marc—even if she did leave her chemise on—made her tummy flutter and quiver quite strangely. Fully clothed, she was attracted to him like a kitten to a ball of string. Without clothes, she was pretty certain she would get no sleep at all.

Marc watched her and then stepped closer, lifting her chin with two fingers of his hand. "If you're worried that I will take advantage, I gave you my word on the *Giselle* that I would protect your virtue—"

"I don't think I want my virtue protected," Ilsa

blurted out and clapped a hand over her mouth, stricken by her boldness.

His facial expression changed, his eyes growing darker and beginning to smolder as he swept his thumb slowly across her lower lip. "*Non?*"

His light touch sent prickles of agitated excitement coursing through her. She could not define what it meant, but every nerve ending sang out to be closer to him, to feel his touch on her body. She *ached* for his touch, her breasts suddenly heavy, even as her nipples beaded and something warm and wet formed between her legs.

Lowering her lashes, she whispered, "I want to find out how it is between a man and a woman." She heard his sharp intake of breath and then he was tilting her head up again, making her look at him.

"Do not be afraid to say it or to want it, *chèrie,*" he said as he stroked the side of her face with the back of his hand, "but I want you to be very sure. It is a very valuable gift you are offering me."

"I don't know what will happen tomorrow. I can't stay at the camp any longer with my life in danger. Mr. Lafitte will more than likely send me away. But tonight…" She hesitated and then took a deep breath and looked Marc fully in his eyes. "Tonight, I want to become a real woman."

Marc growled softly and pulled her to him, slanting his mouth over hers in a gentle yet firm kiss. The softness of her lips, as she hesitantly moved them against his, nearly overwhelmed him, and he longed to crush her to him. Instead, he forced himself to lay featherlight kisses along her jaw and in the delicate spot just beneath her earlobe. Ilsa sighed contentedly, and he nuzzled her neck, nibbling gently as his hands began to work loose the hooks on her dress. He felt her tremble slightly when his fingers brushed against the silky skin of her shoulders as he lowered the bodice of her gown, and he brought his mouth up again to claim hers, his tongue lazily swiping along her lips until, with a low moan, she parted them for him and he slipped inside, savoring the taste of her.

Ilsa reeled with a myriad of sensation. Marc's velvety tongue played with hers, teasing her by nearly withdrawing and then filling her again. Tentatively, she pushed her tongue against his lips and he sucked her into his mouth. His heady scent of soap and brine and something uniquely *him* filled her nostrils. She swayed, slightly dizzy.

Cool air suddenly fanned her back and she realized that somehow Marc had managed to divest her of her clothing without her even noticing. Before she could think to be embarrassed, though, one of his large, warm hands slid up her ribcage to cup and gently knead her breast. He deepened his kiss as his thumb and forefinger rolled her already beaded nipple into a hard nub. Ilsa mewled from pure pleasure, instinctively arching her back to press the other aching tip against his hard chest.

Without breaking the kiss, Marc lifted her and laid her on the pallet of soft blankets. His hand roamed down her arm and across her belly and slid seductively along her thigh, his touch tantalizingly slow and easy. He trailed kisses down her throat and flicked his tongue across a taut nipple. Ilsa gasped at the exquisite sensation. Slowly, he licked a circle around the areole, not quite touching the throbbing tip. She became aware of another kind of throbbing between her legs, and her entire body burned for his hands to continue their relentless roaming. She arched her breast against him, desperately wanting some relief, but he just grinned at her and moved to the other breast to begin tormenting it with his talented tongue. Just when she thought she would scream from pure need, he took the nipple in his mouth and began to suckle. A low moan escaped her lips, and she pressed his head close against her. Never in her entire life had she imagined something could feel this good.

Almost as if he read her thoughts, his hand skimmed up her inner leg, gently pushing her thighs apart. He separated her sleek folds, stroking the warm, creamy fluid from her core along them and coating the little bud that quickly became erect as he fondled it. Someone moaned.

Through his mind-fog of desire, Marc realized that the sound came from him. *Mon Dieu*! In all his years of indulging in lustful play with experienced women, he had never come this close to pure ecstasy. Ilsa was untrained, her touches tentative, but somehow that made her all the more alluring. She was unpretentious, giving herself to him without realizing how her little squirms and mewls drove him nearly crazy with total bliss.

Ilsa was so wet with need that he hoped the pain of his entry would be small.

He continued to massage the hard, little nub with his thumb, loving the feeling of her warm, soft body writhing against his. He slipped a finger into her tight sheath and began to stroke. Ilsa's eyes suddenly widened and her hips lifted, nearly rolling him over. He slipped a second finger in and thrust hard and felt her tighten around him. Her body went rigid and a great shudder took her.

"*Mein Gott*! What happened?" she asked in a raspy

whisper.

Marc's mouth quirked up. "I think you've found the pleasure of being a woman."

Ilsa gave him a big smile. "It felt good. Will you do that to me again?"

This time he laughed outright. "*Bien-aimée*! My love, I am not through yet." He moved over her, spreading her legs with his thigh and positioned himself against her opening. Marc inserted the tip of his painfully hard erection, watching her eyes grow big at the feel of him. He forced himself to move slowly, allowing her time to stretch and accept him. She was so hot and so tight, even with the climax she had just had. He butted up against her womanhood and stopped. He was nearly mad with desire, but he had to be sure…he had to offer her a last reprieve.

"I am about to take your maidenhood," he said through slightly gritted teeth. "If you wish to remain a virgin, you must say so now."

She gave him a smile that any French courtesan would have envied and for an answer, she wrapped her legs over his thighs. With a fervent mutter of thanks to all the gods, he leaned down to savage her mouth in a kiss as he thrust fully into her. For a second, her body stiffened, and then it softened against him. Ilsa wiggled her hips, adjusting to him as he began long, slow strokes inside her. She matched his rhythm perfectly, as though they were long-time, familiar lovers. Marc thrust faster, plunging hard and deep as Ilsa's body silently begged for more, bucking beneath him in glorious, undulating motion.

Her body was on fire. She could feel the flames sweeping through her veins, igniting every nerve ending into a blaze that was building… Her body twisted and gyrated of its own accord and yet she wanted more…more…something bubbled just below the surface of her consciousness, something totally foreign and yet a part of her…she was a part of this man. She had no idea where she ended and he began. They were one…the flames leapt all around them, a raging inferno, and then, suddenly without warning, she exploded, tiny sparks of light all around her. Dimly, she felt something warm and liquid shoot inside her, and then Marc was lying beside her, an arm possessively holding her to him.

They lay in silence until their breathing finally returned to normal. Marc swept a damp strand of hair away from her face. "How does it feel to be a woman?"

Ilsa snuggled contentedly against his shoulder. "Wonderful. I will be sorry to have to leave tomorrow."

He crooked a finger under her chin, tilting her head up. "I don't want you to leave. Not now, when I've just found you."

"I won't have any choice, I'm afraid," Ilsa said in a small voice. "Your men blame me for the slaves' escape. And Ashantee—"

"Don't say her name," Marc interrupted and put his finger across Ilsa's lips. "She is—was—my mistress. We had an agreement. She means nothing more than that." He shook his head when Ilsa tried to speak. "I love you, Ilsa. I was just too stubborn to allow myself to recognize it."

Her eyes widened and she kissed the finger he still had against her mouth. "I love you, too, but what can we do about it? I will be sent away."

Marc frowned, then tilted his head. "Do you still want to work the land your parents came here for?"

Ilsa nodded. "It would be a fitting memory to them."

"Then it's settled. I will take you to your people."

This time she frowned. "And leave me there?"

Marc shook his head. "I think not. You're going to need someone to help you farm that land, and I've been out to sea long enough. I would be your husband, if you'll have me."

Ilsa gazed into his eyes and then gave him that seductive smile that would make any boudoir-lady in New Orleans envious. Slowly, she sucked his finger into her mouth, her warm tongue making his groin tighten again. "I'll have you as my husband," she said, reaching down to stroke his manhood into full hardness. "This comes with it, doesn't it?"

Marc growled as he rolled her over onto her back. "It definitely does," he said as he entered her. Somehow, he had the feeling that his innocent *fräulein* was going to turn into one very sensuous, sensual vamp that would totally blind him from seeing any other woman with lust in his eyes again. Surprisingly, he found he didn't care. Ilsa was all that mattered.

Chapter Ten

Marc put an arm around Ilsa's shoulders as they peered through the scrub oak on the outskirts of Campeche. "The *Pride* is back," he said in relief as he scanned the harbor. "The *Enterprise* didn't follow her in."

"How are you going to convince Jean that I didn't free those slaves?" Ilsa asked in a small voice. "I still think you should have let me stay—"

"No, my love. The Carancahua roam here too, and they haven't forgotten that one of their squaws was once stolen by a privateer, and the Battle of Three Trees followed." He covered her small, smooth hand in his. "With Jean back, you'll be safe until I can gather our things and collect my coin and ration."

Even though he proceeded with caution as they approached the gates, no one seemed to notice them. The entire village bustled about, the men baring the shelves of the shops while the women carried bundles of goods toward the ships tied up at the dock.

"I suspect Lieutenant Kearney is going to be paying us a visit," he told Ilsa as they entered Maison Rouge and slipped into the room that he used. "Jean will make it look like we're readying to leave."

"Isn't that going to a lot of trouble?" Ilsa asked.

Marc grinned and gave her a kiss on her forehead. "If the lieutenant thinks we're really going, he won't be back any time soon. It'll buy Jean some time to relieve a few more Spanish ships of their burdens. Now sit down while I pack some things." He saw her eye the bed, and his grin widened. "Much as I would love to fulfill that wish I see in your eyes, I need to talk to Jean."

Ilsa smiled impishly but took a seat by the unlit hearth. "You shall have to make it up to me, then."

"With pleasure," Marc said and began taking things out of his wardrobe. He felt a small object at the bottom. Pulling it out, he frowned.

"What is it?" Ilsa said as she moved toward him and glanced over his shoulder. "A doll!" She gave a little giggle. "Why would you—"

"It's not a doll," he said in a voice like brittle ice. "It's an effigy."

Ilsa wrinkled her brow. "What's that?"

"It's a voodoo custom to make a likeness of an enemy and place a curse on it." He turned the thing over in his hand and inhaled sharply. "I think these may be your blonde hairs woven into it."

Ilsa's eyes widened. "Why would anyone curse me? And how did my hair—" She stopped. "Ashantee's ring got caught in my hair that first day…"

"Yes. I think I'm beginning to see." Marc narrowed his eyes, then stuck the effigy in his pocket and moved to the door. "Stay here. Lock the door when I leave and don't open it unless it's Andre or me. Understand?"

She nodded numbly, and he only hoped that, for once, she would obey him.

Thirty minutes later, he pushed open the door to Jean's study and ushered a subdued-looking Ashantee inside. Jean looked up from where he was stuffing papers into a leather pouch. "I don't have time to settle domestic disputes, Rochelle. Kearney's delivered an ultimatum. We surrender by dawn or he fires on Campeche. We're leaving."

It took Marc a minute to comprehend. This was no bluff. He nodded slowly. "We knew the day would come." He motioned toward Ashantee. "She has a confession to make." He pulled the effigy from his pocket and threw it on Jean's desk. "Go ahead," he said to Ashantee.

Jean picked the token up and frowned. "What's the meaning of this? Unless you want to be left for Kearney's men, you had better talk. "

She turned ashen. "I only placed a little spell on it. Just enough to make the men not like her."

"Haven't I been clear on not practicing voodoo?" Jean asked.

"It wasn't…" She stopped and swallowed hard. "It's not fair that the witch come in here and take my man away."

Jean tossed the effigy down and looked at Marc. "I said I didn't have time for domestic problems. Can't you handle your women?"

Marc felt a muscle twitch in his jaw. "There's more," he said and reached into his other pocket and pulled out a small leather pouch. "Henbane. I found it in her room."

Lafitte's eyebrows lifted as he fingered the sack. "How did you come by the surgeon's stores?" he asked her and then shook his head. "Never mind. No doubt you used your feminine wiles. But why?"

"It calls up evil entities," she said in a small voice.

"Tell him the rest," Marc said grimly.

She flashed him a look of hatred and then lowered

her lashes. "A small amount might have gotten mixed up with the nutmeg. I'm not sure."

"You're sure," Marc said.

"But why?" Jean asked again. "Why would you want to poison the men?"

Her head came up defiantly. "I wanted them to think it was *her* so they would make you send the German whore away."

Marc's brows lifted. "You should be careful about the labels you choose, *ma prostituée*." He looked at Jean. "She also concocted the scheme with Jacques to let the slaves loose."

Jean's eyes turned obsidian as he glanced over to Ashantee. "If Kearney weren't hovering off shore, I'd hang the both of you for this treachery. Why would you do something so stupid?"

Ashantee looked at the floor and Marc answered for her. "Yesterday afternoon, Ilsa took some food from the kitchen to the slaves. She was discovered, and it created quite a row. Ilsa has not hidden the fact that she thinks slavery is wrong. Ashantee figured the men would blame Ilsa for letting the slaves go. It almost worked." *Merde.* They'd barely escaped, as it was.

"Where is Jacques?" Jean asked.

"Andre and Louis confined him to the guardhouse," Marc replied.

"Good. Ashantee can join him there until we're ready to sail. I'll let you decide their fate once we're out to sea."

"I'm afraid you'll have to do that, Boss. I won't be going."

Jean frowned. "You're going to surrender rather than sail?"

Marc shook his head. "I'm going to take Ilsa south to her people. She wants to work the land her parents gave their lives for. I figure she can probably use a man's help."

"*Protecteur,*" Ashantee muttered. "*Menteur.*"

"*Taisez-vous!*" Jean snapped at her. "Not one more word." He turned back to Marc and studied him for a long moment. Then he nodded and held out his hand. "*Adieu, mon ami.* I shall miss you."

****

Marc halted the gelding Jean had given him, and Ilsa reined in her mare alongside him. He looked back at the village. The sun had set, and in the dusky twilight, he could barely make out the ships quietly slipping out of the harbor. No lanterns had been lit aboard, for Jean didn't want to alert the *Enterprise* anchored out at sea.

"Any regrets?" Ilsa asked as she watched him.

He leaned across the small space between them and kissed her. "Only one," he said, "that I didn't meet you sooner."

She smiled at him, and then suddenly her eyes widened as she looked over his shoulder. "What's that light?" she asked.

Marc swung his head around. "*Mon Dieu*! Jean's set Campeche on fire!" He watched in silence as the flames took hold and the wooden buildings turned into balls of flame. Then he tapped his horse's flanks with his heels. "We'd better go before the Carancahuas decide to pay a visit."

As their horses made their way along the sandy path through the sawgrass, Marc looked back once more. Lt. Kearney would be mightily disappointed in the morning to find the settlement a smoldering heap of ashes and the ships with Campeche's treasure gone.

Fair winds and following seas, Boss, to wherever you go. Marc turned back to the path ahead of him. The wide-open spaces and blue skies of Texas awaited him…and a new life with his wife. He leaned across his saddle to kiss her and was rewarded with that smile that made him not want to wait until they found suitable quarters for lovemaking.

For Marc, Ilsa was the true treasure of Campeche.

A Pirate Of Her Own: Chapter One

Having forgotten her parasol once again, Emily Clayton sat on a bench under the merciful shade of a magnolia tree and watched as a majestic schooner slowly glided through the quiet waters of Charleston Harbor toward the wharf. She swatted at a mosquito and lifted her coppery hair from her damp neck. Although it was not past noon, the day was already hot. Little waves of humidity danced in the air, causing the ship to shimmer slightly, as though it might not be real. Indeed, with its dark hull and tanbark sails, it could sail stealthily at night, unnoticed, like pirate ships of old.

She smiled a little to herself. Mama—rest her soul—had always said Emily was over-fanciful. The golden age of piracy was in the past, over for nearly a century, but she wondered how it must have been to sail the high seas, free to seek adventure in new and exciting places…and to relieve the Spanish galleons of their stolen gold from Mexico. Anne Bonny had done it. A pirate had swept her off her feet, stolen her from her husband, and sailed for Cuba. She became a pirate herself, skilled with both pistol and rapier. How Emily envied the woman's freedom and courage. Of course, she was eventually captured and her father ransomed her, brought her back to Charleston, and forced her into a sedate marriage to some landowner, but at least Anne had had the thrill of venturing beyond the confines of the prim and proper society where she'd grown up.

A large, dark cloud obscured the sun, bringing deep shadows to the stately mansions lining the Battery behind her. The air hung heavy and still as Emily turned her gaze away from the ship to the park across the way. Its old oaks were laden with tendrils of dripping moss, but as a slight zephyr of a breeze stirred, she saw not the moss moving but the bodies of Stede Bonnet's twenty-nine pirates swinging from those trees for four days nearly a hundred years ago. She could almost smell the stench of rotting corpses over the briny scent of the sea.

Stede Bonnet had been known as a gentleman pirate, an educated, wealthy French plantation owner in Barbados. The story always reminded her of the rumors of the infamous Jean Lafitte, who disappeared over a year ago along with his ships and treasure. Before Papa had been killed in the war, he'd fought alongside Captain Lafitte in New Orleans and been proud to do so. How she wished she could have met the pirate!

The sun poked back out, erasing the faint images of long-dead pirates, and Emily gave herself a little shake. She would not allow herself to become morbid. She should be grateful Mama's second husband had given her a home these past two years and even a Season, although she suspected, since she was already eight-and-ten, that he'd been hoping one of the young swains at the various balls and soirees would offer for her hand and relieve him of his responsibility. Unfortunately, none of the young men interested her. They were too conventional, too proper, too willing to accept society's many rules of decorum.

She looked again at the ship. It flew no flag. Where had it come from and what was its cargo? As she watched, two men emerged from the aft cabin and made their way down the gangplank. One appeared to be middle-aged, with slightly graying, dark hair. The other nearly took her breath away.

His hair glistened blue-black in the sunlight and curled against the scandalously open collar of a white shirt that stretched across broad shoulders. The sleeves were rolled up, baring strong, tanned forearms. How totally improper. How totally intriguing. The soft doeskin breeches he wore were almost indecent, hugging well-muscled thighs that rippled as he walked. Emily could just imagine the ladies at one of the many social societies choking over their lemonades, swooning in shock over such a display of pure maleness. Her breath hitched again, wondering what it would be like to dance the waltz with *him*.

She gave herself another shake. Her thoughts really were running wild today. Such a man would never be received by the matrons of Charleston's elite.

"There you be, child! I should have knowed you'd be by the water." A rather plump, middle-aged black woman huffed her way toward Emily. "Your step-pa ain't none too happy that you were gone this morning."

Emily sighed. Aunty Maisie had been her mother's servant, more friend than slave, and had taken it upon herself to keep Emily under her wing after Mama died of the yellow fever. Or at least Maisie tried.

"I'm sorry, Aunty. I just couldn't take another morning of calling on those pretentious old biddies, leaving little cards on silver trays and hoping they were receiving."

The other woman frowned. "It's the way of things if you want to catch a rich husband."

Emily turned her head toward the dock, but the dark-haired stranger had disappeared. "What if I don't want to catch a rich husband?"

Maisie snorted. "'Course you do. Your mama would want you to have the best."

Emily blinked back tears. Her soft-spoken mother had always seemed so happy with her Army husband, even if it meant traveling to different posts. Sometimes she thought her mother had married Mr. Jamison simply so Emily would have a place to call home…a house in Charleston and a plantation to retreat to during the summer months.

"I'd rather be happy than rich."

"Ain't no rule you can't be both, child. Now come along, before the master tans my hide for not keepin' a better eye on you."

Emily stood reluctantly. Mama had never allowed any of the slaves to be flogged, but her stepfather had a temper. As a magistrate, he also favored Mayor Hamilton's militant approach to controlling slaves.

"All right. Tell Mr. Jamison I shall return shortly and attend the Library Society's luncheon at two o'clock." At least, a few of those women actually read books and could carry on a conversation.

"He said I was to bring you myself."

Emily smiled. "You know you don't like to get anywhere near a horse, Maisie, and I brought my mare." She motioned over to a rail down the street where several horses stood, patiently swishing their tails at flies.

The slave's eyes widened to show white all round. "Lordy. You rode here by yourself and not in a carriage? And no escort? Not fittin' and not proper. Lordy, lordy! I be in trouble now, Missy."

"It was a nice morning and the carriage is so stuffy," Emily replied. "I will explain to Mr. Jamison that I slipped out while you thought I was in my bath." Which was true anyway. "It's only a few blocks, so run along. I'll catch up to you before we reach the house."

Maisie looked as though she were about to argue and then sighed. "You come straight home? No ride in the park first?"

Emily smiled. "I promise." She watched as the servant left, shaking her head and muttering to herself. Then she walked down the street, unhitched her horse, and led it to a mounting block. She had ridden at various Army posts and even rode by herself on the plantation; surely, riding a few blocks in the city in broad daylight should pose no problem. She reined her horse around. She wouldn't ride in the park since she'd promised not to, but it wouldn't hurt to ride along the wharf to Queen Street and then back on Church before heading home.

Emily had just passed one of the three churches the street was named for when she looked up at the Planters Hotel. It had a reputation for goings-on that weren't entirely proper. For women... She blinked. A woman dressed in a man's shirt and trousers stood by the window at the end of the second floor. She certainly didn't *look* a strumpet. Not that Emily knew exactly what a lady of ill-repute would look like. But this one had short hair and no painted lips or kohl around her eyes. The woman watched her, a thoughtful expression on her face.

Was she scrutinizing Emily? Did she disapprove of a woman riding alone on the streets? Emily lifted her chin and continued to ride, turning down Chalmers Street.

Southern society had too many rules.

****

Andre Dubois cast a glance toward the titian-haired girl on the bench before he and the captain rounded the corner of the wharf house and she was lost to his view. For some odd reason, he was relieved to see an older black woman talking to her. He was unfamiliar with Charleston, but in New Orleans only one kind of woman would sit by herself, near the docks, with no chaperone. The girl hadn't looked like a lady-for-hire.

"Sizing up women already, *mon ami*?" His friend shook his head. "You've barely set foot on dry land."

Andre grinned. "And how long do you think it will take you to have a new mistress on your arm, *Monsieur Clement*?"

"Not long, I suspect." His companion patted his waistcoat pocket. "I have all the proper letters of introduction to the *crème de la crème* of Charleston society."

"Forged, of course," Andre replied, "since your name isn't Clement."

Jean Lafitte shrugged. "It worked well enough with Governor Claiborne's wife, didn't it?"

"More than well-enough." Andre laughed, remembering. "She lauded you as the most handsome and charming man she had ever met at society events for at least a month. Right in front of Claiborne, no less. If only he'd known—"

"Yes," Jean interrupted, "I'll admit that was a part of the intrigue. She was not without certain charms herself."

"I'm sure."

He hid a grin. "I meant that she very kindly did not

219

give my identity away when she discovered it."

"Of course that's what you meant. Far be it from me to tarnish a lady's reputation," Andre replied with mock soberness.

"At any rate, it behooves us to keep my alias in place and let the authorities think I've disappeared. No doubt Lieutenant Kearney was furious that I burned Campeche and left no spoils for him."

"Not to mention President Monroe might not be too happy that you didn't obey orders to leave the Spanish ships alone."

"Well, that," Jean said, his black eyes flashing with humor, "would be like leaving that red-haired beauty back there all alone. Sinful, almost."

Andre frowned. "I don't think she's that kind of girl."

Jean eyed him. "It's not like you to be so protective, *mon ami*. Not when you haven't even met her."

Protective. Strangely enough, that was almost what he felt. Andre began to wonder if the southern heat was getting to him. Better to change the subject. He pointed up ahead. "That should be the slave mart there...in that complex of buildings."

Jean pulled a paper out his pocket and smoothed it out. "We should get a good price for the thirty slaves we have on board. They've all been civilized."

"A good thing," Andre said drily, "since only American-born slaves are still legal trading commodities."

Jean looked at him with a poker face. "But it says here they are quite legal. I even generously supplied the names of their previous owners."

Andre was about to respond to that when a loud

commotion near the entrance of the slave mart caught his attention. A huge slave, naked except for a loin cloth and dragging part of a leg shackle behind him, had broken free of the guards and raced out into the street. He paused but a fraction of a second and then leaped for a horse and rider trotting down the street toward them.

The red-haired girl from the bench screamed as she was pulled from the saddle and flung through the air.

Chapter Two

Emily hit the ground with a thud that jettisoned the air from her lungs. A fuzzy, gray mist surrounded her. She tried to sit up, but warm, strong hands held her down. A rich, baritone voice, slightly French, came from somewhere behind her.

"*Soigneux!* Be still, *mademoiselle,* until I see if any bones have been broken."

Emily blinked, her vision becoming clearer as the man moved around to her side. Dear Lord, it was the black-haired stranger from the boat! Carefully, he traced her collarbones and ran his fingers down her arms, leaving a pleasant warmth in their wake. His hands closed gently over her ribcage and a strange heat began to stir deep inside her, but when he felt the length of her legs, the tingle moved decidedly to a spot between her thighs. Never in her life had she had such a reaction. She really should protest, since she doubted the man was a physician, but her body felt suddenly weak as a newborn.

He looked up. "I can't feel anything broken. Do you want to try to sit?"

She nodded. Somehow, her mouth was too dry for speech. His eyes were sea-green and so clear she felt like she was swimming in them...or drowning.

He put an arm around her and lifted her slowly. "Are you dizzy?"

She wasn't sure what she was. Her head was

certainly spinning, but she didn't think it was from the fall. His masculine scent, along with the slight smell of soap and leather, filled her nostrils and she inhaled, breathing him in. She felt so safe with him. A perfect stranger.

"How is she?"

It was the middle-aged man who had accompanied him that asked the question as he stood holding the reins to her mare.

"I…I'm fine," she finally managed to say. "I'm not sure what happened…"

The older man narrowed his eyes. "Escaped slave. He'll hang for this."

Emily widened hers and sat straighter. "No! I don't want him killed."

The handsome stranger who still had his hand protectively on her back, frowned. "Is it not against the law in Charleston for a slave to assault a white person?"

"Well, yes, but…I don't want to be responsible for someone's death!" She knew all too well how quickly "justice" could take place and struggled to stand. The stranger's strong hands lifted and steadied her on her feet. "I must go in there!"

"*Mademoiselle*, the slave mart is no place for a lady."

"My name is Emily Clayton. My stepfather is a magistrate here. Perhaps if I can explain—" She stopped, for the two men had exchanged wary glances. "What is it?"

"It is nothing. Forgive us. We are new here and may not understand your ways. My name is Andre Dubois," he said with a slight bow and raised her hand to his mouth to graze her knuckles with a kiss.

Such a brief touch…the merest brush of his lips sent liquid fire through her veins. She stared into Andre's eyes, momentarily forgetting the recaptured slave.

"And I am Jean Clement," the older man said in an amused tone. "If you care to make my acquaintance, too."

She felt herself blush and withdrew her hand from Andre's. "Forgive my manners, Mr. Clement. It was so kind of both of you to come to my aid, but I must try and stop this senseless killing."

Jean frowned. "The slave also stole your horse, *mademoiselle*. That is a hanging offense, no matter what color the man."

"But I have my horse back! That man shouldn't have to hang for that!"

"Are you opposed to slavery, then?" Andre asked quietly.

Emily paused. "I can't change the law. Slave ownership is a way of life in the South. The plantations need the workers and the slaves seem immune to the yellow fever and heat. But they are *people*, not beasts. I am unhurt. I have my horse back. I don't want any killing."

Andre studied her. "You are a most unusual woman." He looked at Jean for a long moment and then back to her. "If you will allow me, I will see what I can do. Please let Monsieur Clement escort you home."

"That's not necessary. I live only a few blocks from here—"

"And does your stepfather know you are out and about without an escort?" Jean asked. Emily looked guiltily down at the street and he continued. "I thought not—"

He was interrupted by the clatter of a carriage rattling toward them. The driver pulled the horse to a stop and Mr. Jamison jumped down.

"Into the carriage at once, young lady," he said in a furious voice. "No back talk either. We will discuss your atrocious behavior when I return from taking care of this matter."

Emily had never seen him so angry. Some vicious gossip had wasted no time in finding her stepfather. She knew that, in his eyes, she had created a scandal. She cast an anxious look at Andre.

"You should do as your father says, mademoiselle," he said in a soothing voice and then tilted his head so her stepfather would not see the wink he gave her. "I will relay your request to the proper authorities. Trust me."

Emily cast one more glance at Mr. Jamison and then reluctantly climbed into the carriage. As it gave a lurch and moved away, she leaned back against the seat and closed her eyes to pray.

She would have to trust Andre Dubois. There was nothing else she could do.

****

Jean swirled the cognac in his snifter and studied Andre as they sat in the aft cabin of the schooner. Andre tried to ignore his intense look, but he knew Jean was waiting for him to explain what had transpired at the slave mart after Emily left.

He tossed back the last of his brandy and set the glass down. "I didn't see any other choice."

Jean raised an eyebrow. "We are in the business of selling slaves, not buying them. *Non*?"

"*Oui*, but you don't believe in vigilante justice any more than I do. That crowd was ready to lynch the man from the rafters and the magistrate, Mr. Jamison, wasn't much inclined to stop them, angry as he was."

"Agreed. A man who can't rein in his temper has no business being in the position of meting out punishment." Jean shrugged. "We've dealt with it before, *mon ami*…at Barataria and Campeche. Law doesn't always equal justice."

"Buying the slave gave me the right to punish him myself."

"Ah. Making a gift of him to Mademoiselle Clayton is your idea of punishment?"

Andre grinned, remembering how the slave—Juma, he said his name was—had stood there, gaping in disbelief, when Andre told him there would be no beating. And how the big man had nearly cried when Andre told him it was Miss Clayton's wish that he not be harmed. His debt would be to protect her with his life. "I have an idea trying to keep Mademoiselle Clayton safe from her own escapades will build his character."

Jean's mouth quirked up. "The *petite fille* has whetted your interest, *non*?"

Andre felt an unexpected warmth creep across his face. He couldn't deny he was attracted to Emily Clayton, even though she wasn't the voluptuous type of woman he was usually drawn to. Emily was small, with gentle curves—albeit in all the right places—and there was no sense of coy flirtatiousness about her. Her ginger-brown eyes snapped with lively interest, and he had an idea her temper might match her fiery hair, if today's passionate plea to spare the slave was any indication. But she was an eligible lady, and he normally avoided getting involved with one of those, avoided like the plague, for single young ladies had devious ambitions of luring men into the parson's trap. A place where he had no wish to be. He still couldn't believe their longtime friend Marc Rochelle had decided to stay in Texas with the German *fräulein* and farm.

"I only did what any Frenchman would do in the circumstances."

Jean laughed and stood. "It's been a long time since any of us claimed allegiance to France, *mon ami*. But still, your generous 'gift' calmed troubled waters, and Mr. Jamison did invite us to St. Michael's church supper this Sunday. It is an excellent way to break into Charleston society."

"Given that they don't know what we do," Andre said.

"Slave trade is a legitimate business," Jean replied. "Besides, we have Spanish goods to trade as well. Our papers are all in order." He grinned. "I paid the man in Cuba quite handsomely to make them so."

Andre didn't fear that they would be caught bringing in foreign slaves, either. Jean was too experienced with slavers—and other lucrative booty that Americans were hungry for—to make any mistakes. Still, even if the slaves were legitimate, he didn't think Emily Clayton would approve.

He frowned, wondering why that should matter.

Chapter Three

"Oh, I done plan to swoon, Miss Emily, I do." The maid fanned herself with the linen napkin from the lunch tray in Emily's sitting room. "The devil musta had a hand in makin' that man downstairs all male."

"Cyrah, you do tend to run on about things." She knew she should reprimand the young slave for such a remark, but truth be told, she found Cyrah's passionate outbursts about whichever man took her fancy at the moment much more interesting than polite conversation about the weather or someone's new bonnet. "I'm still not sure I understand all of this." Emily frowned slightly as she looked at the bill-of-sale in her hand. Evidently, Andre Dubois had purchased the large slave, Juma, to keep him from being hanged, but why had he transferred ownership to *her*?

"Well, it's clear as them crystal glasses in the master's liquor cabinet," Cyrah said with a hint of impatience. "You own one of the finest slaves in Charleston. Big and strong and good-lookin' to boot—"

"Cyrah!" Emily tried to hide a smile. "Didn't I hear you describe Denmark Vessey the same way last week when he came to put those shelves in the library?"

"Ooh! That one is nice, too, Miss Emily, but he be a free man of color. What chance would I have with him? But *this* one...he can even cipher some, and read, too."

Emily raised an eyebrow. "And how do you know

that?"

Cyrah blushed and then giggled. "I heard him tell Mr. Jamison."

"You know you're not supposed to eavesdrop," Emily said absently and turned back to the bill-of-sale. "If Juma is educated, perhaps I could give him his freedom."

The maid's eyes widened and she shook her head. "The man that delivered him—and he was done worth lookin' at too, with that coal black hair and them green eyes—he made sure the overseer understood that Juma was to be your personal bodyguard and nothing else."

Emily stared at her. Bodyguard? She wasn't sure if she should be flattered that Andre Dubois thought of her safety or whether she should be furious that he was arrogant enough to saddle her with someone who would follow her around. It was hard enough eluding Aunty. "I'm not sure that's even proper," she said.

Cyrah nodded vigorously. "Oh, yes'm. Word's already spreadin' among the coloreds. You'll be safe from renegades anywhere in the city. Once the master lets the white folks know, Juma can protect you from anyone."

"I really don't think—"

"You'll be able to spend more time by the water," the maid interrupted slyly. "Maisie won't get in no more trouble for you slippin' away like you did this mornin'."

Well, *that* was a thought to consider. Emily loved the harbor and watching the ships, wondering where they were bound to next. Dreaming of adventure... She sighed and put the paper down. "I suppose I could meet with him—"

Her maid jumped up so fast she upset the chair.

"Yes, Miss Emily." She gave her ebony curls a pat to make sure they were in place. "Are you ready?"

Emily laughed inwardly. Cyrah was obviously a lot more "ready" than she was. Still, if having a hulking guard at her back meant she had more freedom to roam the city, it might be worth it. But she had a feeling that Cyrah may have just developed a taste for being near the water too.

****

Standing beneath the large tent on the lawn of St. Michael's Sunday evening, Emily watched as Cyrah heaped Juma's plate high with fried chicken and sweet potato pone. St. Michael's was one of the few places that provided a repast, albeit separate, for the slaves who attended the white guests to the supper. She felt her lips curve into a smile as Juma offered Cyrah the first choice of a morsel. In the three days that the big man had been in their household, Cyrah had not wasted time in attaching herself to him.

"What do you find so pleasing, *mademoiselle*?"

Startled, she turned to find Andre standing behind her. When had he gotten there? She'd searched for him earlier, quite blatantly scanning the crowd, although she knew she was expected to keep her eyes cast demurely down lest some man think her too bold. What silly rules! And now she probably was supposed to act like seeing him wasn't important and simper behind a fan. Well, blue blazes! He intrigued her. She flashed a smile at him. "I'm glad to see you here."

An eyebrow raised imperceptibly and a corner of his mouth quirked up. "And may I say I was hoping to find you here as well? Have you quite recovered from your fall?"

"Just a slight bruise," Emily replied, "on my…" She stopped, feeling herself blush. Aunty would give her a sound scolding if she said "my backside" to a man she hardly knew. She didn't want to sound like a strumpet. "I mean…that is…"

Andre grinned. "Not need to explain, Miss Clayton. I saw how you landed. I was there, remember?"

She remembered only too well the feel of his strong fingers gently stroking down her arms and ribs. Warmth flooded her at the memory and she felt her face heat even more. Even now, although a respectable distance separated them, she felt the urge to move closer to him, almost as though she were being pulled toward him by some invisible bonds. She needed to focus on something besides the sight of him in snug, buff breeches and a roundabout jacket that hugged his broad shoulders and buttoned across a flat belly. A strand of his inky hair blew across his forehead and Emily resisted the urge to reach out and brush it back. She blinked. Dear Lord, where were these thoughts coming from? A hint of amusement glinted in his sea-green eyes and she forced herself to look away.

"I wanted to thank you for saving Juma," she said.

He glanced across the way to where the colored people sat. "Has he been taking care of you?"

Emily laughed and nearly rolled her eyes. "Only too well. If Mr. Jamison allowed it, he would sleep outside my door."

"I'm glad to hear it," Andre replied. "He owes you his life."

"It was you who saved him. You're a true hero, like the gallant knights of old."

Was that a faint blush that crossed his cheeks?

He shook his head. "I've been called a lot of things, but a knight hasn't been one of them, Miss Clayton."

"Please call me Emily."

His eyebrow arched slightly again. "Is that proper?"

"Probably not," she replied, "but I find some of society's rules too imposing. What on earth is wrong with addressing someone by their given name?"

Laughter floated in his eyes. "You are very different from the rest of these Southern belles."

"Papa was an Army man. We lived in different places. I've even been to Texas."

"Ah. Did you like being on the outskirts of civilization?"

Emily nodded. "There was nothing pretentious about the frontier. I was young at the time, but it seemed like an exciting adventure to me."

"And you like adventure?"

"Very much. It's one of the reasons I like to go down to the harbor. I sit and imagine where those ships have been and where they're going next. Where did your ship come from?"

A fleeting look of hesitation crossed his face before he answered. "The West Indies. We picked up a shipment of goods there."

"What sort of goods?"

"A part of the shipment was Spanish merchandise that *Monsieur* Clement had arranged for," he answered and then changed the subject. "Tell me more about you. Where else was your father posted?"

"New Orleans was interesting," Emily said. "I was only ten, but I remember talk about the black magic the voodoo queens practiced. Mama always made sure I never went anywhere near them, though. And then, there were the pirates."

His gaze intensified. "Pirates?"

"Yes. A thousand pirates lived in the swamps and bayous. Jean Lafitte was their leader. Governor Claiborne tried to make him sound like a scoundrel, but Papa said he wasn't."

"Your father knew Jean Lafitte?" Andre asked.

Emily nodded. "They fought at the Battle of New Orleans. Papa said if it hadn't been for the pirates, the English would have won. General Jackson was far outnumbered." She tilted her head to look up at Andre. "Mr. Lafitte vanished last year. Just sailed away and hasn't been heard from since. It's a mystery." She frowned slightly. "I hope his ships didn't sink."

"A lot of people probably hope they did," Andre said quietly.

"That's awful! Why would—" She stopped as she noticed his friend, Jean Clement, heading their way. "Here comes your friend."

Andre glanced toward Jean and then turned his attention back to Emily. "If seems I must go." He gave a little bow and lifted her hand to his lips. Turning it over, he gave her a mischievous grin and kissed her palm. Deliberately, his gaze holding hers, he gave the sensitive area of her wrist a soft, slow lick before he straightened. "I've very much enjoyed talking with you. We'll have to do this again…Emily."

She stared after him as he left to meet the captain, the impression of his warm, velvet tongue lingering on her arm and causing strange areas of her anatomy to tingle.

Chapter Four

"The sale went well," Jean said as he and Andre walked back to the Planter's Hotel where they had rooms. "Louis said we got top dollar for each man, so maybe you'll still have a fair sum after I deduct the price of that slave you bought for the *petite fille*."

Andre nodded. He wasn't that concerned about how much money he made. Over the past few years, he'd saved most of his coin and had it safely deposited in Cartagena.

Jean glanced over at him. "Problems, *mon ami*?"

"No. Just thinking." Thinking about the silken texture of Emily's delicate skin beneath his tongue and the alluring, slightly spicy, scent of her perfume. It reminded him of the Caribbean—of clear waters and balmy nights scented with exotic aromas. So different from the rose and lavender and jasmine that most women wore.

But Emily was different from most women. He found her forthrightness refreshing. She was straightforward and almost blunt, yet he found her more feminine and appealing than all the sausage-curled debutantes who giggled behind lace fans and batted eyelashes at him. While she was, no doubt, a virgin and guileless, the slightest touch from her made his blood heat hotter than anything the most experienced whore could do. To have Emily lying naked beneath him, gasping and panting with built-up desire while he pleasured her…showed her, with his mouth and hands, all the delights of lovemaking before actually indulging… His erection grew painfully hard and he groaned.

Emily Clayton was not for someone like him. She deserved a man who made an honest living and had both boots firmly planted on dry ground.

"Such deep thoughts on such a pleasant evening," Jean said as they entered the lobby and moved toward the bar area, "makes me think you may finally have heard the *chanson d'amour, non*?"

The song of love? Andre forced a grin. "*Non*. Such stuff only makes a fool willingly put his neck in the parson's noose. I will not be snared."

Jean shrugged. "Marc said much the same thing before he met the little *fräulein*."

"Different circumstances. He was ready to settle down." Andre gestured to the barkeep to bring them their usual brandies. "What about you, *mon ami*? I saw you talking to that enticing little piece of southern hospitality. She hardly noticed the gaggle of suitors lingering around after you left her side."

Jean's eyes lit up like dark coal. "She was a beguiling wench, wasn't she? All too aware of her beauty and how to use it, though."

"Do I sense a challenge coming?" Andre asked.

'Perhaps. Her name is Beatrice Tolliver, and her father is an influential planter. If we're going to set up a trade base here, it might be beneficial to further our acquaintance."

Andre grinned again, naturally this time. "Is that what we're calling it this time?"

Jean laughed and raised his snifter. "To women: The most pleasant diversion a man can indulge in…before the sea calls again."

Before the sea calls again. And she would. She was their real mistress. Andre doubted Emily Clayton would tolerate any competition.

****

One benefit of having her own personal bodyguard slave was that it allowed her more freedom to travel about. Mr. Jamison had not once threatened to flog Maisie for not keeping an eye on Emily since Juma had joined their household.

Emily smiled at the sight of him, dressed in his new livery, sitting stiffly in the groom's seat at the back of the curricle as the driver headed down Church Street toward the wharf. Juma glanced fiercely to his right and then his left as if daring someone to approach. He certainly was protective of her. Or maybe it was Cyrah he really wanted to protect. Her young maid had cow eyes whenever she was near him. Even now she kept twisting around in the seat to look over her shoulder at Juma. Emily didn't have to see to know he was grinning foolishly back at the girl.

"I hears tell that them Frenchmen from da boat be stayin' here," Cyrah said as she pointed to the Planter's Hotel nearby.

Emily looked at the elegant entrance. Again, she wondered what really went on behind those doors. Many of the wealthy plantation owners kept rooms there during the racing season. Even though its doors and architecture were stately enough to blend in with three majestic, neighboring churches, the hotel was known for its licentious atmosphere of wild parties, gambling, and heavy drinking. She'd even heard that wanton strumpets, dressed in little more than chemises, strode boldly through the halls. Emily's heart felt like it dropped to the pit of her stomach. Had Andre taken one of them to his bed? The thought of his magnificent chest and broad shoulders bare, his well-muscled arms holding one of those harlots… What would it feel like to be pressed against him? To have him do more than just kiss her wrist? Emily's breasts suddenly swelled and her nipples hardened. She felt her face heat. What was she thinking?

"They've certainly not been seen much since the church social a week ago," she said to Cyrah.

The maid slid a sideways glance at her. "Do you miss him?"

Emily felt her face grow hotter. "Certainly not! Why should I?"

"Hmmm. There's a ball comin' up at the Tolliver's, ain't there?"

"Yes. Next Saturday. What makes you think he'll be there? Not, of course, that it's important, but traders are seldom invited to such things."

"Umph." Cyrah grinned slyly. "Maybe not most traders, but I hear tell from the Tolliver's parlor maid that Miss Beatrice is mighty taken with Monsieur Clement."

Might it be possible? Emily's pulse began to race. Andre Dubois intrigued her, even more than the *Revenge II* that flew no flag. She still didn't know what its cargo was or from where it sailed, only that Mr. Clement looked and acted more like a landed gentleman than a sea captain. And Andre…

She glanced up at the second-story windows of the hotel, wondering which room might be his. She was about to look away when a curtain fluttered. A face appeared, and Emily nearly gaped. It was the woman again...the one she had seen dressed in men's clothing the day of the incident. The woman, now dressed in what looked like a simple linen shirt, stood by the window and watched as they drove by, her face devoid of paint and impassive. She didn't look like a harlot. On impulse, Emily raised her hand and waved.

"Who you be wavin' at, Miss Emily?" Cyrah asked.

Emily turned to her. "That lady up there. I saw her the other day. She seems rather sad."

Cyrah craned her neck to look up. "Ain't nobody there."

She turned her gaze back. The curtain was still pulled back, but no face showed. "Well, she probably stepped back," Emily said, even as her body gave a slight shiver from a sudden gust of cold air that descended from the direction of the window.

The hair on her nape rose as the carriage moved on down the road.

Chapter Five

Andre watched from his second-floor room as Emily's carriage passed by. The slave he'd sent her seemed to be doing a good job, staying alert on the coachman's seat of the curricle. Andre frowned a little as Emily waved at someone in another room. Who could she possibly know that stayed *here*? The only women who loitered about were of ill-repute. Would Emily be so bold as to wave at a man? He fought back the impulse to lean out the window to see.

Jean came up behind him and tossed an envelope on the small table near the window. He peered out. "Ah. The *petite fille*. Have you not made your move yet?"

Andre felt a muscle in jaw twitch. "No."

Jean's brow rose. "It is not like you to be so patient, *mon ami*."

"I have not had the opportunity to see her," Andre replied. He had deliberately avoided the possibility. Never had he desired a woman as much as he did Emily. Never had a woman been so completely wrong for him. He would wager his entire savings that she was a virgin. Neither he nor any other man had the right to take her maidenhead, unless his intentions were entirely honorable. He was a pirate. And, while he was growing tired of dealing in the slave trade, that is what he had done. And even now, they would be setting sail within the month to bring back another shipment from

Cartagena, along with whatever else could be pillaged from ships on the high seas.

"Well, the Tolliver's ball is next Saturday. It should be simple enough to beg a waltz and find yourself in need of some fresh air on the darkened balcony, *non*?" Jean grinned and sat down in one of the two chairs near the table. He pushed the envelope toward Andre. "Your share of the slave sales."

Andre took the envelope and slipped it inside the satchel he kept by the bed without looking at it. "We must be doubly sure our papers are in order with the next group," he said as he took the other chair and opened the decanter of brandy to pour drinks. "I've heard rumors about a slave uprising."

Jean shrugged. "A lot of slaves are discontent. Most don't know how well off they are."

Andre shook his head. "This involves a free man of color."

"Why would a free Negro want to get involved in an uprising?"

"I don't know. The man's name is Denmark Vessey, a carpenter. He was a former slave, but somehow won a lottery and had enough money to pay for his freedom years ago."

Jean paused in raising his snifter to his mouth. "If he's been free for years, why would he get involved in something potentially dangerous like that?"

"I think it has something to do with the African-Methodist church being closed down again. Seems this happened several years ago also when too many slaves started attending services and started grumbling."

"Well, it doesn't concern us," Jean answered as he finished his brandy and stood to leave. "We just sell them. We don't own them."

Andre looked back at the empty street after Jean left and wondered if Emily would see any difference in that.

****

The hackney came to an abrupt halt in the middle of Chalmers Street, causing Emily to slide across the leather-covered seat. She stuck her head out the window of the hired coach and looked up at the driver. "Why are we stopped?"

"Sorry, ma'am," he said and pointed ahead of him. "Road's blocked."

She craned her neck to see. About twenty slaves—men, women, and children—were being led toward the slave mart. Led wasn't quite the right word, though. The women and children were literally being dragged down the street, crying and wailing, while whips hissed at the black men attempting to help them.

"What's going on?" Emily asked the driver.

"None what's our business, Missy," he answered. "Just stay in the carriage."

But Emily had already opened the door and jumped down. Her stepfather would be expecting her at the church—she'd already overslept—but that would have to wait. Why on earth were slaves being taken to the mart on a Sunday morning?

As the slaves were wrestled inside the gates, different noise drew her attention. Coming down the street were more men—planters and businessmen from their dress—and all sounded angry, judging from the volume of their voices.

"Damn fools!" one of them said as they went by. "Trying to start an uprising!"

"We've been too lenient, lettin' them get by with

meetin' at that church without whites present," another said.

"That's what you get for trying to treat them like people," a man brandishing a riding crop added. "Time to put them in their place."

Ignoring the driver's warnings, Emily slipped through the gates behind the men. They were too upset to even notice her. She stayed close to the shadowed wall.

"We'll split them up," the riding-crop man announced.

A fresh chorus of wails went up from the women as children were yanked from their arms. The cracking of the whip against flesh made Emily wince. She watched with a sickening feeling in the pit of her stomach as the families were divided. Coin exchanged hands as the slaves were traded among the white men and carted off. She clenched her fists into balls, wishing she could do something.

"What are you doing here, *Mademoiselle*?"

Emily started at the sound of Andre's voice, and she turned to find him standing behind her, his face grim. "I was on my way to church when the road was blocked with…with… Did you see what happened? It's not right, dividing families that way." A tear trickled down her cheek as a crying child was pulled, none too gently, toward the door on the other side, while his mother shrieked to let her go with him.

"*Chèrie*." Andre put his hand on her shoulder and turned her toward him while his thumb lightly brushed the tear away. "You cannot save every slave."

His touch was so gentle, she wanted nothing more than to fling her arms around his neck and have him hold her and keep her safe. Then she felt shamed as the last mother was led away, weeping. She, Emily, had no right to feel sorry for herself. She sniffled and straightened her shoulders.

"I may not be able to save every slave, but I can give Juma and Cyrah their freedom. Aunty, too."

Andre raised a black brow. "An admirable thing, but I doubt they would leave you."

"Perhaps not, but at least they could if they wanted."

"And your stepfather? Would he be amiable as well?"

"Aunty belonged to my mother. Cyrah was given to me shortly after my mother married Mr. Jamison. He may not like it, but there isn't anything he can do."

"House slaves are expensive property."

"But should they be *property*?" Emily asked. "I know I sound like a heretic since the South is dependent on slavery, but Papa was in the Army. We didn't own slaves. Free men of color fought beside him."

Andre studied her. "I think you are a woman wise beyond your years," he finally said, "and I admire you more than you know." He offered his arm. "And I also think I had better escort you to church before your stepfather comes looking for you."

She accepted his arm, grateful for the strength of hard muscle beneath the superfine of his morning coat as they moved to the street. He didn't speak during the short ride in his cabriolet to the church and as she glanced over at him, she wondered at his silence and the dark look on his face.

Chapter Six

Andre had been right. When Emily gave Juma, Cyrah, and Aunty their freedom papers, not one of them would leave. Aunty cried, Juma looked dumbfounded, and Cyrah, for once, was speechless, but none of them wanted to go elsewhere. Mr. Jamison had been furious with her and adamant that they would not get wages if they stayed, but their former situation seemed to suit them just fine.

The only small change was that Juma had begun apprenticing with Denmark Vesey in the mornings, but he always returned before Emily needed to go somewhere.

She was fairly sure that once he was able to work as a carpenter he would be asking Cyrah to marry him. She glanced over at her maid as Cyrah took out of the wardrobe the pale blue, watered silk gown that Emily would wear to Tolliver's ball later. Cyrah wasn't smiling.

"Is something wrong?"

Cyrah looked up, her dark eyes suspiciously bright. "No, Miss Emily," she said, her voice shaky.

Emily tilted her head to one side. "That doesn't sound like everything is all right. Did you and Juma have a disagreement?"

"Oh, no, Missy. Nothin' like that." The maid hesitated. "Well, nothin' has been said, least wise."

"Come sit by me on the bed." Emily moved her skirts to one side and beckoned Cyrah to take the empty spot. "Tell me what it is."

Cyrah laid the gown carefully on the other side of the bed and then joined Emily. "It's just that he's working with Denmark Vesey."

Emily frowned. "You don't want him to be a carpenter?"

"Oh, no, it's not that. I want him to have a good job and proper wages and all." Cyrah's toffee-colored cheeks colored. "I mean, I'm hopin'…"

"I'm hoping too," Emily said with a smile. "I think Juma would make a very good husband for you."

Cyrah looked down at the floor. "If somethin' don't happen to him first."

"What do you mean?"

This time there were tears in her eyes when she looked up. "What happened to them slaves last week…the ones who all got split up and sold off…" Her voice trailed off.

Emily had tried to put that picture out of her mind. "Juma is a free man. That can't happen to him."

"I knows. Denmark Vesey is a free Negro, too, but there's talk, especially among the freed men…they ain't happy with what happened. There's been some meetin's white folks don't know about. Denmark's been at them."

A leaden lump settled in Emily's stomach. Rebellious slaves were always a danger, especially on the plantations where they easily outnumbered their white owners and overseers. It was one of the reasons that punishment was swift and sometimes cruel. If Mr. Jamison or Mayor Hamilton found out…

"You must warn Juma to be careful," Emily said.

"June will be here soon and we will be leaving for the country. He won't be attending any meetings there."

Cyrah looked doubtful, but she nodded as she went to pick up the blue gown. "I hope so, Miss Emily. I truly does."

****

Andre accepted the mint julep from the waiter's tray, wishing to God it was brandy the Tollivers were serving at the ball. Southern gentility obviously didn't want their guests getting snookered while the music still played.

He searched the ballroom for Emily. Surely she would be attending. He stole another glance at his gold pocket watch. Nine o'clock. She wasn't even fashionably late yet. If Tolliver hadn't insisted that Jean and Andre join them for a light supper before the dance—supposedly to talk about importing some Spanish goods, although he suspected that Beatrice's father wanted to size up Jean—Andre wouldn't be here this early either. He watched now as Beatrice coquettishly opened and closed her fan while batting her eyes and hoped Jean wasn't really falling for the silly chit. Indeed, it seemed odd that Jean would take an interest at all, since he usually preferred the quadroon beauties of New Orleans.

Andre slid a glance back to the door and then breathed a sigh of relief. Emily had just entered the room, accompanied by her stepfather. Her gown shimmered with the various hues of a Caribbean sea, the red and gold of her hair a brilliant sunset to set it off. He wanted to thread his fingers through that hair and spread the curls over her creamy shoulders and then lose himself in the exotically spicy scent of her. Andre started toward her and then stopped abruptly as some young swain bowed low in front of her and Mr. Jamison handed her to him with a smile. They moved onto the dance floor.

Of course, he should have expected it. She was the daughter of a wealthy plantation owner, just as Beatrice was. No doubt Emily's dance card was already full. Andre watched as she laughingly stomped and clapped to a vigorous reel. A man would be insane not to want her. The swell of her breasts against the low neckline of the dress tantalized him even from here. The soft silk skirt flowed over the gentle curve of her hips and made Andre want to cup her rounded buttocks and press her up against him. A definite ache began to grow inside his pants.

"You're glowering, *mon ami*," Jean said as he stepped up beside him.

"I am not. The light is just not good in here."

Jean laughed. "I don't think you're having any trouble seeing *la petite fille*."

At that moment, Andre was truly sorry for all the times he had ribbed Jean and Marc about the women in their lives. Especially Marc. Andre had a wary feeling that these strange emotions warring inside of him were what Marc felt for his little *fräulein* in Texas. Only Ilsa didn't have obligations to society. Emily did. And one did not take a well-bred lady to his bed without a marriage proposal.

"She seems to be enjoying herself," he said. Indeed. She had changed partners for another dance.

Jean slanted a sideways glance at him. "I think you really have heard the *chanson d'amour.*" When he didn't answer, Jean sighed. "What are you going to do, *mon ami*?"

"Nothing. My life is on the sea. Hers is on land."

"Have you told her what we do?"

Andre shook his head. As opposed to slavery as she was, she would truly hate him if she found out he plied in the slave trade. Even though they only brought young adult males unencumbered by families, she still wouldn't understand. Quite frankly, witnessing the mothers and children being separated last week hadn't set well with him either. Jean would be setting sail next week to pick up another shipment, and Andre was contracted as first mate. Perhaps it would be his last trip. He had his own ship, the *Giselle*, waiting for him in Cartegena. He could make a decent living transporting goods other than humans.

He looked over at Emily again, this time dancing with an older man who looked like he couldn't quite believe his luck. As spunky and spirited as she was, she still belonged to Southern society. In another year or two, she would no doubt be married to some landed gentry and have a *bébé*. A sharp, knife-like pain sliced through his belly at the thought of Emily having a child…and how that child would have gotten there. His jaw clenched. *Mon Dieu.* He was jealous. It was a totally foreign emotion to him and one he didn't like. *Merde.* This had to stop—and he knew how to stop it. He would sate his lust for her tonight. He couldn't ruin her, of course, by taking her maidenhead, but he could kiss her senseless in some secluded garden spot and let his hands roam over her body, exploring all the delightful mounds and valleys while he ravaged her mouth. Once he had tasted her, held her, given her pleasure…the rest of his "need" could be taken care of later with a few coins.

The orchestra began a waltz. Perfect. "Excuse me,"

he said to Jean, "but I believe they're playing Emily's song."

He ignored Jean's laughter behind him.

****

Through lowered lashes, Emily watched Andre cross the dance floor toward her. She had begun to think he was going to spend the entire evening talking with Monsieur Clement, rooted to the spot by the potted palm. But he really needed to hurry. This was a *waltz*, and old Mr. Thompson was already looking hopeful as he began to put an arm around her waist.

Andre tapped him on the shoulder. "I believe this is my dance," he said and held out his hand to Emily. A scowling Mr. Thompson reluctantly let her go. Gratefully, she placed her hand in Andre's, his slightly calloused fingertips closing warmly and firmly over her own. He slipped a strong arm around her waist, drawing her closer than was proper and she should have protested, but she didn't. Instead, she found herself moving her hand from his large, hard bicep to his broad, equally hard, chiseled shoulder. Was everything about his body hard? It would seem so as he expertly turned her, a solid thigh brushing hers fleetingly as he did so. And then again at the next twirl. Emily was almost sure this wasn't proper either, since none of her dance partners had ever dared to be so close. But it also felt *right*. As though they had a will of their own, her fingers grazed the inky hair that curled slightly against his collar and lingered there. One of his eyebrows raised and she blushed, jerking her hand back to his shoulder. What in the world had gotten into her? She'd never touched a man's hair before. And yet, her fingers itched to run though it much more thoroughly.

"You are looking warm, *mademoiselle*. Perhaps a breath of fresh air would do you good?"

She was certainly warm. In fact, it had suddenly gotten excruciatingly *hot* in the ballroom. Too many people. Much too stuffy. For once, she wished she had a fan.

"Yes. I must have danced too much. Perhaps some air…on the terrace…"

"Your wish is my command," Andre said and offered his arm to lead her through the open French doors.

There were several other couples standing about, and no one paid much notice to them. The heat didn't seem to be affecting any of them. "There's not much breeze here," she said, wondering why in the world she still felt so terribly warm.

A corner of Andre's mouth quirked up. "There's probably a better breeze in the gardens, if you dare to venture there with me."

Oh, Lord. She could hear Aunty's voice now, admonishing her about taking unchaperoned walks in gardens. Especially with an attractive man who was practically a stranger and had an air of something a bit wild about him as well. Unlike the dutiful, well-mannered sons of Charleston's society. Usually she found these balls dull and boring, but tonight—well, at least since the waltz—she felt alive and quite…feminine. As though she had some sort of delicious power.

Besides, the garden paths were well lit with lanterns. Tolliver meant for his guests to stroll there. "I'd like that," she said.

His sensual mouth quirked up again as they moved down the steps. Had she noticed before how full his lips were? What would they feel like pressed to hers? She glanced away quickly, but not before an amused glint came into Andre's green eyes. "You must not be afraid of me, *mademoiselle*," he said in a husky whisper.

She forced herself to meet his gaze. "Something tells me I should be very much afraid…and yet, I'm not."

He threw back his head and laughed. "You amaze me, *madem*—Miss Clayton. And you are right. You probably should be afraid, for I want nothing more than to draw you behind some shrubbery and kiss you, among other things."

Her entire body tingled at the thought of "other things." For some strange reason, her breasts began to swell and an odd throbbing began between her thighs. She'd had only one kiss before. Last year, at the South Carolina Society's boxed lunch and social, Bobby Joe Fowler drank some rum-laced punch and planted a sloppy kiss on her cheek as she turned her head away.

Emily had a feeling there would be nothing sloppy about kissing Andre.

She smiled up at him. "What if I said yes?"

He nearly tripped, a startled expression on his face. "*Pardon-moi?*"

"I said, what if I said yes? I think I might like to be kissed." She frowned slightly as he began to grin. "Just kissed, you understand. Nothing more."

"*Oui.*" He glanced around, took her hand and led her behind a rose trellis. "This should do for kissing, *chèrie*." And then he gathered her in his arms and bent his head to hers.

His lips were warm, the pressure firm but gentle, as his mouth slanted over hers, kissing, nibbling lightly at the corner of her mouth before drawing her lower lip between his lips, teasing her, encouraging her to open for him. He felt glorious. Her lips parted and he slipped his tongue inside, its velvety texture exploring her.

With a moan, Emily pressed her aching breasts against his broad, hard chest and entwined her fingers in his silky hair. Andre groaned and his hold tightened, his arms slipping down to cup her buttocks and bring her up against the swell of his erection. Instinctively, she rubbed against the hardened ridge, and he growled.

"I hate to intrude," Jean said from the other side of the trellis, "but Monsieur Jamison is looking for *la petite fille*."

With a gasp, Emily pushed back from Andre. "He will confine me to my room for weeks if he catches me out here with you," she said in a shaky voice.

Andre cursed under his breath and guided her back to the walkway. To his relief, Jean was waiting. "Not if he sees that you've been properly escorted by Monsieur Clement and myself, *chèrie*. You have simply been showing both of us the gardens." He looked over at Jean. "Isn't that right?"

"*Certainement*," Jean said with a grin. "I've always liked gardens."

Emily only hoped her knees didn't buckle as wave after wave of delicious heat from their kiss continued to soar through her. What would have happened if they had not been stopped?

Chapter Seven

Andre was still mulling over the delightful episode behind the rose trellis several days later as he made his descent down the stairs of the Planter's Hotel toward the lobby. Emily had surprised him, not only with her boldness in asking to be kissed, but also in the heated response she had given him. There had been no hesitation on her part in accepting his tongue into her mouth or in meeting his tongue with hers. He wondered how many men she had kissed before.

Her body had melded perfectly with his too. Again, there had only been eagerness on her part to have them pressed close together…and the way she had tantalized him by rotating her hips and teasing his shaft with her belly…it was something an experienced woman would do.

He frowned. Was Emily not a virgin, after all? Given the strict Southern code of honor regarding daughters of the gentry, it would seem highly improbable that she was not a virgin. Yet Emily didn't exactly fit the picture of decorum. She had admitted to liking adventure. Did that include finding out what went on between a man and a woman when they were alone?

The sound of her voice stopped him at the landing. He must be imagining things. Whatever would she be doing at the Planter's Hotel? A certain organ began to swell in anticipation. Was she here to see him? Would she really be *that* bold? He poked his head around the corner to see the counter. There she was. Alone. His groin began to ache, and then he cursed. Where in the hell was Juma?

"I'm telling you," Emily said to the clerk, "that the woman just waved to me from her window. Not five minutes ago."

"We don't have any women here now. It's daylight." The young man turned red and stammered. "I mean…er, there aren't any women staying here."

"And I'm telling you there is a woman on the second floor, the end room. I've seen her before when I've driven by." Emily paused and then smiled suddenly. "She dresses in men's clothes. Maybe that's why you haven't noticed her."

The clerk's face drained of color. "We don't rent that room unless we're full."

"Why not?"

"Folks say they hear strange things at night."

Andre could almost see Emily's ears prick up, like a terrier scenting a rabbit.

"Are you saying the room is haunted?" she asked.

The clerk shook his head. "No one has ever seen anything. Just heard noises…sounds like might come from a ship. Laughter and cussing, too."

"That could come from your own gaming rooms, couldn't it?"

"Not in the wee hours before dawn," the clerk said stubbornly. "Besides, what folks hear is bawdy, seagoing talk…not the likes of the gents that stay here."

Emily's back straightened and Andre nearly laughed, almost giving away his eavesdropping spot. If Emily had a tail, it would definitely be stiff, pointing at her prey. Then he sobered. He had a certain stiffness himself that was straining at his breeches.

"Like pirates?" Emily asked.

The clerk looked dumbfounded. "Ain't been pirates around here for years."

Pirates? It was Andre's turn to snap to attention. Better he intercede now than let this particular path of conversation go on.

"*Mademoiselle* Clayton! What a coincidence to find you here," he said as he stepped out from the shadows.

Emily whirled. "*Monsieur* Dubois! You're just the man I needed to see."

Andre bit back a grin as the clerk's mouth dropped open and he stared at her bug-eyed. Luckily, Emily was not looking at him. She probably had no idea of how loose and wanton that sounded. Or did she? She was either the most guileless ingénue or the most skilled courtesan he had ever met. In either case, discretion would be the best course here.

"How might I be of assistance?" he asked formally.

"I want you to take me up to the room on the second floor."

The clerk made a strangling sound and even Andre had to feign a quick cough. There was nothing he'd like more than to take her to his room and finish what they'd started behind the rose trellis. But he forced those lecherous thoughts down. Even if she wasn't a virgin, there was no reason to tarnish her reputation purposely.

"Perhaps a cup of tea in the sitting room would be better?"

Emily stared at him as though he'd gone daft. "Tea? Why would I want tea? Oh!" A rosy blush stained her cheeks as comprehension dawned. "I didn't mean—"

"Of course not," Andre said smoothly. "I'm sure I misunderstood. Please forgive me for even entertaining such an idea."

Her blush deepened and, for just a fleeting moment, he thought he saw raw desire in her eyes. His groin tightened. Surely she wouldn't...

Emily's chin came up. "I merely want to look inside the end room on the second floor. I am sure a woman is staying there. Since the clerk doesn't know anything about it, maybe the poor woman is being held a prisoner or something."

The clerk managed to find his voice. "The room's empty, but I'll take you up there and show you myself." His look turned sly. "Not much to do around here right now anyways."

Andre resisted the urge to put his hands around the clerk's scrawny throat and strangle him. Instead, he snatched at the key. "We will be back in precisely five minutes," he said and took Emily's elbow. "This way, *mademoiselle*."

Emily was thankfully quiet on the way up the stairs, and Andre didn't trust what sort of totally inappropriate thing would come out of his mouth if he spoke. Silently, he turned the key in the door and swung it open.

Emily stepped inside and he followed her in, careful to leave the door open. The double bed with its plain white cotton spread was all too appealing, and Emily's exotic scent filled his nostrils. He clenched his fists at his side to keep from touching her.

"It's empty," she said.

"The clerk said it was," he managed to say in a somewhat even tone as he watched her drop to the floor to look under the bed, her perfectly rounded rump perkily aimed up at him. *Mon Dieu*. Was she deliberately trying to be provocative? If she did just one more thing that was suggestive, he wasn't going to be accountable for his actions. There was only so much a man could take.

Looking disappointed—and not at all like someone bent on seduction—she took a quick look in the wardrobe and then moved toward the door. For a moment, Andre was tempted not to step aside. She would have to brush up against him…

Merde. Was he going mad? There was a leering clerk downstairs just waiting to see how long they would be gone. Andre took a step back. "After you, *mademoiselle*."

He handed the key back to the clerk with a glare that made the young man blanch. Walking Emily outside, he saw Juma frantically coming toward them, Cyrah running by his side to keep up.

"Oh, Lordy," the big man said as he stopped in front of them. "Cyrah and I only stopped to buy an ice—"

"See to it that you don't lose her again," Andre said grimly as he handed her over to her bodyguard. Juma looked properly chastised and even Cyrah hung her head guiltily. Andre had a suspicion that the purchase of an ice may have extended into something more, but then, it wouldn't take Emily more than a minute to elude her chaperones and hightail it to the hotel.

Andre watched as they moved down the road, with a servant on each side of Emily. She certainly was not conventional. She probably had not even given a thought how it might look to show up at a hotel that had a somewhat dubious reputation. After all, the first time he'd seen her, she had been sitting by herself at the wharf without a chaperone either.

He frowned, wondering again just what amount of feminine expertise she might really have. He would love to find out.

Chapter Eight

Mama—rest her soul—had always said she had the curiosity of a cat. Papa had called her tenacious, but he always smiled when he said it.

The visit to the Planter's Hotel two days ago had only whetted both traits. A room that was empty—she *knew* the woman had waved to her from there—well, something was off. Could the room possibly *be* haunted, like the desk clerk implied?

Emily looked at the ladies of the Charleston Library Society that were gathered in the parlor of Mrs. Hamilton, the mayor's wife. Perhaps one of these ladies would know something of the history of the hotel. They were, after all, the most intellectual of society's lot.

"I beg pardon, but I have a question," she said.

"Yes?" Mrs. Hamilton answered pleasantly. "What is it?"

"Have you heard anything about the Planter's Hotel being haunted?"

One of the other ladies almost snorted. "The place should be haunted by the guilt of those strumpets who lure men upstairs."

Mrs. Hamilton leveled a gaze on the woman and then turned her attention back to Emily. "Why do you ask?"

"Well, I've ridden by there several times, and a woman has waved to me from the second-story window.

Day before yesterday, she was there again. Only this time she beckoned me to come in, so I did—" Emily stopped at the collective gasp of most of the ladies.

"You…went…*inside*?" one of them asked incredulously.

"Yes, I did—"

"My dear, wherever was Maisie? Or that large bodyguard that follows you around?" Mrs. Hamilton put a hand to her bosom as if to catch her breath. "I can't believe they would let you go in there, even escorted."

Emily looked down at the floor. It wasn't Juma's fault she had slipped away while he was buying an ice for Cyrah. And Aunty Maisie—especially if she found out that Monsieur Dubois had taken Emily to the room, even though *nothing* had happened—would no doubt swoon dead away. She didn't even want to think what Mr. Jamison would do. As usual, curiosity had overruled common sense.

Taking a deep breath, she looked up. "I thought it would be quite safe in the middle of the day—"

"But your reputation," one of the single ladies twittered, "something like that could positively ruin—"

"Oh, stop it." Mrs. Johnson, the elderly matron of the group, thumped her cane on the floor. "Don't tell me half of you wouldn't like to know what *really* goes on in there." She looked at Emily. "It doesn't appear any harm's been done."

"No, ma'am. The clerk let me have the key to look in the room…" Emily paused as several ladies gasped again and decided not to mention being escorted there by Andre. "But it was empty and I went right back downstairs." She looked at Mrs. Johnson. "The clerk said noises and voices have been heard coming from that room in the early hours of the morning and when it was supposed to be empty."

"No doubt," a young married woman sniffed, "some harlot plying her favors."

Mrs. Johnson's cane thumped again. "It seems some of you are mighty interested in those harlots." She turned to Emily. "What did this woman look like?"

"She had reddish-brown hair," Emily replied, "but the odd thing was, she was always dressed in men's clothes. A white shirt and trousers."

"Doesn't sound like a harlot to me," Mrs. Johnson said and glared at the two young women who sniggered. "Charleston has its share of ghosts, of course." She closed her eyes, thinking, and then opened them. "There was an incident…before I was born, actually, that created quite a scandal. A man named William Cormac moved here from Ireland and bought a plantation. His daughter—so my own mother said—was quite pretty and could have had her choice of suitors, but she married a pirate."

Emily felt her eyes grow round. "A pirate?"

Mrs. Johnson nodded. "Her father disowned her, of course, and that might have been the end of things, but word came back that she and her second husband—another pirate named Calico-Jack-something—had been captured in Jamaica. They were sentenced to hang. Her father relented and ransomed her. Brought her back to Charleston. Forced her to marry a respectable man." Mrs. Johnson shook her head. "Rumor had it she never lost her love for the sea…or pirates. She, um, 'visited' the sailors that stayed at the Planter's Hotel." The old lady smiled at Emily. "Anne Bonny was a headstrong girl. Rather like you, I imagine."

Anne Bonny. Emily suddenly felt lightheaded. As a child, she had read stories about Anne Bonny and her ship, the *Revenge*, in the cheap novels and felt a strange bond, although she had attributed it to her love for adventure.

Andre was staying at the hotel and his ship's name was the *Revenge II*. Was it merely a coincidence? Could the woman that no one else seemed to see really be the ghost of the infamous Anne? And, if so, what was she trying to tell her?

****

Emily tapped her toes impatiently, although her satin slippers on the rich Aubusson carpet of the library made no sound. The dinner party her stepfather hosted had been a long and drawn-out affair with more courses than were necessary, but it seemed he was interested in investing in Monsieur Clement's next expedition to the West Indies and possibly exporting cotton, as well. At any rate, he'd seated Emily, as hostess, at the far end of the table, and she'd not had a chance to speak to Andre.

And she wanted to tell him about the ghost. Let him know she wasn't daft and had a reason for going to the Planter's Hotel. She hoped he'd understood her signal when she'd tilted her head and slanted her eyes in the direction of the library. His eyes had seemed to darken and he'd smiled slightly.

She did wish he'd hurry. The ladies had been served sherry in the parlor, but she would have to return soon. Surely, the men must have finished a brandy by now, in the billiard room, and he could get away.

To her relief, the knob turned and Andre stepped inside. After closing the door quietly, he walked toward her, a corner of his mouth lifted in a lopsided smile. Her heart fluttered at the sight of him, his inky-black hair curling against the collar of the black dinner coat that did nothing to diminish the broad expanse of his shoulders. His eyes sparked green fire, and as he came near, she caught his scent…soap and leather and something more. Something heated. Something that was essentially *him*.

Before she was aware of what he intended, he'd drawn her into his arms, pressing her against the hard muscles of his chest. His lips came down on hers, hungry and demanding. His tongue plundered her mouth, taking, wanting more, totally consuming her. His hands slid down to cup her buttocks, and she gasped, managing to lean back slightly.

"What are you doing?"

He grinned. "What does it feel like I'm doing? I'm continuing from where we were so rudely interrupted behind the rose trellis." He bent to nibble a path along her neck and she made a soft mewling sound. His mouth brushed softly over the swell of her breasts above the neckline. Emily moaned, her fingers kneading his shoulders, half-pushing him away, half-pulling him closer. He chuckled and let his hand trace a slow path up her back and over her shoulder. Slipping a finger under the strap of her gown, he lowered it enough to expose a rosy, budded nipple. "Beautiful," he whispered and then covered it with his mouth, suckling.

Emily gave a small shriek.

Andre straightened instantly, a hand over her mouth. "I have no objections to your screaming, *chèrie*, once I have you in my bed, but since you have guests not far away, perhaps it would be wise to—"

She pushed away from him, tugging her gown up over her naked breasts, albeit very tingling ones. "This is totally improper, *monsieur*!"

"You don't look angry, though." He tilted his head and grinned. "In fact, your face is flushed, your eyes are glowing, and your lips swollen. I would say you very much enjoyed what I just did." He held out his arms. "Shall we continue?"

Emily stared at him as though he'd suddenly grown antlers or something. "We can't continue here!"

His grin widened. "Do you have some place else in mind?"

"No, of course not!"

Andre lifted an eyebrow. "You invited me in here for an assignation, *oui*?"

"No. I mean, yes. I invited you…" Emily suddenly clapped her hand over her mouth. "No! Not for…not for what you're thinking!"

He dropped his hands to his sides. "*Mademoiselle*. It is not wise to trifle with a man's…affections. I am slow to anger, but you might not be so lucky with the next man you ask to meet you like this."

Emily's eyes narrowed. "I don't invite men to be alone with me."

Andre looked around. "There is no one else here."

She bristled. "I wanted to tell you about Anne Bonny, but never mind. You wouldn't believe me anyhow." She turned and flounced out, slamming the door.

Andre stared at the closed door, wondering why Emily would want to talk about a woman pirate who'd been dead for years.

And what in the hell had just happened? He had very little experience with virgins, but he was pretty sure they didn't respond like Emily did with her whole body melding into his.

The little vixen must be teasing him. Wanting him totally enamored with her.

His lips curled in a tight smile. He'd warned her not to tease him. The next time he wouldn't stop until he had her naked, panting beneath him, begging to be taken.

Chapter Nine

The day after that episode, Emily wandered about the townhouse in a daze, touching her lips frequently as though she could still feel Andre's kisses. The bodice of her day dress felt much too tight, her nipples sensitive against the fabric that seemed to rub at them. The truth was that she *had* liked everything he had done, especially…she felt her face grow heated at the thought of him suckling at her breast. Dear Lord. She'd had no idea a man would do that to a woman. And the sensation! Fire had seared through her stomach and straight to a throbbing place between her thighs.

What had happened was *totally* improper. She should be scandalized that he had even thought to take such advantage of her. She probably should have slapped him, just so he understood that. Indecent. Indecorous. Infelicitous…and *intriguing*. As much as Emily tried to stir up a righteous outrage to such an affront, the most she could muster was…*curiosity*.

Well, that was over. It had been more than a week since the dinner party and, although both Andre and Monsieur Clement had come several times to the house to discuss business with Mr. Jamison, Andre had behaved as a perfect gentleman. Not once had he alluded to, in look, gesture, or speech, that the event had even taken place.

Damn it. Was he so used to carousing with women

that he'd forgotten the whole incident?

Emily heard the back door by the kitchens open and the sounds of Juma and Cyrah's voices. They sounded agitated, and Emily hoped they hadn't had a fight. She moved from the sitting room where she had been trying to read a book and found them in the hall. Juma's expression was stern and Cyrah, for once, looked serious too.

"Is something wrong?" Emily asked.

"Can we speak to you in private, Miss Emily?" Juma answered.

"Of course. In here." She opened the door to the sitting room and indicated that they enter.

Juma closed the door behind him and waited until she was seated before he sat down beside Cyrah on the sofa. He twisted his hat in his hands.

"Just tell her," Cyrah said.

"Tell me what?" Emily looked from one to the other. If they hadn't been so solemn, she would have half-expected to hear they were engaged.

"I been to Denmark's this mornin'," Juma said.

"Yes. You go there nearly every morning to learn carpentry," Emily replied.

"Well, this mornin' there were some folk there…" Juma hesitated, glanced at Cyrah and then went on. "Colored folk ain't happy. Ever since them families got split up. There's talk of stoppin' the next ship that brings more slaves here."

Emily frowned. "I don't like seeing slaves arriving either, but how can they be stopped? American slave trade is legal."

"Some is. Some isn't," Juma said. "Don't matter. The free coloreds gots boats and weapons. There's enough slaves willin' to slip away and fight. The next trader will never make it to harbor."

Emily widened her eyes. "How would they stop a large ship?"

"Element of surprise, I reckon," Juma said. "Fishin' boats look harmless enough. Ain't no one expectin' fishermen to attack and board a ship or kill a crew."

Just like pirates of old. Emily felt a small chill run through her. *Like Stede Bonnet or Anne Bonny...* She gave herself a little shake. Pirates had been on her mind ever since Mrs. Hamilton's luncheon.

"But these men...the runaway slaves will be punished and the free coloreds hanged if they're caught." She leaned slightly forward. "They will be caught. There aren't many places you can hide a big ship."

Juma shrugged. "They can sail her up the coast and disappear into the swamps and rivers by the Chesapeake. Hard to find a man there."

Just like Jean Lafitte's men had hidden in the swamps of Louisiana. Only in the end, Papa had said the pirates helped the U.S. Army. Pirates again. Emily shook her head to clear it.

"Mr. Jamison is a magistrate." Emily hesitated. "I don't know if I should tell him or not. I don't want to see men arrested for owning fishing boats. I haven't heard of any runaway slaves, yet—"

"That's not why we came to you," Cyrah interrupted, her chocolate eyes serious. "Go on, Juma. Tell her the rest."

"There's more?" Emily asked.

Juma looked miserable. "Yes'm. Master Dubois' boat is gettin' ready to sail."

"I know. They're leaving for the West Indies

tomorrow. Mr. Jamison has been talking to *Monsieur* Dubois and *Monsieur* Clement about investing in a sugar cane plantation there and importing rum. They'll be bringing back some along with spices and—"

"Slaves," Cyrah interrupted again.

"Slaves?" Emily repeated. "What are you talking about?"

Juma hung his head even lower. "They're slave traders."

Emily felt a shock of ice water flood her veins. Andre dealt in the slave market? "They can't be. Mr. Jamison would never…" Her voice trailed off. Her stepfather believed in slavery. Was the sugar cane and rum merely a foil? "Are you sure?" she asked in a near whisper.

Juma nodded. "There was a batch of new slaves sold about the time the *Revenge* arrived. Man name of Louis handled the transaction. Denmark made some inquiries about the new slaves. They came from Cuba."

Andre was not only a slave trader, but an *illegal* one. The ice suddenly froze hard in her veins. She gulped air. Dear Lord. What was she going to do? If her stepfather knew of this, she couldn't go to him. If he was unaware, could she go to him anyhow? The thought of Andre being arrested and imprisoned… But if the free coloreds were successful in taking the ship when it returned, Andre would be killed, along with *Monsieur* Clement. Dear, sweet Lord.

She had to talk to Andre.

Juma and Cyrah were both watching her with worried expressions. After the Planter's Hotel incident, Juma had stuck to her like a honeybee to the comb. And she had heard *Monsieur* Clement tell Mr. Jamison they'd be back on board a good two days before sailing to check everything. She knew Juma would not allow her to go to the docks. She had to elude him.

Emily had never swooned in her life, but she'd seen other ladies do it. With a shuddered breath, she swept her hand across her forehead and pitched forward.

Chapter Ten

"Are you sure that's what you want to do?" Jean asked Andre as they sat across the desk from each other in the aft cabin of the *Revenge II*.

Andre nodded. "*La Diligent* will have brought the slaves to Cuba. I'll sail her back to Cartegena and pick up the *Giselle*. This will be my last slave trip."

Jean poured them both a brandy. "Is this decision the influence of *la petite fille, mon ami*?"

Andre accepted the snifter. "Perhaps." He really didn't know if it was or not. The distress on Emily's face when those families were separated had started him thinking. In Barataria, they had all been free men. Outlaws, perhaps, but free. The lucrative slave trading had begun after the war. When they moved their headquarters to Campeche, it hadn't been that hard to continue, especially since the Spanish galleons carried slaves to Mexico. Their fate hadn't really affected him. They would be slaves in one country or another. But then, Emily had been horrified that Juma might be hanged for trying to take her horse. She *cared*. And Andre had seen how devoted the big man was to her. Cyrah and the old Aunty, Maisie, were treated more like family than slaves, although now they were legally free. Thanks to Emily.

"So." Jean swirled the amber liquid and held it to his nose to sniff. "You will bring the *Giselle* back and propose and live happily ever after?"

How he wished he could. "I won't be returning."

Jean raised an eyebrow. "Why not?"

"My life is on the sea," he said. "Emily is gentry. She needs a man who will be home, running the plantation that she will no doubt inherit. Not someone who is gone for months on end."

"Marc gave up the sea to farm with his *fräulein*," Jean replied. "Perhaps—"

Andre shook his head. "Marc spoke many times of missing the home Napoleon had confiscated. A home surrounded by fields, not water. The sea called to me the first time I stepped onto a boat."

Jean set his empty glass down and stood. "Perhaps you will change your mind," he said as he moved toward the door.

Andre sat for several minutes more, letting the gentle sway of the boat bobbing on her lines relax him. He had thought long and hard about telling Emily he wasn't returning. But goodbyes were never easy.

And what good would it do? She was as bonded to the land as he was to the sea.

****

Emily pulled the boy's cap down low over her face and checked to make sure all of her hair was still tucked under it as she peered around the corner of the pier to watch the loading of the *Revenge II*.

Swooning had been easier than she thought. Juma had caught her before she actually fell, thankfully. He'd carried her upstairs and Cyrah had brought smelling salts. She had managed to convince her maid and Maisie that all she needed was to rest in bed for the rest of the day.

The door had barely closed behind them before she was out of bed and digging in the depths of her wardrobe. She still had a linen shirt and a pair of men's trousers that she'd used when she rode astride in Texas—how much more freedom she'd had then!

Now, she gave one more tug at the shirt, loosening it enough to hide any hint of her bound breasts. Masquerading as a boy was a lot safer than walking on the streets as a girl unescorted. And she could hardly expect to be welcomed on board in hoops. Besides which, sailors had strange superstitions about having women on board to begin with. She'd read that in one of the cheap novels about Anne Bonny. Much better not to attract attention while getting to the aft cabins where Andre and Monsieur Clement would more than likely be.

Emily took a deep breath and sauntered over to the warehouse area. Picking up the smallest crate she could find, she moved up the gangplank.

"Put 'er there, matey!" One of the sailors pointed to where other crates stood mid-ship.

Emily set the crate down and then glanced quickly around. There was a lot of shouting and movement, but no one seemed to take notice of her. She moved toward the port gunwale, past the main mast, and then along the companionway that led to the quarterdeck. She glanced around once more, but every hand was busy, stowing items or carrying them below.

She tried the knob on the first cabin. A silver decanter sat on a small desk, along with two brandy snifters. Most likely the captain's cabin. Emily tried the second door and saw Andre's cloak lying on the bed and breathed a sigh of relief. His cabin. She would wait here.

Settling in the chair near the bed, she became aware

of the gentle rocking of the ship, almost like a baby's cradle. If she weren't careful, it would lull her to sleep. It really was peaceful and cozy in here. She could still hear men shouting, but the thick teak door made the sounds muffled. Hopefully, Andre would appear soon. She wanted to appear indignant, if not outraged, that he had not told her he was a slaver. The more the ship bobbed, the more relaxed she was becoming.

Emily yawned in spite of herself. It had been a very stressful day, come to think of it. Her eyes slowly drifted shut.

A very stressful day.

****

Emily awoke with a start as someone lifted her from the chair. Andre's startled face came into focus. She swayed, but his hands on her arms steadied her. Slowly, she became aware the ship was moving.

"What are you doing here?" he asked, his mouth a tight line.

"I needed to see you." She swayed again as the ship pitched. "Are you moving the ship to another slip?"

"Hardly. We've been underway for nearly four hours."

Emily felt her eyes go round. "I thought you weren't leaving until tomorrow."

"We got everything loaded and the tide was turning. Jean didn't see any reason to wait. How did you—" He stopped and glanced at her clothes. "Why are you dressed like that?"

"I thought it was safer to look like a street urchin that a lady alone on the streets."

He lifted an eyebrow. "And how did you elude Juma this time?"

"I pretended to swoon so I could come to see you."

His mouth softened just a bit. "You could have sent a note. I would have come to you, *mademoiselle*."

"Yes, well. I didn't know if you'd get it before you sailed."

"*Merde*," he said, his mouth hard again. "Sailing. I've got to go tell Jean to turn the ship around and get you back to port before your stepfather thinks we've kidnapped you." He started toward the door when Emily stopped him.

"Wait. We've got to talk."

Andre hesitated by the door. "About what?"

"Where this ship is going."

"Cuba. You knew that."

"Why?" she asked.

He frowned. "I thought you paid attention to your stepfather's conversation. He's investing in sugar cane production. We're handling the paperwork and picking up some cargo."

"What kind of cargo?"

Andre's face became guarded. "Various products."

He wasn't going to admit to slavery. Emily felt like she'd swallowed a lump of hot coal. If she confronted him, he'd deny it. And, if they turned the ship back now, she wouldn't have enough time to convince him not to bring slaves back. Even if he believed her and they were prepared for the planned ambush at sea, the uproar from such a battle would surely see them arrested for importing foreign slaves. She needed more time. She had to stay on the ship.

"I want to see this sugarcane plantation Mr. Jamison is investing in."

"Don't tell me your stepfather sent you on this

mission." He looked at her clothes again. "Not dressed like that. Not that he would allow it under any circumstances."

"You're quite right," Emily answered, trying to think quickly, "but it is my inheritance that is being used for funding, is it not?"

"Perhaps. But Jean is a good investor. You have no reason to fear you're being duped."

"And I've heard my stepfather say it's always wise to check things out himself."

"He doesn't even know you're on board, *mademoiselle*."

"That's not exactly true," Emily responded. "Of course, he wouldn't have given me permission to go, since I'm a *woman*, but I *did* leave a note." It was only a half-lie. She had left a note propped on her pillow for Cyrah, saying she'd gone to the docks and would be returning soon.

Andre looked skeptical. "And where, then, is your luggage?"

"I told you I felt safer traveling as a boy. I thought maybe Monsieur Clement kept some things on board that I could wear."

His mouth quirked up. "Anything feminine that Jean keeps on board would probably shock you, *chèrie*."

She raised her chin. "I doubt it."

His eyes began to smolder. "Such garments would hardly keep you safe from any man, myself included."

Emily felt her face warm. His heated gaze was bringing odd, fluttering sensations to her tummy as though a dozen butterflies didn't know where to land. Her breasts grew heavy as he momentarily shifted his gaze there and suddenly, she wanted him to kiss her again, like he had in the library.

"I really am going to need a change of clothes, I think."

He made a funny sound low in his throat. It sounded like something between a growl and a groan. "Do you have any idea of what you're saying?" He glanced toward the bed and then back at her. "It's insane for me to even think of letting you stay on board."

She glanced at the bed too and then back at him. "*Monsieur* Clement won't be pleased at having to turn back," she said, "and I do want to see the plantation. Couldn't I just stay here with you? I can sleep on the floor if you want me to."

Andre made a strange, choking noise. "*Mademoiselle*. If I allow this madness—and Jean doesn't kill me in the morning—you will be sharing that bed with me every night of the journey." He put a finger under her chin and forced her to look into his eyes. "Sharing it the way a man and a woman do. *Est-ce que vous me comprenez*? Do you understand me?"

She trembled slightly from his touch. If sharing his bed meant having more of those wonderful kisses that made her knees feel like melted butter and her insides go all mushy and quivery, then yes. And it would give her more time to convince him not to bring slaves back. She took a deep breath.

"I understand," she said.

****

Andre stared at Emily, not quite sure he'd heard correctly. Then he shook his head. At least, now he had his answer. She was no virgin.

Not that it really mattered to him. Virgins had to be *taught* to accept pleasure from a man, how to be

277

comfortable with being touched and *to touch* as well. And virgins—thanks to the stupidity of prim-and-proper society—actually thought it *wrong* to experience pleasure from their bodies.

Much better that Emily had already learned to be responsive. It wasn't Andre's business to know who—or how many—had taught her. An unexpected surge of anger whipped through him, though, at the thought of another man being inside her. Where had that come from? He should be grateful that the idiot didn't have enough sense to keep her attached to him. Whoever he was.

Andre fingered a curl that had spilled over her shoulder. So silky, just like her creamy skin.

"Come here," he growled and, in a deft movement, pulled his shirt over his head and reached for her.

Emily's eyes widened, but she didn't draw back as he started undoing the buttons of her own shirt. The rough callouses on his fingertips grazed the tender skin at the base of her throat and swept lightly across the tops of her breasts as the buttons came undone. His large, warm hands slipped under the fabric to slide down her ribs and around her back. He pulled her to him, her naked breasts crushed against his bare chest and slanted his mouth over hers.

The kiss was full and sensual, his lips brushing hers lightly, nibbling, pressing, alternating the pressure, teasing her, making her want more. Her lips parted in open invitation and he thrust himself inside, claiming her tongue, her mouth…claiming *her*.

Andre's hands cupped her buttocks, and she felt a hard ridge press against her belly, oddly sending tingling sensations like shooting stars everywhere. She rubbed her body against his, longing to be even closer, and was rewarded as his groin moved against her. Instinctively, her hips rotated against his. With a moan, he straddle-walked her to the bed, and she found herself on her back, looking up at him as he loomed over her.

He tugged off his boots, his eyes never leaving her face as he removed his pants and kicked them aside. He made no move to cover himself. Emily's breath hitched at the sight of a very thick, very stiff shaft sticking out from a nest of black curls. She'd never seen a man's privates before. Fascinated, she reached out to touch him. He felt so hard, but the skin was warm and smooth as satin. She ran her fingers slowly and lightly up the length of him and felt his member grow even thicker. Even more curious, she closed her hand around him and he moaned deeply. She jerked her hand away.

"Did I hurt you?"

"No, *chèrie*, you did not." He joined her on the bed, kissing her deeply, as his hands made quick work of removing her own trousers.

She felt the cool air on her bare skin and realized she was totally naked and Andre was draped half way across her. She should really be scandalized—or at least embarrassed—but his warm tongue was already trailing kisses down her throat and toward a breast while his fingers gently kneaded the other one. In anticipation of what had happened in the library, she arched into him.

He grinned and slanted a look at her face. "So eager? So soon?" A finger flicked lightly over her nipple and then again from the other direction. He bent his head to run his tongue around the aureole of the other breast, and she arched more, wanting him to take her in his mouth.

"So you like this?" he whispered as he laved the

round mound of breast and then stopped.

Emily wiggled. "Yes… More…"

"More please?" He flattened the nipple with the broad sweep of his tongue.

"Ah! Yes! Please! More!"

With a smug chuckle, he rolled one tight bud between his finger and thumb and closed his mouth over the other, drawing deep. Emily mewled contentedly. The sensation was exquisite…an achy need being soothed…and yet, another need was throbbing and swelling between her legs. She felt herself growing wet as Andre alternated breasts and suckled on the other one. One of his hands glided down her belly and tangled in the short curls at the juncture of her thighs. She gave a slight gasp as his finger stroked through her folds, massaging the wetness toward the hard, little tip that thrummed.

His mouth traced kisses down her ribs and across her stomach. Switching positions, he spread her legs, opening her. Her body felt boneless, melting to his will.

And then he dipped his head.

Emily whimpered in pure ecstasy as Andre slowly and deliberately licked his way along her folds, stroking her over and over. She writhed and he clutched her hips, pressing them tightly to the bed, holding her still while he worked his magic torture on her. His tongue swirled around the hard nub that was aching for his attention. He placed a light kiss on it and she moaned, trying to arch off the bed again, but was held fast. His tongue delved into her center, causing waves of heat to sear through her as he lapped at her. She felt ready to explode…so close…she needed… Oh, dear Lord! His devilish tongue had found the pulsating nub. He was teasing it…licking round and round…she needed….just a little more… Ah, God! There… Oh, *yes*… Right there… and then she shattered, shrieking as his mouth closed down on it and he sucked hard.

Emily panted, gasping for air, and then felt her legs pried wider and the thick edge of his shaft pressed against her hot, swollen core. She felt herself being spread open…and then he drove himself into her.

She cried out, then bit her lip. The pain was sharp and searing.

Above her, Andre stilled.

"*Mon Dieu*. You're a virgin."

She opened her eyes, hoping the tears wouldn't spill over. The pain was beginning to subside. "Of…of course I am. Wha…what did you think?"

Guilt flooded his face. "I thought…the way you responded in the garden…the day in the library…you being here…" His hand stroked her cheek. "Ah, *chèrie*, I am sorry. I would have gone more slowly if I'd known."

He had thought her not a virgin. Did he think she would do…do *this* with just anyone? This is where she should slap him. Society demanded it.

Andre must have read her expression for he sighed and begin to pull out of her. She grabbed him. "Just stay where you are."

He raised a black eyebrow and a corner of his mouth lifted. "I don't think I've ever had an argument in…er, this position," he said.

Emily wrapped her legs around his, snugging him to her, and felt him grow inside her. "I should be very angry, I suppose, but…well, I haven't exactly played by society's rules, have I? Can we discuss it later? I think

I'm beginning to like the feel of you inside me."

Andre grinned. "I think I love you, Emily Clayton. And yes, we will have much to discuss *later*. But first…"

He began a slow, easy thrusting, allowing her to adjust to the rhythm, but his Emily—his precious, one-of-a-kind Emily—quickly matched him, urging him on, gyrating her hips to allow him to go deeper and harder. A fire began to burn in him, igniting every nerve ending, rousing a frenzied desire he didn't know he had, as the flames within him blazed into an inferno. Beneath him, Emily writhed in her own throes of passion, her nails raking across his back as she called his name, and he felt her powerful contraction a split second before he exploded inside her.

They lay still as their breathing slowed. Finally, he rolled off her, pulling her backside against him, an arm wrapped around her waist. Emily was *his*. Whatever hell he might have to face in the morning, he was in heaven tonight. Emily was *his*.

Chapter Eleven

Jean looked from one of them to the other, and Andre almost flinched. He and Emily had been sitting across the little desk from Jean for what seemed an eternity.

"I can see that I underestimated you, *mademoiselle*," Jean finally said. "You are quite resourceful." He switched his gaze to Andre. "And you chose not to tell me when we still had time to turn around?"

Andre straightened his shoulders. It had been sheer lunacy on his part to allow Emily to stay, but obviously his head—the one above his shoulders—hadn't been in charge last night. *Mère de Dieu*! He'd wanted Emily and he'd had her, not once, but *trois* times. He would not apologize for that.

"She wants to see the plantation that her fortune is being invested in," he said.

Jean's eyes glimmered like obsidian. "Do you remember how the men reacted when we had Ilsa aboard on the short trip up the Texas coast?"

Andre set his jaw. "The storm wasn't her fault. We both know that."

"We may," Jean answered, "but what of the crew? They're superstitious. We're a good six days from Cuba, and that's in fair winds."

"I don't know who Ilsa is," Emily interrupted, "but if your men think having a woman on board is bad luck,

I'll tell them about Anne Bonny. She was a woman *and* a pirate!"

"If I'm not mistaken, she was spirited away," Jean replied and then lifted an eyebrow in Andre's direction. "Is that what you did, *mon ami*?"

"He didn't know I was on board," Emily protested, "but I will admit, I hadn't come to see him because of a sugar cane plantation."

Andre actually felt himself blush and his groin grew tight. *Mon Dieu!* Emily had stowed away to warm his bed?

Jean raised both brows. "I don't think you need to explain the real reason, *mademoiselle*. More than one woman has tried to lure Andre into the parson's trap. I must say, though, you took a peculiar approach to it."

Andre watched as Emily's face flushed, first from embarrassment and then in anger as her eyes blazed. "I did not—" She stopped abruptly, her face the color of sunset. She turned to Andre. "I never intended to lure you—"

"Stop, *chèrie*," Andre placed his hand over hers. "You don't have to explain anything."

"But I do," she insisted. "I know you're slave traders, and illegal ones, at that. You must not bring any more slaves to Charleston."

Andre stared at her. She had *known* and still she had given herself—her virginity—to him? A warm feeling of protectiveness swept through him. It should have been an alien emotion, but if felt strangely right.

Jean grimaced. "I know your soft sentiments about slavery, *mademoiselle*, but this is business. If South Carolina didn't have a need for slaves, we wouldn't be selling them. However..." He held his hand up as she opened her mouth to speak. "Perhaps you will be relieved to know that Andre has already told me he's given up the slave trade. He won't be returning with us."

"But that's not—" Emily halted and then turned big, accusing eyes on Andre. "You weren't going to tell me goodbye?"

Andre felt as though one of the yardarms had just struck him squarely in his stomach. *Merde*. It didn't help that Jean was suddenly trying hard not to laugh. "*Chèrie*. I—"

"We will talk about this later," Emily said, her voice strangely sounding like she was on the verge of tears. She swallowed hard and then turned back to Jean. "It's not safe for you to return, *Monsieur* Clement."

"And why not?" Jean asked.

Emily told them what Juma had related. "So you see," she finished, "even if you've been warned and are prepared to fight them off, you'll only be arrested once you dock. It's not safe."

Jean inclined his head. "I thank you for your concern, *mademoiselle*, but I've managed to elude the long arm of the law for some time."

"Well, I'm sure you have, since foreign slave trading has been illegal for years. But you're also looking at fighting men who will be armed."

He shrugged. "I've battled ships far better prepared than a few fishing vessels ill-equipped with an assortment of crude weapons. It's a way of life on the high seas. The stakes are high, but so is the bounty."

"But…" Her voice trailed off as she looked from him to Andre and then back again and frowned. "Are you telling me you…you're pirates?"

"Privateers would be a better word," Andre

285

corrected. "Jean has always carried a letter of marque when he's commandeered another vessel."

Her frown turned into a look of puzzlement. "There is no reason to carry a letter of marque these days. The United States isn't at war any longer. Whose flag did you fly?"

"Cartagena when she sought independence from Spain. American against Britain in the war. Then Mexico…" Jean shrugged again. "…although Spain had the distinct opinion I was carrying *their* marque."

Emily bristled. "You make it sound like you're Jean Lafitte, *Monsieur* Clement."

He grinned. "At your service, *mademoiselle*."

She widened her eyes and looked at Andre.

"Emily, I'd like to introduce you to the privateer Jean Lafitte," he said.

****

Jean Lafitte. The pirate who was both famous and infamous. Who had become a legend in his own time. Emily still couldn't quite believe she had met him and was actually on his ship.

The other thing she couldn't believe was that Andre had intended to leave—forever—without telling her.

"You weren't even going to say goodbye," she said to him once he'd returned her to his cabin. Tears stung her eyes, but she blinked them back. She would not let him see her cry.

He reached out to touch her, but she shifted away. His mouth tightened. "What good would it have done to tell you I was returning to Cartegena? It's well over a thousand miles from Charleston."

Why did he have to sound so cool and logical? It made Emily want to stamp her foot in frustration. "A gentleman would have taken his leave in a proper fashion."

He lifted an eyebrow. "Since when did you become concerned about what was proper?"

Heat flooded her face. She certainly had not worried about being proper when she stole on board. Nor last night... Involuntarily, she glanced at the bed. It was much too close in this small room. Her face grew even hotter.

"I stand corrected. You must think me not better than the...the harlots that visit the Planter's Hotel." She looked away from him as a tear slid down her cheek. Angrily, she wiped it away.

"Never call yourself that, *chèrie.*" He touched her shoulder, turning her, and tilted her chin up with his fingers. "What we shared in that bed was unique. Nothing like... You made me feel things I've never felt before." He wiped at a second tear with his thumb. "Please believe that."

Emily sniffled and he handed her a handkerchief. She dabbed at her eyes and swallowed hard. "So why didn't you say goodbye?"

Andre sighed. "I wanted to. But I was afraid you would do just what you're doing. I wanted to remember you as independent and strong. As the girl who rode alone without an escort, even though it wasn't wise. I wanted to remembered the fiery tempered woman who cared nothing for society's rules, yet cared for *people*. Your people—Maisie, Juma, Cyrah—giving them their freedom. You've even made me see that I no longer want to deal in slavery. So do not underestimate yourself. Ever."

"You could have asked me to come with you."

His eyes widened. "Ah, *chèrie.* You are a lady of southern society, even if you don't care to be. The summer plantation season will begin soon, and when you return to town in the fall, there will be a round of balls and parties, theater invitations… No doubt you'll find a very suitable husband from among society's elite and soon be a grand hostess at your own town house and plantation."

"That sounds like drudgery to me," Emily replied. "Besides which, as I'm sure you're aware, I am officially ruined by being on this ship. I doubt I'll get an invitation anywhere."

Andre shook his head. "It is amazing what society will overlook, given the proper incentive. You stand to inherit your stepfather's holdings, which are quite vast. Jean checked into them. A beautiful woman with a large dowry can be forgiven for almost anything." He gave a little shrug. "Jean can be very persuasive. He'll have all of Charleston believing he escorted you to Savannah for a short, well-chaperoned vacation."

"I don't want to spend my life on a plantation. I crave adventure. I want to see new places, experience new things. Take me with you to Cartagena."

A fleeting look of desire smoldered in his eyes and then disappeared. "Life at sea is hard. There is always danger. If not from pirates"—a corner of his mouth quirked up in a smile—"then from the sea herself. She tests men constantly. Davy Jones' locker holds many corpses. A ship is no place for a woman."

Emily set her jaw. "Anne Bonny did it."

"And she was captured and would have hanged except she was pregnant, and that bought her father time to ransom her." Andre brushed the backs of his fingers along Emily's cheek. "Would Mr. Jamison do the same for you?" When she didn't answer, he continued, "Besides, sailors are a superstitious lot. Having a woman aboard is bad luck. They would never accept you."

"I heard some of the men talking yesterday while I waited for you," Emily answered. "They were saying they would be going back with the other boat."

Andre nodded. "That's true. *La Diligent* will return to Cartagena, taking some of this crew home. Others, coming from there, will take the *Revenge II* to Charleston. Why?"

"If I can convince these men that I can do the work—just like any other sailor—and I'm not bad luck, you won't have a reason to refuse me."

"Be careful, *chèrie*, that you do not anger the sea with such boasts." He moved away, taking clothing out of drawers and stuffing the items into an empty valise.

"What are you doing?" Emily asked as she watched him.

"I'll be moving into the boatswain's quarters," he said as he snapped the bag closed.

"But why? You said we'd share every night... Oh!" She felt her face heat again and she looked down at the floor. "I didn't...satisfy you."

The bag dropped with a clatter, and then Emily was in Andre's arms, clamped tightly to his chest while his mouth claimed hers, hungry and demanding. His tongue swept into her mouth, filling her, stroking deep, letting her know of his desire. His hands swept down her torso, cupping her buttocks, pressing her against his rocklike erection. Then abruptly, he ended the kiss and set her apart from him.

Emily gasped for air, slightly dizzy, her eyes out of

focus.

Andre's voice was husky. "Don't ever think, *bien-aimée,* that you don't satisfy me or that I don't desire you."

"Then why—"

"Because you must return to your home. I don't want to get you with child. If I stay here, there is no way I can resist you." Andre picked up his bag and opened the door. "Jean will make sure every man on this ship leaves you alone."

Emily said nothing as he closed the cabin door. There was no way she would be returning home. She looked into the mirror fastened to the wall above the shaving basin and smiled. She had felt Andre's desire. He wanted her.

The mirror wavered in front of her and, for one brief moment, the face of the lady from the second floor of the hotel smiled at her. Anne Bonny? Emily blinked and looked again, but only her face looked back at her. Had that been her imagination?

She straightened her shoulders. Anne Bonny had sailed the high seas with a male crew. All Emily had to do was convince these sailors to accept her. How hard could that be?

****

Harder than she imagined. The first night, when Jean escorted her to what served as a dining room below deck, the sailors not on duty had given her dark looks that made her all too aware of how sharp their eating utensils were. She even heard mutterings about "damned females" and "the luck of the damned" before Jean silenced them all with a glare that they seemed to understand.

Andre did not put in an appearance, and she spent a lonely night, with the door securely bolted, listening for any sound of him, so that she might let him in.

The next morning she knocked on Jean's door. He alternately frowned and seemed amazed as she told him of her plan to become part of the crew and show Andre she wasn't some southern magnolia that needed cosseting. And she told him about Anne Bonny's ghost…that Emily thought it was Anne who had appeared at the hotel and again on the ship. She thought he would laugh, but he was surprisingly serious.

"Some of the *camarades* aboard have sworn they've seen the spirits of dead friends, often helping them in times of crisis, which, given the life of a privateer, happens frequently." He paused, studying her. "The sea is a hard taskmistress. She is unforgiving and not prone to second chances. Are you sure this is what you want?"

Emily took a deep breath. "I want adventure, to be able to explore new places and not be fettered by silly rules society makes."

"Sometimes, *mademoiselle*, those rules are for a reason. Like protecting you. Even at sea, we have a code we follow. Perhaps it is even more stringent, in its own way, than southern society. At sea, you can't afford to make mistakes."

"I know. But…and this may sound silly of me, since I've only been aboard two days, but I feel like I'm *home*. This is the life I want."

"I can't fault you for that, *ma petite*. On more than one occasion, I've had the opportunity to be a lawful part of society. I always return to the sea." He studied her. "I just hope Andre realizes what a gift you are."

So did she. As the next few days passed and the

sailors grudgingly began to accept her presence, Andre kept himself apart. He took the night watch and slept most of the day. Emily would have joined him on watch, but Jean had taken her at her word and she was assigned daytime duties as any other crew member and fell into bed exhausted after the evening meal. Occasionally, Andre's path did cross with hers, and he was always polite. Once she caught him watching her intensely, his eyes seeming to smolder with desire from across the room, but when she smiled, he nodded curtly and turned away.

She had not lied when she told Jean she felt at home on the ship. The creaking of the wooden hull and the sharp crack of sails filling were music to her ears, as was the lapping of the water as the bow sluiced through huge waves. When the boat pitched, running close-hauled, it felt like a horse's canter. The slow rolling of swells in dead calm was like a baby's cradle. The boatswain showed her the difference between direct and apparent wind by turning her face and when she finally understood, she realized that was how the helmsman held his course. But, best of all, was when the wind was on the beam, heeling slightly, and the ship seemed to find herself and accelerated through the sea as though being pulled by an invisible string.

Emily breathed in the familiar tangy, salt smell as Cuba loomed on the horizon. The one thing she hadn't been able to do was convince Jean not to take on slaves, although he had assured her he would put into port in Savannah first, to see her safely off the ship.

She had no intention of going back. Once they docked, it would be a mere twenty-four hours to take on supplies, exchange crews and load their human cargo.

She had to see Andre. Tonight.

****

Andre had given orders that under no circumstances was Emily to be allowed to leave the boat. The burly sailor who accepted the gold sovereign from him had nodded grimly and folded huge arms across his barrel chest. Even now, as Andre turned on the dock to look up the gangplank, he could see the man standing beside it. Unless Emily suddenly developed mermaid tendencies, she would not be getting off the ship. He looked aft to where Jean stood near the gunwale and raised his hand in a farewell salute. Then he turned and quickly walked away.

He had thought parting ways with Jean would be hard, and it was. Lafitte had rescued him in New Orleans, where at the ripe age of four-and-ten, he'd nearly had his throat slit dallying with a woman who had a jealous lover. Jean had taught him the ways of the sea and of the Louisiana swamps as well. They had fought together at the Battle of New Orleans and downed several bottles of fine French cognac afterward, much to General Jackson's chagrin when he couldn't keep up. And Andre had been with Jean when he made the decision to burn Campeche rather than let the Army have it. Leaving his friend, who was also his mentor and almost a father to him, would be hard.

Leaving Emily was harder.

"*Merde*," he muttered as he strode toward *La Diligent* farther down the pier, "what magic does she possess to make me feel like this?"

He moved along, caught in the flow of the rest of the crew, who would be going back to Cartagena with him. He was doing the right thing. Even though Emily had proved herself admirably in the week at sea, not once complaining or becoming sick, she belonged on land. Her home—her inheritance—was in South Carolina. Even though she might chafe at the rules imposed on her, in the end, she would see that the genteel life of Southern aristocrats was much better than being tossed about on stormy seas and swamped by salt water.

Still—the memory of Emily's soft, pliant lips opening for him, the taste of her mouth, the silky feel of her tongue as she swirled it around his—*Mon Dieu*! He had kissed women before, thousands of times, and never felt like that.

Worse, he could feel the satin smoothness of her full breasts and the puckered skin circling nipples that pebbled for him at just the flick of his finger. And the little mewling sound she made when he suckled her or the way her back arched up for him as he lapped at her core, making her groan with pleasure when he nibbled the hard, little pulsating nub. He closed his eyes and felt her writhing beneath him as he thrust into her hot, wet, tight sheath…

Someone thrust an elbow into his ribs. With a grunt, he opened his eyes to find the boatswain grinning at him.

"We're here," the man said.

Andre blinked and looked up. *La Diligent* bobbed gently, tugging at the lines securing her to the dock. He didn't even realize how he'd gotten there.

He couldn't allow Emily to torment him any longer. Their lives were on different courses. When he arrived in Cartagena, he'd find some raven-haired beauty who looked nothing like Emily and make her his mistress. Eventually, he would forget Emily.

He had to.

"Be ready to cast the lines at daybreak," he told the boatswain. "The sooner we get home, the better."

****

Emily stood by the rail in the pale dawn light the next morning, trying to peer through the patches of fog and mist that curled up from the sea. She would not cry. Andre had left the boat yesterday afternoon without a farewell and that…that monster sailor had prevented her from getting off the ship.

She had tried so hard. Even the cynical Louis, who had complained loudly about women being bad luck, had acknowledged that—for a female—she hadn't gotten in the way. Why couldn't Andre at least have said goodbye?

She knew the reason. He didn't see any use in having her create a scene. God's blood! Was he so cold-gutted—she realized suddenly that she had picked up some colorful vocabulary—he could leave without a farewell?

She closed her eyes, trying to keep the stinging tears away. Did their night together mean nothing? How could he have kissed her like he did with such passion that she felt boneless? His touch…those big, warm hands and calloused fingers so gentle and easy, kneading her breasts, stroking between her legs until she was sure she would shatter? And his mouth…where he put it…

"I am sorry, *mademoiselle*. I thought he would come."

She took a deep breath and opened her eyes. Jean Lafitte watched her silently, his eyes obsidian in the pale light. Unable to help herself, she glanced down the pier.

"He is gone. *La Diligent* sailed an hour ago, as soon as the fog lifted."

Emily swallowed hard and lifted her chin. "Thank you for letting me know. I'll get about my duties, Captain."

He nodded and turned away. Within minutes, their lines were loosened and the *Revenge II* slowly made her way to open water.

Emily busied herself, stowing small items in the cabin. Once they were underway in heavy seas, anything that wasn't secured would fly across the room. She heard a shout, and she went up on deck.

"Ship approaching, port side. Looks like they're hailing us," the sailor up in the crow's nest shouted.

Jean appeared by the helm. "It could be a trap. We carry a lucrative cargo."

Emily shivered. Pirates? *Real* pirates who would try to board the ship and overcome the crew? She looked around. Every sailor suddenly had a sword by his side, and several were readying the small cannons on the bow. Was there going to be a battle? She watched as Jean lifted his spyglass and walked over to him.

"I can fire a musket, if you have an extra one," she said. "My father taught me."

Jean lowered the glass and smiled. "I don't think you're going to have to, unless you decide to shoot Andre."

Emily frowned. "What?"

Jean pointed to the rapidly approaching ship. "It's *La Diligent*." He gave the order to luff the sails and the *Revenge II* slowed.

A grappling hook skittered through the air as the ship approached, catching neatly on the gunwale. More lines were thrown as the two ships came abreast, and Andre leaped onto Jean's ship.

Andre came toward her and bowed formally, taking her hand and kissing it. "I couldn't leave you after all, *chèrie.* Will you forgive me?"

Emily stared at him, not knowing what to say.

"You may just want to shoot him," Jean said. "He deserves it."

She strove to find her voice. "Is forgiveness all you want?"

"No." Andre looked deeply into her eyes and went down on one knee. "I want you, Emily. Your heart, your body, your soul. No one has ever made me feel like you do. With you I am complete. Without you, there is a vast hole that not even the sea can fill. Will you marry me? I'll return with you and purchase a plantation somewhere. I have the money—"

"No," Emily interrupted.

Andre swallowed hard and looked down. "I guess I deserve that answer, but—"

"I'll marry you on one condition," Emily interrupted again.

His face brightened and he brought her hand to his lips. "Name it."

"That you take me to Cartagena instead."

Andre's eyes widened. "You mean that?"

Emily tried to look solemn, but a corner of her mouth lifted anyway. "Of course I mean it. I love the sea almost as much as I love you—"

She didn't get to finish her sentence, for Andre stood and swept her into his arms for a resounding kiss that took her breath away.

Not caring that they had onlookers, Emily put her arms around his neck, her fingers tangling in his hair as she opened her mouth to take his tongue, amid the cheers of the crew. Andre tasted wonderful…sweet and salty and…*him*. Finally, she had a pirate of her own.

Emily opened her eyes slightly to see if his were closed and then noticed a tendril of fog lingering in the air between the two boats. Slowly, it began to take shape. Anne Bonny's apparition smiled and then faded away, leaving only clear, blue seas.

Author's Note

An interesting correlation can be drawn between Anne Bonny and Jean Lafitte—both disappeared from the pages of history.

Anne Bonny, the daughter of an Irish Charleston plantation owner, married a small-time pirate named James Bonny, who hoped to inherit her father's wealth. Instead, her father disowned her.

While in the Bahamas, Anne met her true love, "Calico Jack" Rackham, and she left her husband to become Calico Jack's pirate mate. Eventually, in 1720, they were captured and sentenced to be hanged, although Anne's sentence was delayed since she was pregnant.

There is no evidence of what happened to her after that. One theory is that her father did relent, ransomed her, and brought her back to Charleston.

Many accounts of the life of Jean Lafitte are available. Suffice it to say, he lived as an outlaw—albeit a privileged one—in the swamps and bayous of Louisiana until he came to General Jackson's aid in the Battle of New Orleans. President Madison pardoned him and, for a while, he and his crew lived as "honest" men. But the call of the sea was great, and Jean set up a second fortress on Galveston Island, supporting Mexico's fight for independence from Spain. Since the United States had declared a truce with Spain, the government did not take kindly to Spanish galleons being seized and ordered

Jean and his men to leave. It took a year of persuasion, but finally the ultimatum was given: Surrender or be fired upon.

So, one evening in May 1821, as the brig *USS Enterprise* sat waiting offshore, Jean set fire to Campeche and disappeared, along with his ships and crew.

Theories put him in Cartagena, the West Indies, and Charleston, but no one knows where he went, what he did, or when he died.

Anne Bonny and Jean Lafitte may have lived a century apart, but both of them sailed away into legend.

A word about the author…

Cynthia Breeding lives on the Gulf Coast of Texas with a very non-spoiled poodle-mix and enjoys walking and horseback-riding on the beach, as well as sailing.

www.cynthiabreeding.com

Thank you for purchasing
this publication of The Wild Rose Press, Inc.

For questions or more information
contact us at
info@thewildrosepress.com.

The Wild Rose Press, Inc.